A Novel by
Heather Melo

Copyright © 2022 Heather Melo
All rights reserved.

The characters and events portrayed in this book are fictitious. Any similarity to real persons, living or dead, is coincidental and not intended by the author.

No part of this book may be reproduced, stored in a retrieval system, or transmitted in any form or by any means, electronic, mechanical, photocopying, recording, or otherwise without the express written permission of the author.

ISBN: 979-8-88831-916-1 (ebook)
979-8-88831-917-8 (paperback)

The cover is by the Author.

For Tom,
who always told me that I could,

And for Jake,
who shut up long enough
so that I could get it done.

Wednesday, April 5th

1.

The steel doors of the elevator slowly converged, and Liz started to feel the quick downward pull of gravity that, despite its daily assault on her body, would always give her a little lurch in the stomach. She hid her hands behind her back and white knuckle gripped the rail that ran along the back of the elevator. She realized that the rail shouldn't really give her a sense of safety; after all, the descent to the lobby from her office was nineteen floors, and she once made the mistake of watching an episode of some show or another that demonstrated how the human body would fare after even a moderate elevator fall of, say, five or six stories. Yet, despite this fact, she continued to grip the rail every day, twice a day, sometimes more, as she escaped her office and entered the world outside. If she didn't enjoy a high heel so much, she might consider hoofing it up the emergency staircase every day, but we all make our choices in life, she thought.

Beth yapped away as the elevator stopped first on floor eleven, then floor four, before finally reaching its ultimate destination of the lobby. Liz was used to Beth's yapping, and truth be told she appreciated the distraction of, "Did you see Carol's weirdly unnatural new hair col1or or "How in the hell did Joanne get engaged before me?" as it kept her mind off of the irrational fear that she and her elevator mates were one faulty cable away from plummeting to their deaths down a murky, dark elevator shaft. Today, their elevator-car companions did not seem to notice Beth's chatter, but on more than one occasion Liz had spied an eye roll or a shocked expression, usually from a female building associate.

The doors opened and bright light poured into the elevator from the huge glass lobby windows. Liz exhaled and released her hands from the rail. She swung her large brown work tote over her left shoulder and adjusted the small shopping bag that had been looped around her wrist. It was Wednesday. Liz and Beth always took an extended lunch break on Wednesdays because their direct supervisor, Martin, had ceremoniously announced earlier that year that he would be switching to a four-day workweek, for reasons unknown. While both ladies thought it was slightly suspect that Martin could get away with working a thirty-two-hour workweek and still collect the same paycheck (facts they assumed but could not definitively prove) they'd decided about six weeks ago that each Wednesday, Martin's day off of choice, they would take an extra-long lunch break, and fit in any errands that may have taken their time after work. Shouldn't they, after all, be able to pick up their prescriptions and return those too-tight white pants on the company dime? They sure believed so.

Liz glanced into the small shopping bag. It contained a truly beautiful silk scarf that she had purchased at a weak moment. The navy scarf was intricately decorated with a floral motif in cream, brown, and a deep burgundy. It was truly a work of art. A work of art that Liz could not justify, after some introspective moments at home starting at her checking account balance, spending three hundred dollars on. She planned to return it after lunch that day and pray that nothing else in the store caught her eye and taunted her into making an unnecessary purchase.

"Let's do wraps today. I feel like something Greekish," Beth stated, as she looked down at her watch. She, too, had an errand to run today. Today was date number three with Brandon and she wanted to grab some new undergarments, just in case, as she put it, "I get liquored up enough to show him the real estate." Never once had Liz considered that a female body might be likened to a house, or a barn, or a twenty-three-acre field, but Beth seemed more excited about this potential suitor than she had been in a long time, so Liz was happy to help her friend peruse Victoria's Secret and pick up something a little bit sexy. But she giggled at the thought. Beth was just not a girly girl at all. Liz had seen her underwear drawer practically a million times and it was chock-full of Fruit of the Loom and Hanes.

 They strolled along and made their way toward The Greek Garden, a small place on West 46th Street that was a favorite of both ladies. They made a killer Greek salad, and Liz was known to order a giant plate of French fries as well. The Garden never disappointed. They were also one of the few places around, at least as far as Liz knew, that still used "fake" chicken for their souvlaki, the kind of processed product that spun all day and all night on a spit at the front of the store. Every time they passed by it Beth would turn to Liz and exclaim, "Wheel...of...MEAT" in the grand style of Wheel of Fortune. Liz didn't have the heart to tell her that it wasn't really a wheel. Beth thought it was funny and she didn't want to burst her bubble. Liz loved that rotating wheel of what passed for meat. Most people went out of their way to look for actual grilled white meat chicken, but for her money Liz much preferred the fake stuff. It would be a souvlaki day for her for sure. She'd soak her ankles later to combat the high sodium content.

 They sat at an interior table as an added precaution—who knew where Martin really lurked and skulked around on his day off. They'd hate to be sitting at a window table enjoying a midday full-course meal and have their weirdo boss give them the stink eye.

"My favorite lunching ladies! How are you both doing today?" Nic, a waiter with whom they'd come to have an easy and friendly rapport, dropped two menus at the table, as well as a plate of pita and hummus.

"Hey, Nic. You know. Here for our weekly spin on the Wheel...of..."

"I know, I know. If I didn't work for tips, I might point out that your joke is getting a little bit overplayed," he teased. Beth laughed and blushed slightly. Liz suspected that she had a budding crush on their waiter friend.

Beth feigned utter despair, covered her eyes with her hands, and joked back, "My burgeoning comedy career is over! A-starving-actor-slash-waiter doesn't approve of my joke!"

The trio laughed. It was an easy and comfortable feeling whenever the ladies came to The Greek Garden and chatted with Nic. It was a midday respite that Liz especially enjoyed. "Any performances coming up that we might want to know about?" Liz inquired. Although they had not yet crossed the bridge from "diner waiter and patrons" to "friends," she felt like she would like to support Nic if he had a part in a local play or whatever he might be up to. She knew he also played bass in an indie rock band, but as far as she knew it was more of a passion project that hadn't yet yielded any fruit—or any performances at an actual venue. He felt like a kindred spirit to her, so affable and genuine. She appreciated it.

"Big big audition coming up next weekend for a swing in a musical that I'm not supposed to mention. Let's just say that if I get this role, someone else might be the ill-fated recipient of Beth's meat jokes." They all laughed.

"Well, although you've cut me deep, I will still send all of the good audition vibes your way," Beth said, as she dipped a wedge of pita bread into the creamy beige hummus.

"Much appreciated, ladies. I can use all of the vibes, prayers, good thoughts, and whatever the hell else you want to send my way. Just takes one little moment to sort of change the path you've been walking down, and for the love of God I'm hoping this is one of those moments for me." He said it with a smile, but Liz thought that his eyes looked tired. He must work there all day, she thought, and then spend his evenings doing whatever he could to keep his craft alive somehow. She thought she understood. Obviously, she wasn't an actor, so she didn't quite understand the feeling of success possibly being around the corner, and also equally possibly never surfacing ever, but she did understand how tiresome the monotony of regular life could be, and how, as he said, one moment might alter your path forever.

He took their orders and left the ladies to their luncheon. Liz tapped her fingernails on the hard surface of the table. She'd loved that sound since she was a little girl. Long fingernails clicking on a table top always seemed like the ultimate emblem of what it meant to be a woman. That, and walking loudly in high heels, which she certainly did due to an entire lack of grace. She'd been told by a coworker once that she sounded like a stampede of ponies walking down the hallway. She'd stared long and hard at Jay that day, unsure how to react. She'd smiled, and at a later date made sure that she slyly removed his peanut butter and jelly sandwich from the lunchroom fridge, lined the bread with dill pickle chips, and deftly placed it back into the fridge. She credited the summer she spent at theater camp with her ability to remain stoic as she sat at a nearby table and watched Jay take a huge bite of the sandwich, spit out the offending bite, and then proceed to dry heave over the sink.

She hadn't told Beth about any of this, but as soon as Jay cried, "Who the hell put pickles in my sandwich?" she shot Liz a knowing look and mouthed, "You?" Liz just shrugged. Beth was all too privy to some of the truly immature antics Liz had participated in during her college years. Although she had most definitely matured and would likely no longer, say, fill her ex-boyfriend's mailbox with wet cat food, she wasn't above a little innocuous payback as the need dictated.

"So, black-panty night, huh? Seems like you're getting invested in this one?" Liz asked as she took a bite of the fries that Nic had placed in the middle of the table.

"I guess. I mean, he's not the greatest for sure, but I'm going through a bit of a slump, and at the same time I could most definitely use a few new pair of underwear. And for future reference, promise me that you'll never use the word 'panty' ever again? It makes me puke in my mouth a little bit."

Liz laughed because she knew that Beth had a list of words "never to be spoken aloud" and panty was, for sure, in the top five, probably only slightly more acceptable to her friend than the dreaded "moist."

"Wow, and I thought you were excited about this one! I'm not one to lecture you, but why waste your time if this guy is... How can I put this? Below par? Non-panty-worthy?" Beth threw a fry straight at Liz and it bounced off her nose onto the floor. This made both ladies break out in a fit of laughter.

"I have only been out with him a handful of times, and to answer your question, I have been hanging in there because I have no other prospects to bring to Jenna's upcoming nuptials. I don't want to have to point out the obvious, but you've been dating—no engaged—to Pete for about forty-eight years and he's... What did you say? Below par. Like, answer the damn window."

Beth was referring to a story Liz had told her about an event that had happened last week. Liz and Pete had brunch together nearly every Saturday. Nothing fancy— typically they'd head to a diner or a small bistro near Liz's apartment that had great croissants. Liz had driven over to his parents' house on Saturday, into which he had recently moved back, at eleven, as usual, but there had been no answer at the door. She'd called his phone; nothing. She'd called the house phone, because she'd had a slight pang of worry kick in. No answer. She'd walked to the side of the house, had climbed atop a garbage can, and had looked into his childhood bedroom. He had been sound asleep in his bed. Liz had banged on the window full force, but despite her efforts he hadn't even budged. She'd thought she might break the glass, but he'd been dead to the world. She had been so incredibly livid that she'd gotten in her car and had driven home. Two whole hours later Pete had called her. He'd been up all night playing an online role-playing game, and he'd guessed he just didn't hear her attempts to rouse him from the dead. He hadn't even been that apologetic.

Liz began to spin the ring on her left hand. "I would be lying if I told you that I haven't been having second thoughts. Often. But I think that's normal, right? I'm embarrassed to say that I wasn't really that surprised that he chose some sort of all-night Dungeons & Dragons bullshit to spending time with his real-life flesh-and-blood fiancée. But the thought of starting over now? Frickin' going on a dating app or whatever? It's just exhausting. Plus, I feel like I've invested eight years of my life here. I'm not quite ready to admit that a huge chunk of my adulthood was a failure."

"Well, now you know why I'll be picking up some new underwear for my date. The path of least resistance. Long live complacency!" They laughed, but it wasn't the carefree giggle that they'd shared earlier. There was a sense of disappointment in how each lady relaxed into a sigh and slumped in her chair. At least their meals had arrived. They could direct their energy toward food, a much less complicated topic for the time being.

Then Beth's phone vibrated on the table, shaking the ice-filled glasses and startling the girls into the present. Beth picked up the phone, looked at the caller ID, and rolled her eyes before placing it back down onto the table unanswered.

2.

Ben couldn't remember the last time he'd seen hail quite like the chaos that was currently rocketing down from the darkened sky. He opened the side door to take a peek, and also because he was genuinely concerned that one of the ice balls might shatter the windshield of the truck parked in the driveway. He loved that truck. His wife didn't quite understand his affection for it, now nearly thirteen years old, but it was the first and only large purchase he'd made in his lifetime. Even growing up he'd never lived in a home that his family had owned—they'd always rented apartments, moving every few years—and as an adult, he and his wife, Adeline, had fallen into that cycle as well. They never seemed to be able to get ahead of that eight ball. But the truck symbolized something for Ben. Adulthood? Maturity? He couldn't put his finger on it, but he knew that every time he hoisted his body up into the truck he felt a solidity that just didn't seem to permeate any other area of his life. Confident that the truck appeared unscathed, he pulled the door closed and walked back into his home office.

He fell back into his brown leather office chair and allowed the force of his fall to roll the chair back toward the bookcase slowly. This had been his favorite room in the condo, and probably the only reason Adeline had been able to lure him out of Los Angeles proper and into the more casual, beach-centric community of Manhattan Beach. He could absolutely understand why many people, his wife included, loved this area; this rental was only three short blocks to the ocean and a ten-minute walk into town. Typically, this type of real estate would have been incredibly out of their tight budget, but this had been a six-month sublet, and due to the last-minute nature of the previous tenant's departure (their landlord had implied heavily that she had been spending an extended vacation in the hoosegow) they had been able to afford it. They were already closing in on the fifth month of the lease, and Ben was looking forward to finding something in Los Angeles. Suburban living didn't suit him, and part of him thought, perhaps, his next move would likely be alone anyway, given the atmosphere of the home lately.

 Although the location had more than doubled Ben's commute to the office space that he shared with his writing partner, he'd still had a shred of hope that this particular change of scenery would serve as a glue, or at least heavy-duty masking tape, for his perpetually crumbling marriage. Adeline had grown up in a beach town further down the coast, and in the early days of their marriage, when they had still treated each other as more than mere roommates passing in the hallway, they would often enjoy an afternoon cup of coffee together while she opened up about her seemingly idyllic childhood. She'd grown into an angry person all of these years later, alternating between silence and rage. Maybe much of this was his fault, Ben often thought, but perhaps the proximity of the beach would help her hearken back to those early days of marriage when she had still been open to sharing her heart as she reminisced about her toes in the sand as a little girl.

 Now that it was only the two of them, the silence in the house had grown deafening. Their only son, Jack, was in his third year of college and, having grown up in a volatile environment, Ben doubted he would come home after graduation. He seemed to look for every excuse to busy himself elsewhere during school breaks—hiking in Oregon with a friend, working long hours at multiple jobs during the summer. Ben had a special relationship with Jack, and it made him very sad that his own difficult marriage kept his son from spending time at home. He'd taken to driving to visit him at college once a month; truth be told, he was nearly equally happy to see his son as he was to be away from his wife and her icy ire for a weekend.

The beach town didn't exactly appear to save the marriage, but Adeline was certainly out of the house more, spending every day at the ocean. Ben knew that her constant absence was a sign that things had been getting worse, and although he wouldn't admit it to himself, at this point he might value the quiet peacefulness of an empty house more than his marriage.

He slid back over to the desk and flipped open his laptop. He scanned through some emails: one from his accountant, asking something about retirement account contributions; one from his brother-in-law, which was probably just some sort of political meme; two from a sender named "Wild African Shaman" promising him that he could, indeed, learn the secret to pleasing twelve women in one evening. He wasn't really interested in any of these. A final email, which had been sitting in his in-box for a week, was an email forwarded to him by his agent from Adam Spink, a Senior Development Executive. This one interested him more than any email he'd ever received in his lifetime, and he had "kept it as new" so that he could, perchance, feel the excitement every time he looked at his email box that he'd felt the day it arrived last week.

Ben and his writing partner, Joe, had experienced some nominal success trying to break into the business. To date, they had sold two pilot ideas to smaller networks, but neither had been ordered to series. Their most recent project, a somewhat popular semi-scripted/semi-reality show had been gaining a cult following. Basically, the two of them worked as staff in a seedy motel, along with a few other aspiring actors; the everyday goings-on of a mostly "short stay" motel was somewhat interesting, but admittedly they had to prod the action a little bit with some injected story line. It had a small but loyal fan base and had been good enough to pay the bills for the last two years, but to Ben's slight relief, as he didn't love being in front of the camera, it hadn't been renewed for a third season. None of these projects were really Ben's passion, though. He'd had a screenplay for a feature film rattling around inside of his head for years. One night after writing some new storyboard for the following season, Ben and Joe had stopped off to have a few drinks. Ben hadn't been ready to go home that evening and face whatever happened to be waiting for him, and Joe was perpetually single and only had to worry about getting home to feed his cat.

One drink had turned into two, which then turned into both guys requiring an Uber in order to get home, but somewhere around beer number four or five, Ben had unexpectedly unburdened himself to Joe all about his unrealized screenplay. It all, slowly and with slurred speech, tumbled out of his mouth. And Joe, who was half in the bag himself, thought that it was probably the most sensational story he'd ever heard.

The next day they'd gotten to work.

That had been fourteen months ago. Ben knew the age of his screenplay the way a mother marked the age of her infant child. It was, after all, his baby.

By all means, Joe had been a true partner in getting the plot intricacies and the character nuances out of Ben's head and onto paper, but the heart and soul of the script was 100 percent Ben. He had put so much stock into this script that it simply had to come to fruition. He'd once heard a performer—maybe a comedian or some actor—say that the best way they knew how to succeed in "the business" was to take away any safety net. Then you had no choice. Succeed or maybe you won't eat dinner that night. Right now, Ben was poised to leap off of the cliff with nary a net in sight.

He reviewed Adam's message for the one hundredth time. His screenplay—their screenplay—was one of a handful being considered for production. It was still a crapshoot at this stage in the game, but his agent, Brit, had been trying hard to secure a second meeting with Spink, after an initial last-minute lunch meeting in Los Angeles had been less than successful.

He closed out his email and stared blankly at the wallpaper on his laptop. It was one his favorite photographs of all time, taken at least thirteen years ago, maybe more. They had been on a family outing at Disneyland. Jack was on his shoulders, enjoying one of those giant circular all-day sucker lollipops that inevitably end up 2 percent eaten, and 98 percent in the trash. Ben wistfully remembered how hard it had been to wash the candy out of his hair that evening, and how he'd wished that he'd appreciated that moment more at the time than he did. In the photo, Adeline had been smiling widely—the kind of smile that engulfed a person's entire face in the joy of the moment. He believed that the split second that had been captured in this one photograph was the happiest he'd ever seen her. Maybe the happiest she'd ever actually been. It had been a silly, happy-go-lucky day for a family who had been anything but.

Ben and Adeline had met in college, and if they were both being honest, their initial reaction to each other was one of playful annoyance. They had always seemed to find something to debate, and this playful banter eventually had given way to some pretty strong sexual tension. Ben would say, and he'd bet a million dollars that Adeline would agree, that they had been deep in lust, but never in love. Not even for a minute. Unfortunately, or fortunately depending on how you approached the situation, about seven months into their tumultuous relationship Adeline had found out that she was pregnant.

Ben had grown up with an absentee father, and he knew that despite the fact that he had been merely twenty-one years old, and a senior in college without an actual job, there was no way he wouldn't be front and center in his child's life. He had proposed to Adeline that night and they'd eloped about two months later. It had probably been the worst decision either had made in their life, and he knew now, with maturity and many years of life behind him, that he could have been a fantastic father and co-parent even if he hadn't remained in a loveless relationship with his son's mother.

They'd tried to make the best of it for a few years, but it had been evident by the time Jack was about three or four that Ben and Adeline had been poorly matched. To the onlooker, it wasn't even clear whether or not they'd liked each other. They'd been on the brink of divorce at least half a dozen times throughout their marriage, but neither had ever pulled the trigger and visited a lawyer. By the time Jack was a young teenager they'd settled into routine; they had been cordial roommates, and both had focused the majority of their love and energy toward their son.

At least Ben and Adeline had thought they were cordial until they'd gotten a call from Jack's ninth-grade school psychologist. Ms. Stringer had informed them that Jack had been inquiring how he might expedite the high school experience, with the end goal of possibly going off to college by age sixteen. It had been clear that he hadn't just wanted to leave home; he'd wanted to escape his parents' relationship. They had started seeing a marriage counselor, as well as a family therapist, and they'd learned some skills to help them through their daily lives. But all the therapy in the world couldn't spark love that didn't exist.

Ben sighed. He closed the laptop. The photograph made him melancholy. He missed his son and he mourned for the marriage in the photo, a marriage that never actually existed. He wondered how Adeline felt when she saw this memory, which also sat in a frame on the end table in their living room. Maybe they shared the same feelings about the split second captured there. It was probably the only thing they still shared.

Ben's phone vibrated in his pocket. He pulled it out, looked at the screen, and answered the call. "Hey, Joe. What's up?" he said, leaning back in his chair.

"Hey, man. I have some news. Something big. In-person kind of news." Joe sounded amped up. "Meet me at Sitzy's in like fifteen minutes. I'm busting right now."

"You know how I feel about being told that there is news and then not immediately being told said news, right?" Ben stated, but he was used to this from Joe. Joe loved the dramatic reveal. It was part of what made him a great writer.

"I'll be there in twenty minutes, man. Better be good to keep me hanging like this."

"Aight man, you'll see. I gotta deliver this in person."

Ben jotted down a note for Adeline, then thought about it, crumpled it up, and tossed it in the garbage. He grabbed his keys and sunglasses and walked out to his car.

3.

Ravioli made the epic leap from the top of Liz's dresser and landed most unceremoniously upon one of the piles of clothing that consumed the top of the bed, like a baker punching down a massive pizza dough. She was such a fat little thing, with tiny ears and a belly that rivaled Santa. She circled around a bit, and settled on a well-worn angora sweater as her bed du jour. Midday light poured in through Liz's window and highlighted the chaos currently taking place in the bedroom. It was a scene hard to behold—truly one that would send Marie Kondo and the plethora of YouTube minimalists into a tailspin. But Liz and Beth were used to this scene. It was how most of their trips began. In fact, it was how most of their Friday nights commenced ten years ago when they were still of barfly acceptable age. Now, in their mid-thirties, their nights out were mostly relegated to those horribly contrived paint-and-sip nights, or perhaps twofer margaritas and fajitas at Chili's. Both were pretty sad prospects.

Liz stared at the pile for a few seconds. "Alright, it's all out there," Liz said, and she drew in a deep breath, as if the act of removing all of her clothing items from their respective storage spaces had exhausted her like a runner after a half-marathon. "Tell me again why I needed to pull out all of my sweaters if we're going to visit the hottest place on Earth?" Realization that she had to put everything away after this debacle was through made her arch her back a little bit in premature defeat. Maybe she'd take the opportunity to finally commit to a good old-fashioned closet purge and bag up the majority and drop it off at Goodwill.

"OK, first of all it does get very cold at night in Vegas. And we all know you're going to complain continually about feeling freezing in the hotel, as you are apt to do," Beth noted. "Plus, Rav appreciates it, don't you, pretty little lady?" The cat purred with appreciation as Beth scratched her under the chin.

"I'd kind of just like to throw it all out and start over, actually. Maybe I should just pack my toothbrush and hit the mall when we arrive. That would be some sort of an adventure."

Beth laughed wryly. "Wow. Shopping in another American city. You're becoming quite the daredevil in your old age, Liz."

Liz laughed. If there was one word she would be surprised to hear herself described as it would probably be "risky." Or maybe "outdoorsy," but that wasn't really relevant here, she thought. She was certainly not a risk-taker in any aspect of life. In truth, she did not fully understand people who traipsed around the world with a backpack or flitted from job to job. She was a serial monogamist in every sense of the word. She'd had the same best friend for thirteen years, having met at the orientation for their current job the summer after college graduation. She had been with Pete, or as Beth had just yesterday taken to calling him, Window Boy, for nearly eight years. She worked at the same office since age twenty-two. Hell, she even owned and wore a pair of black pants on the regular that she'd had since college. Long term was just her thing. Truth be told, she didn't even prefer to venture to the pizza place on the other side of town and she certainly wasn't interested in trying out a new brand of underwear.

The upcoming trip to Las Vegas was not on the "things I'm excited to do and/or spend money on" list for either woman, but unfortunately, they were bound by the pesky constraints of long-term friendship; their mutual friend Jenna requested "one last slay" in Vegas before her August wedding. Liz had a problem with much of this, the least of which was the fact that Jenna actually continually referred to the trip as her "last slay," whatever the hell that meant. Liz was embarrassed to be in the room when the phrase was uttered, and Beth literally feigned the dry heaves whenever she heard it.

    This would be Jenna's second wedding, and although they were appropriately pleasant to her face, Liz and Beth were more than a bit annoyed that they had to do the whole "wedding party" thing for a second time. The bridal shower, the dress, the gift...and of course, the requisite bachelorette party. They figured by the end of the ordeal it would cost them each at least a paycheck. When Jenna announced to them, a month ago, that she was engaged again, to Jerry, a man she'd known only three months, they'd assumed that the happy couple would either elope, or at the very least have a small, casual backyard-type wedding. No such luck. Jenna was mentally preparing for and obsessing over another full-on, giant, and typically huge New York wedding. She reasoned that since Jerry hadn't been married before, and since her first wedding to Todd had only lasted two years, she was entitled to it. Beth mused to Liz that she thought they were entitled to the return of the gifts they'd given to Jenna for royal wedding number one. Jenna had called the ladies during lunchtime last week and further informed them that she was planning a "super fun" girls' long weekend over Easter weekend. In Vegas. In a suite.

    "Who the hell goes to Vegas on Easter? Seems like a conflict of interest... Jesus, Vegas... Right?" Beth joked.

"Wow, I've never known you to be a Biblical scholar, and I'd wager that you haven't been to church since Cassidy was baptized," Liz retorted, laughing.

Cassidy was now seven. Beth had to laugh at this, because it was true.

"Anyway, I made a little list of things I'd much rather spend one thousand dollars on. Don't get me wrong—Vegas was fun when we went that time, how many years ago was that? Eight?" Beth scratched at Ravioli's belly and the cat playfully bit at her wrist.

"I think nine," Liz said, as she popped a Hershey kiss into her mouth from the half-open bag on the dresser.

"But seriously, I'm thirty-five years old. I just paid eight hundred dollars for a stupid crown on that molar last month and they nearly talked me into some five-hundred-dollar tooth-whitening tray. Not to mention Ravioli has done a number on your already pretty ugly couch, so I'm just going to flat out inform you that you need a new one."

Beth grabbed a kiss herself and continued, "Not like we can do anything about it. When you get married to Idiot Window Boy someday you'd better make sure she pays up the ass. Pick an extra stupid dress for her." Beth sucked on a second kiss absently as she poked through the piles of clothes on the bed.

Liz laughed and rolled her eyes, "I'll just gloss over the idiot comment, but I promise to make her pay more than her fair share if and when that day ever comes." She lifted up a sundress that hadn't seen the light of day in a few years and dropped it back onto the pile. It wouldn't be making the trip. "I don't feel much like wasting money on this trip, either, but it'll be nice to get away for a bit, even if it's not really on our own terms."

"Yeah, whatever."

Ravioli echoed the sentiment by burying her head beneath her paws. This subject seemed to bore her. She was right. Packing was a dull business.

Liz took a look at herself in the framed mirror that hung over her dresser. She sighed. There were so many moments of introspection lately. She wouldn't describe herself as unhappy with her life. Not really, at least. Her life, on paper, looked pretty swell to the casual onlooker. She was in her mid-thirties. She had a decent job at a law office as a paralegal. It wasn't exactly the career she'd dreamed of, but isn't that the way with most people? At least that's what she told herself every time she had one of those "I need to get out of this hellhole office and away from my irrational boss" moments and started perusing for job openings. It paid well. She had great health insurance, and she had a retirement plan. These were just so unexciting, though. She'd been with Peter for what seemed like a million years, and although it was most definitely not a romance-novel-level relationship, it was alright most of the time. Her job, her relationship, even her haircut seemed to her to be the very definition of "just OK." So, she didn't expect much from this trip. It would be average, she assumed.

"Let's get really crazy on this trip. You know, break out of our comfort zones," Beth suggested, but Liz knew her well enough to know she had zero intention of doing anything more outrageous than possibly getting a little too drunk and choosing a Tina Turner song at karaoke.

Liz raised an eyebrow in a Cersei-esque move. Maybe she needed to throw caution to the wind, maybe they both did, but Beth interrupted this thought and brought her back to earth, "Yeah, let's not pack a sensible pair of sneakers and just go balls to the wall with strappy sandals." A smile slowly spread across Beth's face. Liz threw a pair of socks at her.

"Not where I thought you were going with that. I got lost in the fantasy for a second, but in all honesty, part of me really does want to use this trip...this awful, forced, expensive trip, to prove to myself that I'm not just a boring piece of shit."

"Whoa. Where did that come from? I mean, I know Peter is an unemployed lump, but I thought that was kind of your thing?"

"Jeez, that was a little harsh." It was hard to believe that Beth had liked Peter at first, but it became increasingly clear as the years went on that he wasn't exactly what one would call ambitious. He'd been unemployed for all eight years of their relationship, save for one summer when he worked as some sort of an intern, and had been leaning a bit too heavily on the artist crutch for Beth's liking. She truly felt as if her friend could score much better, and if all else failed, she was probably better off alone than with someone who, she'd been told, didn't even have enough money in his wallet for lunch at Wendy's.

In another one of those many introspective moments, Liz sighed. Lately, more than ever, she had spent many waking hours practically fantasizing about scenarios in which she did not marry Peter. She'd helped an old high school friend, Caroline, work on her dating profile after a particularly messy breakup, and she felt a little bit of misplaced jealousy every time Caroline came back and reported about some of the train-wreck dates the profile had netted her. She often thought to herself about how clean her medicine cabinet would be if Peter was out of her life, along with his stupid Pokémon electric toothbrush. What adult chooses to use a Pokémon toothbrush? The very thought of it seemed to symbolize her growing annoyance toward her fiancé.

"What's up? You look like you went off into space for a second there," Beth inquired.

Liz was quiet for a time. She was not a girl accustomed to sharing all kinds of feelings, even with her best friend, and she tended more toward self-deprecating humor when the topic turned to her relationship, but she had to compose herself this time because she felt the hot tears pool behind her brown eyes.

Beth saw the shift and sat down on the bed. "Really, what is it? You look like you just heard that someone died, and not someone who would leave you a huge inheritance."

Liz chuckled. She was relieved to have Beth bring some levity to the situation, but she also felt like these were feelings that, for a change, she needed to say aloud. Throw them out into the Universe and see what the Universe brought back to her in return.

She took a deep breath. "Beth, I'm just not really sure that I want to marry Peter."

And there it was. Just hearing the words spoken aloud felt at once a little bit like a betrayal, but even more like a cinder block had been lifted from her back. Beth hugged her.

"Well, that's because you shouldn't. I know that I trash on Pete a lot, but honestly, Elizabeth, enough already with you running the relationship and him just showing up occasionally for the free Wendy's."

Liz laughed but was also unable to keep a few tears from escaping.

"You can't commit the rest of your life to someone if you're not, like, ten thousand percent sure. And I don't say this as a catty bitch who is bitter because I'm still single and

I want some miserable company! I reserve that attitude for all of my other friends. Like Jenna. I give her and Jerry eight months, tops. But I hope you know that for you, I really and truly only want the best," Beth was getting a little misty herself, which was also out of character.

Liz knew this to be true and had known it for a while. It was just so easy to say "yes" when Pete had proposed four months ago. It had been the next logical step. But she'd felt disappointed from the start.

Like many girls, she'd been planning her wedding casually since about age four. She knew, from a young age, certain non-negotiables. Circular solitaire diamond, her dress must have straps, and per Beth's demand, the bridesmaid dresses could absolutely not be purple.

The ring that Peter had proposed with had been a family heirloom, as he obviously did not have cash to shell out for a diamond. Liz had been touched, at first, to wear his grandmother's ring, especially because she had known Beatrice before she passed away several years ago and she had been a sweet lady, but it was a marquis shape and had the wedding band soldered to the engagement ring. It did not fit into the vision of the wedding that she'd been planning lo these many years. But, as she had done with many aspects of her relationship with Peter, she'd acquiesced. She'd settled. She'd taken what she could get.

She glanced at herself in the mirror again. Although she may have gained a pound or two, or maybe even ten in the last decade, she thought she still looked pretty good. Definitely not the captain of the cheerleading squad, but a solid seven and a half if she did say so herself, on the slim side with light brown hair that hung in soft waves slightly past her shoulders. Why did she always settle, or maybe the better question was, why was she settling?

Earlier in the day she had spoken to her mother on the phone. She wanted to let her know about the upcoming trip, and also let her know that she would be having a feline house guest for four nights, but her mom always seemed to know exactly which probing questions to ask. And she didn't mince words.

"Good for you. Go and have some fun with Bethy. How does Mr. Fiancé feel about the trip?" Liz could practically hear her mother's eye roll over the phone as she said "fiancé." Her parents' opinion of Peter was no secret. He seemed like a nice enough boy—their words, not hers. He was, after all, thirty-three years old—but he just didn't bring much to the table. It was a phrase they'd used often. "Lizzie," they'd say, "you just bring so much more to the table than he does." How could she argue this point? Unemployed, living back at home...and she hadn't even revealed the window debacle to her mom, nor would she.

"If you want my advice," her mom had continued, even though there had been no indication that Liz had, "cool it with Pete, give him back that awful antique ring, and go enjoy your vacation. But you should be home for Easter dinner. Who hell plans a vacation on Easter?"

Liz had assured her mom that she and Beth had already booked an early flight home on Easter morning, and she would, of course, be there for dinner. And although she had "ok mom'd" her way through the conversation, he mother's words had hit much closer to home than she'd expected. It was a perfect storm of her mom's unsolicited advice, Beth's not-so-subtle jabs, and her own blooming seed of self-doubt.

Now, Liz turned to Beth, who was heavily engaged as the mad puppeteer in an intense sparring match between Ravioli and a dangling purse strap.

"You know what? I'm done. I think that's it. I think I'm going to end it."

Beth dropped the purse strap onto the cat's bulging abdomen and Ravioli clawed at her prey in a frenzy. Beth grabbed a handful of Liz's clothing and threw it into the air in celebration. They laughed, but those bothersome hot tears started to well up behind Liz's eyes again. She understood. She felt guilt, she felt disappointed, but she also knew that they—Beth, her parents, her intuition—spoke the truth. She couldn't sacrifice the rest of her life and her happiness because of a weird cocktail of guilt and complacency. It was about time she gave herself a second chance.

4.

Ben made the left across traffic into the Sitzy's parking lot and quickly found a spot. He saw that Joe was already seated near the window and was sipping a cup of coffee while he scrolled through his phone. Ben hopped down from the truck and trotted inside. It had been unseasonably hot all week, and today the midday sun beat down on his head like a drum. He rushed inside, as anxious for whatever news Joe was about to deliver as he was for the air-conditioned relief from the heat.

Joe waved when he saw his friend walk in the door, and Ben strode over to the table and sat down.

"So, how are you today? Can I interest you in a nice latte, or perhaps some frozen bullshitty drink thing?" Joe inquired, knowing full well that Ben was too curious and anxious for small talk.

Ben laughed, "Fuck you, man. I had to wait a full twenty-five minutes for this news thanks to goddamn LA traffic. Spill it."

"Well...what are you doing next weekend? Aside from getting a haircut, which, in case you haven't looked in a mirror, you need, because you're starting to look homeless." Joe had a coy smile on his face, which he attempted, unsuccessfully, to wrangle into fake stoicism.

"Next weekend? What do you mean? Like, Easter? Get to the point!" Ben was playful but frustrated.

Joe laughed. "OK, I've tortured you enough I suppose. So, I got a call today from Brit. Seems as though Spinky Dinky is very interested in a certain screenplay and wants to have a meeting with the two of us and Britty, next week."

Ben slammed his hand down on the table in excitement and a fairly loud "yes" escaped his lips. It must have been louder than he'd expected, because they experienced one of those moments when it seems like a record screeches to a halt and everyone turns to look at whatever ruckus has just occurred. A little kid at the next table jumped onto his mother's lap and everyone in line turned in their direction. Joe laughed at the reaction.

"Awesome, so where's the meeting? His office? Or maybe Brit can set up something at his place downtown? Any thoughts?" Ben inquired. His mind was racing a mile per minute.

"Actually, the plot thickens. It turns out that Spink—who is clearly doing well for himself by the way, remind me again why we became writers—will be spending the week at his second home in Nevada, and he would like to set up a dinner meeting with us at a location in Vegas TBA. So, pack a bag and clear your calendar."

"Vegas. Alright. Kind of a pain in the ass, but at least if it's a business dinner we can rest assured that his wife won't be making an appearance, creepy-ass lush."

Brit, the agent that Ben and Joe shared, had set up an impromptu lunch meeting with Spink to discuss the screenplay earlier in the year. When they'd arrived at the restaurant for the luncheon, Spink's wife, Vivian, had been there. Vivian's reputation had preceded her, and anyone and everyone in their circle knew that she was two things: a drinker and a grabber. Vivian had clearly been hitting the sauce a little early that day, and unfortunately Ben had been the unlucky recipient of her wandering hands. While Ben was quite positive that Spink hadn't noticed the special attention paid to him by Vivian, Ben was incredibly uncomfortable and came across as awkward and stammering in the meeting. It was devastating. Since then Brit had been trying to secure another opportunity for the boys to pitch their movie, citing excuses such as illness, family issues, apocalypse, meteor showers—Brit was willing to spin any yarn he had to in order to get this deal done. And according to Joe, he'd finally secured the meeting.

"Ok then. So, what's our plan? Are we driving? Flying?" Ben asked Joe as his mind raced. Jack was supposed to be coming home next week for his spring break, and while he hated to miss out on time with his son, this was an opportunity that he could not pass up.

"I'd say let's drive and save a few bucks, but we all know that the 'four-hour drive' might actually take more like ten, so maybe we'll bite the bullet and fly. I'm thinking leave Wednesday, come home Saturday or Sunday? Brit says the meeting will be Thursday evening, so it will give us some time to settle in, play a little craps, have a drink or whatnot," Joe suggested and shrugged casually. Ben could tell that Joe could use a night of something other than writing until nine in the evening followed by TV and takeout with his cat. A night out with his friend, without the distractions of his home life, might be a nice mental vacation for Ben as well.

"Great, get Brit on the phone. Let's do this."

Wednesday, April 12th

5.

Liz fished inside of her giant work bag, which was doubling as a carry-on tote that day, and dug out her pill box. She popped two Excedrin in her mouth and chased them with a few sips of the watered-down fountain Dr. Pepper that she'd grabbed at 7-11 when the car ride had begun almost an hour ago. It was probably the stop-and-go traffic on the Belt that had spawned the slow throb radiating from the center of her forehead, or maybe it was the whining drone of Stevie Nicks' voice as she prattled on and on (and on) about a landslide. Liz had always hated this song. What was it about, anyhow? A divorce? An actual landslide? She didn't really care to give it much more thought. She just wished it would stop, but her mom was a die-hard Fleetwood Mac fan, and she had been nice enough to take time out of her day to sit in God-forsaken Queens traffic so that Liz and Beth wouldn't have to take a taxi to Kennedy Airport. Listening to her mother's musical choices, however questionable, without complaint, was the least she could do. She said a quick prayer that the traffic and the headache would both abate soon.

The gravity of last night's conversation weighed heavily on Liz and she was a ball of mixed emotions today. She wasn't in the business of hurting anyone, least of all people about whom she cared, and so ending things with Peter had been much more difficult than she had ever anticipated. She imagined that it was much like having a family member with a terminal illness; you spent so many of their last days, weeks, or even months mourning for them, thinking that when the time came, and they really left you forever, you'd somehow be more prepared, more ready to accept the finality of it all. But then when that day came, you'd find that the loss was no less acute, no less devastating. She'd played the tape of their breakup over and over again in her head for nearly a week before she finally found the courage to just get the job done, but in the aftermath, she'd felt completely spent and exhausted, in both body and soul.

What she hadn't expected was how hurt he had looked when she'd told him and when she had tried to return his ring, tears in her eyes. She'd been so disconnected from the relationship for so long that she'd just assumed he'd also been on autopilot. What a shock it had been to realize that as apathetic as she had grown toward their union, he was clearly and totally still in love with her. It almost shook her to the point where she doubted she could end things, but in her heart she knew that she had to, at least this once, be true to herself.

He'd urged her to think it through. Hadn't they had good times? Wouldn't she miss him? The truthful answer to both of these was yes, they had, and yes, she would, but it was also true that neither of these factors outweighed the crux of the issue: she just wasn't in love with him. A future with him would mean just going through the motions, and she wasn't willing to sacrifice herself for him. Reluctantly, she'd promised that she would take a good week to reconsider, and he'd practically begged her to please hold on to the ring until she'd made her final decision. It killed her to know, in spite of her promise, that her decision had already been made, and she had no intention of turning back now.

But she'd kept the ring for now as he had entreated her to do, and had promised to do some soul searching on her trip. She looked at her naked finger now, and had no urge to resurrect the ring from its resting place, now in her travel jewelry kit at the bottom of her tote. She didn't think it was fair to have to carry the burdensome task of "soul-searching" with her on this particular trip, and her promise hung around her neck like an albatross. She'd hoped that putting twenty-five hundred miles between yesterday and tomorrow would give her some fresh perspective.

Stevie's words shook her from her reverie, Well, I've been afraid of changin', 'cause I've built my life around you... She silently cursed Stevie for cutting so close to her core, and via a song she'd truly hated, even before that particular day. She wouldn't build her life around anyone but herself going forward. She knew that for sure, Stevie be damned.

"Mrs. D, I appreciate you driving us, but this song sucks," Beth broke through Liz's silence. Liz's mom chuckled and shuffled the songs on her phone until another came through the speakers. "1-2-3" by Gloria Estefan. At least it wouldn't exacerbate Liz's broken-engagement blues. It was a nice distraction. She closed her eyes and allowed Gloria and her peppy beat to take her away to someplace where she might be enjoying a piña colada and wearing some sort of floral sundress. No broken hearts, broken promises, or sad and broken fiancés allowed in this daydream, thank you very much, Stevie Nicks, she thought.

They approached the airport, finally, and Liz's mother pulled into Terminal 5. Both girls had their small, wheeled duffel bags ready to go in the back seat, as despite what the rules may dictate, Liz's mother always insisted on dropping the two women off directly in front of the terminal. They'd have to make an incredibly speedy exit, so as to not cause a backup of traffic or draw the attention of security.

"OK, Mom! I'll give you a call as soon as we land," Liz said, as she tried to make a quick getaway out of the car. Her mom grabbed her hand, and looked her in the eye, "Lizzie, I know you better than anyone, and I know that you feel guilty right now, but you need to find your own way. Now go, get on that plane, and live a little bit. Get a little crazy. And call me when you land." She gave her a kiss on the cheek, and refused to pull the car away, even as the driver behind her leaned on the horn for what seemed like a full two minutes, until both Liz and Beth were safely behind the sliding glass doors.

6.

Ben liked to travel lightly through life, and this naturally extended to the times in his life when he was actually traveling. He reasoned that unless he'd planned on vacationing at, say, a remote cabin in rural Alaska, he could probably run to the closest Walmart and grab anything he may have forgotten. He hated the feeling that he might be leaving something behind when he was away from home, so he reasoned that the less he brought with him, the less he was responsible for keeping tabs on during his trip.

Many years ago, when he somewhat reluctantly had played the trumpet in his high school marching band, he had gone on a three-night school trip for a regional music competition near Bakersfield. Apparently, he'd had such a rip-roaring good time on the trip that it hadn't occurred to him that he should make sure that he'd repacked all of his necessities before the bus trip home. He'd stared blankly and confused as his mother inquired how he could have possibly come home with a nearly empty suitcase, having left two sweatshirts, two pair of jeans, sneakers, and all of his undergarments in the hotel dresser, as well as all of his dirty laundry someplace in the hotel room. He'd literally come home with a huge duffel bag that had been so empty compared to its condition when he'd left for the trip that it had looked like a deflated red blimp. The lesson he'd learned from this experience? Pack less stuff.

He surveyed the clothes that he had neatly arranged on the bed. Three tee shirts, two pair of shorts, and a swimsuit, plus one business casual outfit to wear for the dinner meeting. He had a small case that contained some basic toiletries and a carry-on bag that held his laptop. And that was it. Travel light. All you need is less. He wasn't one for memes or trends, but he'd seen a graphic or two online that echoed this minimalist sentiment, and he always appreciated it. As a bonus, he never had to check his luggage.

He began to roll the clothes and arrange them tightly in his small rolling suitcase when Jack walked into the room. He'd grown up so much in the last year that sometimes Ben didn't quite recognize the adult man standing before him. He looked so much like Adeline, but Ben could see his own eyes looking out at him through Jack's sometimes. He hated that his work had conflicted with Jack's visit. He knew the years were so short.

Jack fell onto the bed and propped himself up on one elbow. "Tell me again why I can't tag along on this trip, Dad? I can be your good luck charm," he teased from his position on the bed.

"Well, first of all, you're only twenty and Vegas is no place for such a sweet and innocent little boy," Ben joked back. Jack looked at him pleadingly, the way he'd looked at his dad all those years ago when he'd wanted McDonald's for dinner or an impromptu trip to Toys 'R Us. "And second, this is a business trip. Uncle Joe may have gotten you all charged up about gambling and girls, but you know that this is strictly business. Get in, get the job done, get home. We're really not going to have much downtime."

"Yeah, yeah. I don't believe for a second tha—"

Ben interrupted, "And third, I don't want you to leave your mother all alone on Easter. I know that she hasn't been back to church since Nan died, and she's probably trying to forget that there is even a holiday coming up, but I know that just having you around the house will be good for her." Adeline's mother had passed away two years ago, and although she had been an active member of St. John's

Episcopal Church for many years, after her mother died she seemed to have lost her faith. Ben had never been religious and had no real opinion on his wife's self-imposed excommunication. On the most basic level, though, he assumed that on a holiday she might be feeling sad and having another human around the house, one that she loved as opposed to one whose presence she merely tolerated, might ease that pain.

Jack grunted his concession. Today's plan involved a father/son luncheon around noon, and then Jack was going to drop Ben and Joe off at LAX for their four o'clock flight.

While their relationship had been especially frigid as of late, Ben still felt that, as her husband, he owed Adeline an explanation about the upcoming events. With a touch of naivety, Ben thought that Adeline might feel happy about the screenplay, despite the fact that she only knew about it vaguely, as Ben had ceased confiding in her years ago. He'd come home last week after his coffee date with Joe and had excitedly explained everything, but in the end she'd merely stared at him blankly, and when he had finished and had sat waiting for a positive reaction, she'd simply turned around and walked out of the room.

He hadn't mentioned it again. He wasn't sure if he'd even spoken to her again.

Jack pushed himself up and stretched. "Alright, we have a few hours so I'm going to play a little Call of Duty and shower. We'll reconverge at noon. Meeting adjourned."

Ben laughed. Jack always seemed to have an air of positivity and he admired it. He wasn't sure from whom he'd inherited this particular trait, as it wasn't one that he saw in himself, and Adeline certainly wasn't a glass-half-full type of person.

He finished neatly packing his clothes, topped them with his toiletry bag, and zipped it closed. He wheeled the suitcase over to the bedroom door, and left it in the doorway. He always felt a little chilly on flights, especially if he and Joe imbibed, which he was positive they would on this occasion, so he decided to grab a hooded sweatshirt and he placed it on top of the luggage.

He walked into the kitchen, filled a glass with water, and took his daily multivitamin. It was quiet in the kitchen and the only evidence that Adeline had been there at all was the washed coffee carafe in the dish drain. Ben wasn't sure why he expected her to be there. Her behavior didn't exactly suggest that she'd want to send him off with wishes of good luck, maybe a kiss on the cheek while she waved a pink hankie in the air as he drove away. It wasn't that the ship had sailed; this was a ship that had never even left dry dock.

He filled the carafe himself and put on a small pot of coffee. It was going to be a long day and he needed all of the help he could get. And that was when he saw it, propped up neatly on the kitchen table against the fruit bowl that sat on a place mat in the center. An unmarked manila envelope.

It never occurred to Ben what the envelope might hold, and his first instinct told him that it probably contained some documents for Jack, maybe something he'd needed to prove family income for financial aid purposes or whatnot, and he'd want to take care of that before he left this afternoon. Ben opened the envelope.

He had to read it twice, because although he should have been expecting the words for many years, he never foresaw actually reading them, especially not today. But there they were: Superior Court of California, County of Los Angeles, Request for dissolution (divorce) of marriage.

7.

The air on the Vegas Strip had cooled down considerably as the day had worn on and it felt much more bearable to Liz to amble about the city without the desert sun beating on her brow. They'd arrived around three o'clock, Vegas time, and between the long plane ride, the arduous breakup the evening before and her headache earlier that morning, when Liz first stepped out into the desert air that afternoon, she'd felt the heat slam into her like a brick wall and nausea had kicked into high gear. Thankfully, after a cool shower and a short nap in the hotel, she did feel better physically, and also felt herself starting to mend emotionally. If it wasn't for the absurd getup, she was forced to wear it might have been shaping up to be a great night. But, alas, she was decked in a bubble-gum-pink tank top that read "Bride's Matey" and featured an obnoxiously large rhinestone anchor on the back.

Her problems with her shirt were myriad. At age thirty-five, hadn't they graduated past the age of matching bridal-party shirts? Once you pass age twenty-nine, she thought people started to look at you a little side-eyed if you seemed to cling pathetically to notions that were unabashedly juvenile, and didn't this shirt clearly fit that bill? She'd argue that it did. Second, why was she a "matey" at all? Was Jenna going to have a pirate-themed wedding? Had she been an avid sailor all of these years and Liz was only just now learning this? Weren't they at that very moment in the desert, with nary a large body of water in sight? She just hoped that everyone they encountered that evening was too drunk to care to read the cursive donning her breast.

They strode at the back of the pack of ladies as they made their way up the Strip toward the Bellagio fountains. Beth got close to her ear and said, "I feel like an asshole in this shirt, but more than that, I feel horrible for Sonia." She nodded her head toward their mutual friend. What a trooper Sonia was. She'd come on this trip despite the fact that she had a four-year-old daughter and was only five months postpartum from the birth of her son. She hadn't yet lost the baby weight—it had only been a few short months—but nonetheless she had been forced to don the pink tank, nursing bra and all.

There had been other demands made by Jenna on this trip that had not been met with the same acquiescence as the attire. For example, Jenna had some sort of vision in which her pack of reluctant mateys would traipse behind her, probably in some sort of 1990s dance-movie formation if Liz knew her friend, and she certainly did. In this vision, which, again, the other ladies refused, she would call out "Vegas, bitches!" and she'd wanted the group of women to return her call with "oww oww," like a bunch of she-wolves, Liz assumed. When she'd explained this to everyone in the suite earlier, she was met with silence and confused stares.

"Yeah, I'm not doing that," Beth had finally spoken up, and there were murmured agreements among the other bridesmaids. They were all women in their mid-thirties and as far as Liz could understand, none had any interest in revisiting the silly antics in which they may have partaken fifteen years ago when they'd still believed acting like a drunken idiot had been adorable. She'd wear the shirt, but she had to put her foot down at "public group chanting" or whatever vision Jenna had for the trip.

Jenna looked both hurt and angry. She was the youngest child in her family and was clearly used to stomping her feet and getting her way. Her sister and matron of honor, Cara, was able to cut through the awkwardness with chatter about their plans for the evening.

Cara looked like a clone of her younger sister, and was nearly as demanding, but as a married woman with two preteen daughters, she must have learned the art of compromise at some point. "OK, let's talk about tonight. When I was walking across the Strip earlier to grab the Chipotle I got an invitation to an event at a bar tonight! Sounds exclusive if you ask me."

Beth shot Liz a look that was a mixture of "why are we here?" and "we both know there is nothing about that invitation that seems exclusive." But Liz and Beth had made a pact prior to leaving, or at least a cursory agreement, that they were just going to go with the flow on this trip, within reason. Yelling in the streets hadn't been on their radar when they'd talked last week, and thank goodness Beth had the wherewithal to shut that down before their other friends had been bullied into it. That being said, they'd go to whatever restaurant, club, or activity that the others had planned, they'd decided. They would try to keep the unnecessary drama to a minimum on this trip.

Beth leaned forward in what only Liz realized was mocked interest, "Super! Tell us all about it!"

Cara was happy to tell them all about it. She'd been walking across the street earlier, with Sonia, to grab a quick snack when two very well-dressed ladies had stopped them and handed them "invitations" to a "special event" tonight at the Lily Bar and Lounge at Bellagio. Obviously, they'd noticed that Cara and Sonia were a cut above, as the event at Lily Bar was, according to the invitation, or flier, as any onlooker could plainly see that it actually was, an escape from the mayhem of the clubs on the Strip. It was geared toward a slightly more mature crowd and promised a sophisticated evening of "cocktails and DJ-spun tunes." The photo on the reverse side of the invite featured some very inviting leather armchairs. It most definitely wasn't a place for drunken exploits and sloppy antics, and for this Liz was grateful. A low-key evening with a glass of wine in a big leather armchair might be what she needed.

Then she remembered the tank top. She could tell from the photo that it was not a bedazzled-pink-tank-top type of establishment. She made a mental note to shove a light cardigan into her cross-body bag tonight, even if it meant eye rolls from the Bride-to-be and her fellow mateys. It's hot. It'll ruin your look! Now we won't all match! She'd just had a feeling that her little black sweater might be her savior tonight.

As they walked in group formation to dinner, Liz patted her bag to make sure she'd neatly rolled the sweater and stuffed it inside. No one, save for Beth, had noticed this maneuver, and Liz had suggested that Beth do the same. Preserve their dignity a little bit. Beth had shrugged it off and laughed and said, "I hope to be so drunk by eleven tonight that I won't care if I'm wearing a bearskin rug."

"That's an odd garment choice to default to, but okay," Liz had laughed. Liz wanted to relax but did not have any aspirations of becoming out-of-control drunk tonight. At her age, the certainty of morning-after vomiting and beer shits heavily discouraged her from indulging in more than two drinks.

Liz and Beth had decidedly different aspirations for this trip. Beth had committed to have the Vegas experience to the fullest extent minus, perhaps, a visit to a prostitute, she'd joked. If she had to dress like a twenty-two-year-old, she'd reasoned, then for four days she was going to act like one.

Liz was merely going through the motions. She was fresh off a breakup from a relationship that had encompassed most of her adult life. She had wanted her freedom, but she wasn't quite ready to jump off the cliff yet. She needed a little mourning time herself, she'd reasoned. Yet, here she was. Glittering pink tank top, strutting down the Vegas Strip. She promised herself that she'd try to enjoy the moment, but, despite Beth's violent objections, she'd put the engagement ring back on her finger. "Just for the night," she'd said. She was not ready to field any potential suitors tonight; the ring was like armor. She felt especially confused and vulnerable and needed to put a barrier between herself and the world right now. She needed just a minute to be left alone, to figure herself out—where she'd been and where she might be going next.

8.

The nearly scalding water pelted Ben's back as the hotel bathroom filled with a dense, thick fog. The water was hot, way too hot for comfort, and Ben knew that he'd likely have a bright red back for hours, but he couldn't bring himself to turn off the water and dry off. He remembered reading A Streetcar Named Desire in college and could never understand how or why Blanche DuBois would continually take hot baths when the summertime weather in New Orleans was likely unbearably hot. Maybe he finally understood; maybe the heat dulled her senses, distracted her from the chaos of her life; singed her nerve endings and burned away all of her pain, at least for a moment.

But Ben wasn't a literary character, and a thousand gallons of scalding water couldn't alter the circumstances of the last twelve hours, let alone the last twenty-something years. He turned around and let the water rain over the top of his head, exhaled sharply, and thought about the knife that Adeline had planted firmly in his back that very morning. He wasn't in denial about the state of his marriage, but he hadn't realized that his wife obviously harbored such hatred toward him.

There was no other reason, at least not one that made sense to Ben, that would cause her to serve him with divorce papers practically moments before he left for the most important meeting of his career as a writer. They had not started on firm footing, and had grown steadily apart in the years since, but he still couldn't imagine going out of his way to hurt her purposefully, and he also couldn't think of what he might have done that would cause her to harbor these feelings toward him. No one, to his knowledge at least, had been unfaithful. There was no embezzlement of money, no abuse, no secret life with another family. There wasn't love, this he knew, but he thought, at worst, there was a festering apathy in their home.

Now he knew she hated him. And he could forgive her for that, in all honesty. He could look past her underhanded attempt to catch him off guard and ruin his potentially life-altering meeting. He could look past the fact that she'd obviously met with a lawyer and had papers drawn up without letting on. He could even forgive her for her complete lack of participation in their marriage. But there was one thing he simply could not look past: when she'd blindsided him this morning, she'd also blindsided Jack.

Like Ben, Jack knew that his parents' marriage was perfunctory at best, but, also like his father, he did not realize that there was an end in sight, at least in the eyes of his mother. Jack had assumed, his father supposed, that they'd just go on like this forever, sharing space and a grocery bill, but not much else. Jack had probably never considered that they might get divorced, even though if he searched his soul, he'd be forced to admit it was probably the best for everyone. But when Jack discovered his father, that morning, slumped in a kitchen chair pouring over an unknown document, the reality of the situation hit him like an anvil, and he'd actually cried in his father's embrace like a little boy.

Ben hadn't been able to get in contact with Adeline before he'd left, but he'd left a voice mail and a string of texts. Once he'd landed at McCarran Airport, he'd called Jack. Jack had decided to self-isolate from his mother, but he did confirm that she'd come home, and she'd tried to have a heart-to-heart with Jack about the divorce papers. Ben knew that although Jack wasn't interested in his mother's reasoning today, that he would eventually come around. Jack was pragmatic and a sensible boy, and after he'd had a few days to decompress Ben knew he'd realize that this was probably inevitable.

But it didn't excuse Adeline's behavior in Ben's eyes. What kind of mother, he thought, completely disregarded their child's feelings, even when the child is an adult? A crappy, selfish one, he thought to himself. In retrospect, he wished he had brought Jack along on this trip. He hated knowing that his son was suffering at home, and that he had somehow been the root cause of it. He let the water burn his flesh a few moments longer.

He turned the shower faucet off and began to towel dry his body. The mirror had turned an opaque grayish color, and he could barely see through the pea soup steam, but he knew that he probably looked exhausted. Or maybe defeated was a better description. He was acutely aware that he could not go into tomorrow's meeting like this. He had worked too hard and come too far to fail. He mused that his current state was a little bit like having a bout of insomnia; you realize that you must wake up at a certain time, and you also know that you must fall asleep. Yet, too often you'd feel your eyes glued to the blue black of the nighttime bedroom ceiling, counting away the minutes, and then the hours, until daylight peaks through the window and you realize that you've lost the battle.

This was a battle he would not lose. Not because of an angry soon-to-be ex-wife. Not because of deep-seated guilt, or sadness, or loss. He felt like he'd had a lifetime of almosts, a lifetime of pretty goods and too many years of "good enough to pay the bills." He was poised and ready for something better.

He heard a knock at the bathroom door, and he opened it a crack, and through the opening a cold breeze from the air-conditioned room rushed in. Joe liked to keep the room at a chilly 64 degrees.

"Just making sure you're still alive in there," Joe said tentatively. Ben knew from experience that Joe hated to see him confused and upset, as he imagined he had appeared earlier today, but he also knew that Joe wasn't the type of friend who would interfere in family matters, and he certainly wasn't the guy you went to to talk about your feelings. He was the type of friend who would take you out for a drink or two and try to help you forget whatever might be weighing on you, and Ben imagined that this was what Joe intended to do tonight; help Ben out of his funk, with a dash of self-preservation. It was, after all, Joe's project also, Ben figured.

"Yeah, I'm hanging in there. I'll be out in a minute." Ben closed the door, dried the rest of his body, and changed into a clean pair of jeans and a button-down shirt. Both had been last-minute additions to his suitcase at Joe's suggestion; apparently some of the nicer bars on the Strip didn't allow you to wear shorts, and what if Brit wanted to take them out for a celebratory drink after they sealed the deal?

He stepped into the room. Joe was sprawled across one of the beds and was absently watching an episode of Seinfeld. It was one of Ben's favorites: the one in which George breaks up with a girl he's been dating, and, at her behest, he fully unloads on her all of the things about her that have brought him to this point: her pretentious demeanor, and, Ben's all-time favorite, the way she pronounces "papier-Mache." He chuckled in spite of himself. Joe looked up at him.

"I figured we could go down to that noodle place we walked past on the way up, get something quick to eat, and then maybe check out that Lily place." He looked up at

Ben, hoping that some food and liquor might, at the very least, distract his friend from the bombshell Adeline had dropped on him earlier. He was going to do everything in his power to try and help Ben get his head back in the game because he knew that if they blew this meeting for the second time, Ben wouldn't be able to forgive himself. Joe didn't wish that type of guilt on his worst enemy, let alone his best friend.

Ben nodded and grabbed all the necessities that he might need for the evening: room key, wallet, cell phone. He tucked the room key into his wallet, and transferred it to his back pocket and, cell phone in hand, he and Joe made their way out of the room and down the hall to the elevator.

9.

Dusk had long since transitioned into evening, and as the hotel lights shone bright against the clear, black desert sky, groups of people of all ages—families, honeymooning couples, but mostly twenty- and thirty-somethings out for the night—milled about the sidewalks in search of something different, some excitement, an escape from their ordinary lives in a city that seemed, to Liz, at once wholly artificial and somehow also palpable with real, living energy. The notion of excitement, something forbidden even, was, after all, the reason so many people escaped to the Nevada city for a getaway.

For many, the evening would rate as average. They'd enjoy a few drinks, stop for a bite to eat, and then, having lost their inhibitions, perhaps grow a little bit careless at the roulette table. They'd go home after their trip was long over and claim that the allure of Las Vegas was fictitious, nothing more than fancy advertising. I lost my shirt and gained five pounds. But for so many, Vegas was an oasis in the desert of a life of boredom. Their one best chance to feel a little wild, a little bit less like themselves.

Liz and Beth hung at the back of one such group as they navigated their way from Margaritaville across the Strip to Bellagio. Safely out of earshot from the bridal party, Beth spoke freely, partly because the rest of the women were several strides ahead, but mostly because they'd all had quite a bit to drink while they'd eaten dinner. Beth rarely bit her tongue under normal circumstances, but if you gave her a few drinks, there was really no holding her back.

She pointed her finger, arm completely stretched outright, toward Jenna and the other women. "Look at these idiots. They're stopping to take a picture in front of a urinal," Beth spoke, slowly and carefully so as to mask her level of inebriation. Liz didn't know what she was talking about. She saw Jenna wave the two of them forward, to pose for a photo, but they were standing in front of the entrance to the Flamingo Hotel and Liz certainly didn't notice anything that could be mistaken for a urinal.

"Wow, you are tanked. First of all, that's a door. Second, why the hell would there be a urinal just out on the street?" Liz had also imbibed, but substantially less. If Jenna and the other women were at a level eight on the drunk scale, and Beth was at a six and rounding the corner toward a seven, then Liz was safely pulling up the rear at a cool level four. She felt loose, but not out of control. She intended to maintain this level of buzz and nothing more, because the only thing worse than having a hangover was having a hangover in a suite with six other chatty people, all of whom were sharing two bathrooms.

They posed for the requisite photograph and fell back a few strides again. Beth stopped short and dramatically grabbed Liz by both shoulders. "List-sin to me," Beth said carefully, but her pronunciation belied her drunkenness, "We…we are just going to go into that leather chair bar tonight and we are going to forget Peter and Brendan and you know…" she trailed off.

"Isn't his name Brandon?" Liz asked. She doubted herself for a second.

Beth shushed her and mushed her index finger over Liz's lips. Liz couldn't help but laugh. She couldn't remember the last time she'd seen her friend nearly losing control like this. Beth was a fun drunk, though, so Liz knew that if nothing else, there would be laughs tonight.

"Brendon or whatever. Tonight, we're single classy ladies, so please take off that ugly ass ring, please!"

Liz glanced at her finger for a moment, "Nah. Tonight I just want to have a drink, dance with the girls, and unwind. The last thing I need is some creep approaching me. Or anyone, really. Just not in the mood for that."

Beth shrugged and leaned in way too close for comfort and sang, off key, in Liz's ear, "I've got a lovely bunch of coconuts..." and then shimmied her boobs back and forth.

Liz laughed. It was going to be a long night.

* * *

THEY STEPPED INTO the Lily Bar and Lounge at Bellagio and Liz was relieved to notice that although the atmosphere was much less "clubby" than most of the nightlife spots on the Strip, there was a decent-size crowd of mostly thirty- and forty-somethings. She was further relieved to notice that there were plenty of other women in glittery tank tops. She had thrown on her cardigan before entering anyhow, because it was chilly in the hotel, but she was glad that her group wouldn't stick out like a sore thumb.

The lounge had an amber glow and Liz appreciated the ambiance. Something about the combination of the soft lighting, the rich leather textures throughout and the lightly back-lit shelves of liquor, backed by subtle mirrors, reminded her of old money; she had a fleeting thought about The Great Gatsby, a book that she was loathe to have pop into her head, as it was not one of her favorites, but it had always exemplified to her the notion of wealth, especially because it was supposed to take place so near to where she had grown up. The amber liquors reminded her of a time when she had been so anxious to appear sophisticated at a bar in her early twenties that she'd ordered a Manhattan assuming, she guessed, that it would taste like caramel based solely on the color and the fact that it contained a maraschino cherry. She'd nearly gagged when she'd taken a sip, never having thought for a second that the brown concoction was mostly whiskey and carried the drink around for a half hour before finally deciding to abandon it in the ladies' room on the sink while no one was watching.

She smiled at the memory of more innocent days. She had a warm, good feeling rush over her, like a breeze on a cool spring evening. It made her shiver for a second, like she'd had a chill, but she wasn't cold anymore, thanks to her sweater. She welcomed the feeling. It had been such a tough few day, and truth be told the last few months hadn't been stellar, either. She thought to herself that it was a little like when you're just in a terrible mood for no good reason, and you can't seem to shake it, but the opposite. She just felt like the veil had been lifted and good things were on the way. It was about time.

Beth grabbed two seats near a table, and Liz went to the bar to order two drinks. She joined her friend a few moments later, with a vodka and cranberry for Beth, and a rum and Diet Coke for herself.

"Cheers, lady. To panties!" Liz smiled at her friend.

"Oh, you bitch," Beth said, but clinked glasses anyway. Liz surveyed the bar. It was not exactly the place she expected that they'd end up on night one of Jenna's epic "last slay," but she was pleasantly surprised. She'd envisioned a loud club, packed to the gills with sweaty twenty-five-year-olds, grinding and flailing all over the dance floor in a display that they probably thought was sexy and fun, but to the sober onlooker just looked pathetic; she imagined deafening music with a thumping rhythm so forceful that it might alter your body's natural heartbeat. Thank God for small victories. She could actually hear herself speak, let alone think.

Beth suddenly grabbed her head by both ears and pointed it toward the left corner of the room. "Oh. My. God. Is that Paul? Tell me that it isn't Paul." Paul had been Beth's on-again, off-again boyfriend in their mid-twenties, and their final breakup had been... Well, to be honest, Liz wasn't sure whether they had ever officially broken up. She squinted her eyes. That most definitely was not Paul, but she did see the similarity: just shy of six feet tall, a little soft in the center, probably enjoys a burger and a beer more often than he should, but who was she to judge? She once ate Taco Bell every day for lunch one summer during her college years.

"It's not Paul, but I definitely see a resemblance," Liz noted. She took a sip of her drink.

Beth downed hers. "Well, I'm going to pick up with this guy where Paul and I left off. You mind?"

"Godspeed, Bethy," Liz said, and clinked her drink with Beth's newly empty glass. Before Beth walked off to "reconnect" with not-Paul, they reviewed some of their "rules" from their barhopping days of yore. Purse on the crook of the right elbow was the universal signal for "come and rescue me immediately" and, come what may, neither would let the other leave with a stranger. The two simple rules hadn't led them astray thus far, and as for Liz, she had no intention of letting her friend leave this club in a strange city with a strange man, even if he was a dead ringer for good old Paul.

Liz settled into a seat at the far end of the bar. She wanted to keep Beth within eye shot, just in case she maneuvered her bag onto her arm and wanted to hide in plain sight. She was more in the mood to people watch than she was to force herself through a conversation with a stranger.

She took out her phone and scrolled a bit through the photos that they'd taken so far on the trip while she sipped slowly from her glass. For the life of her she could not understand, looking at the photo now, what on Earth Beth had mistaken for a urinal in the group photo they'd taken earlier, and she must have laughed out loud at the thought.

"What's so funny?" Her private reverie was interrupted, and she looked up. She felt a pair of dark brown, almost black, eyes, staring hard at her. She wasn't sure how she didn't feel his gaze before he'd spoken, because it seemed evident that he had been eyeing her for a while and had seen an opportunity to make a move.

Liz didn't make a habit of behaving rudely without cause, and she smiled and said, "Just looking at some photographs." She made sure that she placed her left hand over her right wrist so that the ring on her finger was noticeable. A wedding band on her left hand should be a deterrent, she presumed.

"I'd sure love to take a look at some pictures, especially if they feature your sexy smile." He looked her up and down. She inwardly groaned. He had one too many buttons opened on his shirt, and he wore a toupee that was questionable at best. His gaze felt like an X-ray. She pushed her purse onto her right arm in a rapid, exaggerated gesture, but she could see that Beth was heavily involved in conversation with fake Paul, and hadn't given Liz a second thought.

"Thank you, but I'm going to finish my drink and meet up with my friends in a few."

He was undeterred. He moved closer to her and she could smell the liquor and cigarettes on his breath. She stood up off of the stool and tried to back away but realized that in her initial quest for some solitude she had seated herself near the corner and she was all but trapped with this horrible-haired would-be predator.

"Hey, guy, no respect for the ring?" a voice came from behind Toupee Guy and placed a heavy hand on his shoulder. Toupee Guy jumped back, startled, and Liz noticed the source of the voice; he was a nice-looking guy, she thought; his dark hair had some gray at the temples, and it was a little unkempt for her taste, but he was well dressed and he had hazel-colored eyes that seemed friendly. He gave her wide eyes and a quick wink, the universal signal, she thought, for "play along, I'm here to help you."

He held up his left hand as well, which revealed a simple silver wedding band. Toupee Man must have assumed that this newcomer was obviously Liz's husband and stammered, "Sorry, man, I'm sorry, I didn't realize…" and skulked away, defeated.

Liz was incredibly grateful but confused. Who was this evidently married guy out at a bar in Las Vegas, and why did he care enough to even step in? Maybe she should be more concerned about him than Toupee Guy; he was, after all, married according to his left hand. She shouldn't have been on his radar, she thought to herself. She must have looked utterly perplexed and a little skeptical. "That guy looked like he was making some unwanted advances." He glanced toward the ring and back at her. "I saw the ring and I figured I could help you out. My good deed for the day. I hope I didn't overstep." He gave a crooked smile.

She wasn't sure how to respond. "Thank you," she said. "I'm Liz," and extended her right hand.

"Nice to meet you, Liz. I'm Ben."

10.

Ben and Joe arrived at the Lily Bar and Lounge around nine o'clock, before the crowd started to thicken. They secured seats on one of the small couches and sat back to enjoy a few drinks. Ben glanced around. The lighting was low, the ambient noise of the room wasn't more than, at least at that early hour, a low hum, and the atmosphere was what he would have described as mellow. It was warm and settling into the soft leather seat he felt his body relax for the first time in the last twenty-four hours. Ben had to admit that he actually felt glad to be out and about in the world. Both guys had agreed that they didn't particularly want to make it a late night as they'd had such a long day, and tomorrow they wanted to be on their "A" game. A good night's sleep was imperative.

Joe had excused himself to use the restroom. Ben knew that he was most likely also taking a moment to call home to check on Jennifer. Joe would never admit this fact to Ben, but Ben knew that Joe had some anxiety leaving her when they went on short trips and checked in on her often. Jennifer was Joe's eight-year-old tabby. She had shown up on his doorstep as a skinny kitten years ago when Joe had been going through a tough time: a recent breakup in combination with a dry spell at work and the accompanying stress over money. Joe had taken her, a scrawny little thing, into his house that day and she'd been his baby ever since. Ben had thought it was unusual that Joe had chosen to name the cat after the woman who had so recently broken his heart, but he figured that everyone works through grief in their own way. Since that day, Jennifer had been the apple of Joe's eye. He doted on that cat the way a mother dotes on her firstborn child. Joe's parents took care of his beloved while he was away, and they indulged all of his phone calls. It was the closest thing they had to a grandchild, Ben assumed; Joe was perpetually single and his younger brother, Jonathan, lived across the country in New York and often traveled months at a time for business.

When Joe exited the room, Ben looked up and toward the bar. It was then that he noticed the woman's body language, leaning so far away from the man talking at her that she looked like she might fall off of the bar stool. He could tell it was not a mutual conversation. He saw her awkward smile, probably an attempt to gently let the guy down. He hoped the guy would just walk away. When the man grabbed for her phone the hair on the back of Ben's neck stood up and he rose from his seat to walk over. Then, the lights from above bounced off of the wedding ring on her left hand, and he saw his unique opportunity. Ben was by no means an Alpha male, but he felt compelled to step in this time. She was obviously a married woman, and he had always been disgusted by people who showed no respect for the institution of marriage. He may have had a difficult relationship with his wife, but he'd never once strayed.

He got up and walked over to where they sat at the far end of the bar. He placed a hand on the man's shoulder, making sure to apply some pressure on his shoulder blade. He truly hated the altercation, and his heart was beating quickly, but he knew he had the perfect weapon to neutralize this particular scenario: his own wedding band, still on his finger, yet devoid of its meaning, he supposed. As the words fell from his lips, he hoped that his rescue mission would be well received, and that he wasn't just making an ass out of himself.

Then, as quickly as the inclination had come over him a minute before to inject himself into this scene, it was over. The man had slid away like a defeated bully on an elementary school playground, and he'd introduced himself to the woman seated at the bar.

"Well, Ben, that was certainly some sly ring work you had there. Can I buy you a drink to thank you?" Liz said amiably. She had kind eyes, and he could tell she wasn't flirting with him; she just seemed nice. Plus, she truly did seem thankful to be rid of the unwanted attention.

Ben smiled kindly. He saw Joe making his way back from the bathroom and walking toward him at the bar. "I appreciate that but as you can see, I'm still nearly full." He held up the drink that he'd been nursing for a half hour. He certainly did not want her to think he had driven away the other man just to stake a claim on her himself.

Joe joined them at the bar, obviously confused. He stretched out his hand toward Liz, "Good evening to you," he said in a mock British accent, "I'm Joseph." Ben looked at him quizzically and laughed. "Actually, he goes by Joe and he couldn't be less British, as you can probably glean from his horrible attempt at an accent." They all laughed easily, as if they hadn't been strangers mere moments ago.

"Well, Joe...Joseph, it's nice to meet you both. And you also, Ben," Liz said. She spied Beth across the room scanning the bar, obviously looking for her wing man. Liz waved, and Beth cupped her hand opened and closed to call her over. She must have been hitting it off with faux-Paul and wanted Liz to join in the fun. Joe and Ben saw the exchange.

"I think you're being summoned," Ben said to Liz.

"I think you're right. I'd better get over there. Honestly, you were a lifesaver tonight. I can't thank you enough," Liz said, as she slipped her purse over her left shoulder.

Joe looked at his friend sideways, and then back at Liz, confused at the whole interaction. She held out her hand to Ben for a handshake and he accepted. "I'll see you around, Ben. So nice to have met you, Joseph." She winked and walked across the room.

11.

"What the hell was that?" Joe finally asked when Liz was out of earshot. Ben chuckled. "You will never guess what just transpired," Ben said, and then recounted the rest of the story: the man with unwanted advances, her wedding band, him swooping in to save a stranger from God knows what might have happened next. Joe sat, mouth agape. "I left to take a piss for five minutes and you have some sort of weird-ass fairy-tale encounter. Figures!"

They made their way back to the couch. "She was pretty. You should have gotten her number," Joe said once they were seated.

Ben looked at him incredulously, "She's clearly married! Plus, I mean technically, so am I." Although he knew it was over, Ben hadn't signed the papers that morning. He hadn't even read through them. He figured that it was best to meet with his own lawyer and figure out his next move. He'd already put in a call to his entertainment lawyer, Carol Winkler, to inquire if she had a colleague in the field whom she might recommend. He certainly didn't have a divorce lawyer on his speed dial.

Joe shrugged. "Her friend looked cute." Ben ignored him and downed the rest of his drink. He pulled out his phone and sent a text to Jack. He hoped that his son had gone out with some friends tonight and gotten his mind off of the divorce.

"He's going to be OK, you know. He's a smart kid," Joe said, possibly seeing the worry on Ben's face, or maybe just knowing, as a concerned friend, what was probably going on in Ben's inner monologue that day.

"Yeah, I know. But I still worry. I'll always worry. Truth be told I even—" His sentence was interrupted by the approach of three women. They looked mildly tousled, like they'd just walked through some sort of a wind tunnel. Ben wondered if their hair looked that way on purpose, some type of undone style that was supposed to look sexy. He thought it just looked, well, like they'd been caught in a hurricane or something, maybe one of those attractions that mimicked what it felt like to free fall by propelling a person up into the air with some sort of turbine. He didn't particularly think it was a good look.

The blonde in the group started in, "Oh my GOD, it is you. I thought so!" and sat down right between Ben and Joe, despite the fact that there really wasn't enough room between them for a magazine, let alone a woman's rear end. The guys did occasionally draw some attention when they were out and about, but it had been a while since either of them had been approached. Their show had a small following, and it seemed that most of their fan base was on the "younger side," meaning that they were likely too young to legally enter a bar. These women were clearly in their early forties, maybe a tad older. Botox and makeup made it so hard to tell these days, he thought.

She was so close to his face that he could smell the wine on her breath. Probably rosé, he thought to himself. He knew the type. All three ladies smelled strongly like competing perfumes; all three had fake lashes so thick that Ben thought they looked like the business end of a kitchen broom. The one who had wedged herself between the two men had on a leopard-print top and her breasts were pushed up high and pressed together like two rolls placed too close on a baking sheet that had met and been forced to kiss mid bake in a hot oven. The other two women sat down on either side of the guys. Although they were fairly petite, Ben felt ambushed, or maybe more like a feral cat backed into a cage.

Joe caught his eye. His look said something like "I'm too tired for this tonight" and Ben nodded and rolled his eyes. It was true. He was in no mood for this, but he also knew that it was in poor taste to alienate a fan, even if she was at least one bottle of wine in the bag already. He forced himself to make small talk as he sat stiffly on the couch. What brings you ladies to Las Vegas? Where are you from?

He feigned interest and looked down at his empty glass. He shook the ice around at the bottom and tried to sip out some of the melted ice. He could have used another drink to get him through this conversation, he thought to himself. He glanced at his watch. Ten thirty. The blonde saw him and asked, "Have somewhere else to be, sweetie?" as she leaned toward him, brushing his upper arm with her bosom. It was such a presumptuous move and it made him groan inwardly. He could think of about a thousand unappealing places that he'd rather be at that very moment, and only a short hour ago he had felt glad to be out for the evening.

He stammered out an answer, "Actually, tomorrow we have a—" but he was unable to finish, as he was interrupted by a voice from behind him.

"Sweetheart, there you are! I have been looking all over for you. I grabbed you another drink!" It was Liz, along with her friend from across the room. She winked at him, almost deviously. Apparently, she must have enjoyed their theatrical endeavor earlier and saw an opportunity to return the favor. She handed him the drink, which turned out to merely be a coke, but he didn't care. He was ecstatic to have been thrown a lifesaver.

"Thank you, dear. I was just about to mention to these lovely ladies, fans of the show, mind you, that I was about to come and look for you and then head back to the, uh, room for the night." He realized now that Liz probably had no idea what he meant by "the show" but she didn't let on her confusion or surprise. She played the role like a pro.

She extended a hand to the blonde, who now looked visibly uncomfortable at her position next to Ben. "Hi, I'm Liz. I didn't catch your name?"

"Sandra. Nice to meet you." Sandra stood up and adjusted her top so that her cleavage wasn't on full display. It was obviously not how she expected this part of her evening to go. "It was nice to meet you all, but maybe it's best if we take off. Ladies, ready?" She looked at her friends. They all looked a little taken aback. They said goodbye and then moved back to the bar to order another round for themselves.

* * *

LIZ TURNED TO BEN, "Well, now we're even." She smiled. Just two kindred spirits stumbling upon a mutually beneficial situation tonight that turned out to be moderately entertaining in retrospect.

"Mind if I sit for a minute? My feet are pretty tired. Actually, they're pretty...bleeding." Her smile was easy and affable. Ben made room for her on the couch, and she sat back. "I'm not used to these new sandals, and my poor toes are paying the price." She slipped them off slightly and revealed purple indentations where the straps had dug into her flesh. Liz noticed that Ben averted his eyes. "I bet this makes you feel incredibly grateful for your socks," Liz quipped.

"That was some pretty fantastic acting right there," Joe said to her. She laughed, grateful that her feet were no longer the subject of conversation.

"Well, I did go to theater camp one summer in middle school. I'm glad to see my parents' five-hundred-dollar investment paid off."

Beth plopped down on one of the chairs that sat adjacent to the couch. Liz could tell that Beth's buzz was beginning to wear off, and she started to look incredibly sleepy. Friendly, but sleepy. Beth introduced herself to Ben and Joe and turned to Liz. "The rest of them are going back to the hotel, but I'm fricking hungry. I need fries. Can we get fries please?"

At the mention of fries Liz felt her stomach grumble. She could definitely use some fried food. "You guys want to come? Big plate of fries, my treat," she said. She felt like a five-dollar plate of food was the least she could do.

Ben looked at Joe and shrugged, "You want to go? I could eat. And I'm kind of done with this place."

"Sure, why not." Joe turned his attention to Liz. "Are you offering to pay for our fries because you've seen Ben's overgrown hair and you think he might be homeless? Because we fully accept charity of the food variety," Joe said, as he stood up.

Beth threw her head back in a big laugh. Probably bigger than typical because she still had some alcohol in her system. "It could use a trim," she said, and pointed at his hair. Liz considered it. It was a little longer than she was used to, but whoever Ben happened to be, he wore it well. He looked almost like he'd had some life experiences that made him care less about trivial things like haircuts, like it was the last thing he had time to deal with right now. Or maybe he just liked it that way, what did she know? She made a mental note to stop overthinking things. It was exhausting.

She smirked. She locked arms with Beth. "I'm abstaining from judgment on the hair, as I've only known you both for the balance of fifteen sentences. Let's go eat."

The left the bar and Liz could feel the eyes of the big-cleavage blonde woman burn holes into her back like two lasers as they exited.

12.

"So, you mentioned that those women were fans of a show. What show were you talking about? Are you guys actors?" Beth asked as she dipped a well-done fry in a little mound of salt that she'd built on her plate. Liz was intimately familiar with Beth's french-fry-eating habits, and, yet every time she watched her pop a fry into her mouth that was positively coated in salt she shivered a little bit, as if she, herself, had bitten into something incredibly sour. Beth was also the only person that Liz had ever met who ate a hot pretzel without rubbing off even one rock of salt. Just thinking about it made her tongue burn.

Joe took a sip of his root beer. "Ehh, not really. We wrote a scripted reality show, and we were also part of the cast." Beth raised an eyebrow and Joe laughed. "Yeah, I know. Lowest common denominator, but it paid the bills. Apparently both men and women in the eighteen-to-twenty-five age group just can't get enough casual sex, infidelity, and trash in general. Who knew?" He paused for a second and then added, "Well, actually I guess they did have enough, because it wasn't renewed for a third season."

"As you can see, we value our dignity quite highly," Ben added. They all laughed. "How about you guys?" he asked. "What brings you ladies to Las Vegas?" He looked back and forth between Liz and Beth. Beth looked at Liz and laughed. "What?" he asked. "Was it something I said?"

"Well, Liz, I guess we don't look as good as we thought," Beth said to her friend, laughing.

"Jeez, what did I say?" Ben asked, and Liz could tell he was genuinely concerned that he may have insulted them.

"I'm kidding with you, but it's clear you haven't been looking at our racks, because if you had been, you'd realize that we are, in fact, the Bride's Mateys," Beth said, and gestured to her bedazzled top. Ben was at a loss for words, it seemed.

Joe jumped in to diffuse the situation, which was more comical than awkward. "Well, Ben here has only been single for less than twelve hours so he's highly out of practice, and, as for me, I only hold women in the highest regard and would never objectify one." Ben took an ice cube and put it down the back of Joe's shirt.

"Twelve hours. That feels like a story," Liz said, but realized, fresh off a breakup herself, that it probably wasn't a subject that Ben was apt to discuss with a bunch of strangers over a plate of fries at a Denny's on the Strip. Before she could think it through, she followed it up with, "I'm seventy-two hours single myself." She immediately felt stupid when she thought about the fact that she was still wearing an engagement ring, no, a wedding band on her finger. She wished that she could take back the last sixty seconds of her life. She looked at her friend for help, wide-eyed.

Beth threw her a lifeline, "So, tell us more about this reality show." There was a collective sigh of relief, as the topic of conversation reverted back to the superficial. It just felt more appropriate, Liz thought, to chat about television with a group of strangers than to delve into any of their personal lives.

* * *

THE LATE-NIGHT FRIES turned into later-night coffee, and when they'd all realized that it was nearly one o'clock in the morning the men walked the ladies back to the lobby of their hotel. Although it was still pretty crowded, Ben and Joe felt better seeing the women to the door. Liz thought it was a little old-fashioned, but also appreciated the sentiment. They had learned a lot about each other in a few short hours; the guys had a big meeting the following day and were hoping to have their screenplay produced; the ladies were here to see their friend off on her second, and hopefully final, marriage.

When they arrived at the front of Treasure Island, the hotel at which the women were staying, Liz, for the second time that evening, held out her hand to Ben. "This was really an entertaining night, and now I feel like I have a fun story to bring home with me. Seriously, I hope your meeting goes well tomorrow. I have a good feeling about it."

Joe interjected, "We hope so."

Ben thanked her, they all said a final goodbye, and with that, the two duos went their separate ways.

"Weirdest night ever," Beth said as they traversed the lobby, past the concierge, and headed toward the elevators.

Liz laughed. "I know. Weird, but it kind of got me out of my funk, playing a role like that. I feel like now I can take off this ring and just enjoy the rest of my vacation." Beth was uncharacteristically quiet as they rode up the elevator. "What is it?" Liz asked, curiously, as she held tightly onto the rail behind her back.

"Well, at first, I felt a little like I was, oh, I don't know...vibing with Joe? And he was kind of cute and all, but first he got up from the table to call and check on Jennifer and then, like...wasn't it weird that an hour into hanging out he pulls out his phone and said to his friend, 'Hey look at this pic of Jennifer that I just got,' like, couldn't that have waited? Like, is Jennifer just sitting at home sending him pictures? Slut. And why does his friend even care?" She sounded downright angry. Liz hadn't even realized that Beth was interested in Joe. And while she did think it was odd that he brought up Jennifer by name more than once to his friend, who she assumed would have known Jennifer, she figured maybe it was just a new relationship and he was excited. She put her arm around Beth, "This is only day one. I'm sure tomorrow we'll run into lots of guys who are all impervious to the allure of all kinds of Jennifers."

Beth laughed. "You're right. I don't know why I'm so perturbed. I only talked to the guy for a few hours. Tomorrow is a new day. Different Joes, less Jennifers."

They walked down the hallway to their suite, and quietly let themselves in, as everyone else was already asleep.

13.

Ben and Joe walked back to Bellagio after leaving the women in front of their hotel. It was an unusual evening, and they were both quiet for a time, each reviewing inwardly the events of the past few hours.

"I think Beth was checking you out, man," Ben said to Joe as they strolled through the somewhat thinning crowd, breaking through the silence.

"Nah, I didn't get that feeling at all. And I can always tell. Fun night, though."

"Yeah, it definitely took the edge off a little. Made me forget shit for a bit, pretending to be someone else for a second," Ben said, and chuckled almost wistfully. He felt like he needed a subject change, because he had to put the events of tonight behind him. It had been kind of fun to playact at the bar for a little while but now, later in the night, he realized that the issues of yesterday and tomorrow still loomed large. "So, how's the cat? She's hanging in there without you?" Ben knew Joe was always up for chatter about Jennifer.

Joe looked at the wallpaper on his phone at the mention of his beloved feline. "Oh, she's a little cutie. Mom said she's eating fine and she spent all day sleeping on the bathroom floor."

"Oh, the heated tile one? How do they like that? Do think they it was worth the money? I'd hoped this rental would have had it, but no luck."

"Yeah, it's pretty awesome actually. I took a shower there last week after a run and my feet were very pleased."

Ben nodded. They didn't talk for the rest of the walk to the hotel, or the ascent to their room. Maybe they'd reached their small talk limit for the night. As they walked down the hallway to the room they had decided to share, Ben said, "You know what? I think I might get up early-ish and actually go to the gym. Get out a little frustration, prep myself for the meeting or whatnot."

"Well, good for you. I plan on not doing that."

Ben laughed. He probably wouldn't, either, but now, as the clocked creeped toward two in the morning, he felt like tomorrow might be a new day. A clean slate; an hour of sweat might just usher in a new era for him. He vowed to leave the curtains open and let the morning sun decide for him.

14.

It was nearly six in the morning and the sun hadn't even begun to make its debut over the eastern horizon when Ben was startled out of a deep sleep by the shrill ring of his cell phone. He looked at the large red numbers on the alarm clock that rested on the bedside table next to him. 5:54. Four hours wasn't nearly enough sleep. He heard Joe stir in the other bed.

"What the hell, man?" Joe said and threw the pillow over his head. He obviously thought it was the alarm or an errant wake-up call.

Ben looked at the phone and the caller ID startled him awake. It was Brit. His heart sank. There weren't many reasons why Brit would be calling him this early in the morning, and none of them, to his knowledge, were good ones. The meeting is canceled, he thought to himself, and began to feel nausea clench his insides. All of the time he and Joe had put into the script, and all of the years that he'd been molding the plot in his mind. Reluctantly, he took the call.

"Hey," he said, still partially asleep.

"Ben. You know I would never call you this early if it wasn't important." Ben felt his heart drop.

"It's off, isn't it?" Ben asked, crestfallen.

"No no, not that. But, well, actually, I'm not sure how to put this. The meeting is still on, but the venue has changed, sort of." Brit sounded so vague. Ben thought that a change of venue was more of a ten a.m. phone call. What was so emergent about a change of location? Maybe he was missing something, as he was severely lacking sleep.

"Uh, OK. So, what's the change?" Ben asked. He wanted to hear the location change and then force himself back to sleep for another four hours.

Brit hesitated. Ben could tell that he was reluctant to reveal whatever information had been the purpose of the phone call. "Alright, I'm just going to come out with it. Spink is still very interested, and we will still be meeting him for dinner, tonight, but at eight o'clock..." Brit stopped speaking, but Ben felt like there must be more information about to spill forth.

"Alright, so a little bit later. I feel like you're holding back something big, though."

And then Brit let it out like a deluge, "Well, the dinner meeting is going to take place at his house in Summerlin North. It's close by, so I'll send a car for you guys. But, you know."

Ben did know. Now that the meeting had been moved to Spink's home it was a safe bet to assume his wife would be in attendance. Ben's nausea did not abate.

Brit tried to soften the blow a bit. "Is there any chance you can get the wife to come along? Spink mentioned that spouses would be welcome, and I imagine her presence would throw cold water on the Lady Spink."

Ben realized Brit had no idea about the divorce. How could he? Ben hadn't really even admitted it to himself yet, and Brit didn't know too many intimate details of his personal life anyway. He'd never even met Adeline. He probably didn't even know her name. Ben liked to keep a little distance between work and pleasure, although if he searched his soul, which he was not apt to do, he would probably have to admit that he derived more pleasure from his work life than his personal life. "Nah, she won't be able to make it. I'll just have to put up my best defenses solo. Not going to blow this one." Ben's head was spinning. On the one hand, he refused to blow this opportunity a second time. On the other hand, Vivian Spink was relentless.

"Alright, guy. I'll send a car for you boys tonight. Be downstairs around 7:15. You got this!" Brit said, and Ben hung up the phone. He hated that phrase, and he certainly wasn't sure that he had this. Joe had awoken and saw Ben's face.

"What was that?" he asked. Ben debriefed him, and Joe could hear the defeat in his voice. Then, despite the early hour and their shared lack of appropriate rest, Ben watched as Joe's face morphed from disappointed, to pensive, to mischievous. Ben could almost see the cartoon light bulb appear above his head. Joe was often full of fun, cockamamie ideas but he usually relegated them to the page, where they were fruitful and didn't have the outcome of their collective lives hanging in the balance.

"What? You're up to something," Ben said.

Joe was up to something. "OK, hear me out..." Joe began. Neither man would be falling back asleep that morning.

* * *

THE LOBBY AT TREASURE Island was bright and crowded, with elaborate coffered ceilings and a tile floor that was meant to look like an expansive treasure map. It was large, and with the number of people milling around even at nine in the morning, Ben thought that running into Liz, or her friend Beth, was akin to finding the metaphorical needle in a haystack. But the truth was, Ben didn't have a better plan, so he listened to Joe with rapt attention, and then after some convincing agreed that, yes, this might work. Take that leap and hope for the best, or die trying, he thought to himself.

"Hear me out..." Joe had begun early that morning, and carefully laid out a relatively simple scenario. They'd find Liz, which might prove to be the hardest part, they would ask her to reprise her role of unnamed wife for one dinner, that very night, and then they would be indebted to her forever. Or at least maybe take her and her friend out for a nice celebratory lunch the next day, or maybe drinks. Those were details that could be worked out later. Ben wanted her to feel more like an improv actress and less like a prostitute.

Ben hated that his life hinged on a silly scenario like the one last night, but he also had to admit that he didn't have a better idea. The best way, as Brit had even mentioned, to diffuse Vivian Spink was to bring some sand to the beach. As Spink had no idea what Ben's actual wife looked like, he supposed that any old wife would do. There really were just so many variables, and he hated it. "Remember. It's just one dinner. She just has to be present. It's not as if she has to turn out an Oscar-winning performance. Just keep it simple."

And so, there they were. Staking out the lobby of the hotel because as of last night there was really no good reason for any of them to have exchanged phone numbers. It was accidentally revealed that the breakups of both Ben and Liz were hot off the presses, and Joe was too preoccupied with his pet, Ben thought, to realize that maybe, just maybe, Liz's friend Beth had shown some interest in him.

After some debate, they had settled on nine o'clock in the morning as arrival time; they assumed that the women, having had a late night also, were unlikely to be up and at 'em after at least, they calculated, seven hours of sleep. Ben thought, though, that it was feasible that the women might not be down for hours, if at all today. They could have opted to visit the spa, the gym, the pool, the casino—all of which would not cause them to visit the lobby. For all Ben and Joe knew, the women went back out after they walked them to the hotel and might not yet have even returned. Ben mentally crossed that off the list, as he just didn't get the impression that they were "all-nighter" kind of girls. But all of the other options were very viable, he thought, as he sipped his coffee and broke off a piece of a bear claw. Nonetheless they'd cleared their calendar for the day, which was actually pretty empty anyhow, and set up camp in the lobby, hoping that luck would be a lady that morning, or at least sometime today before 7:15 p.m.

* * *

THE SUITE WAS ABUZZ with chatter and Liz found herself unable to tune out the noise anymore, so she gave in and awoke. She glanced at her phone, which lay on the nightstand next to the bed. It was nine. She wasn't hungover, but last night was a bit of a whirlwind and she was glad she'd at least remembered to charge her phone. She could have used another hour or two of sleep, she thought. She looked at the other side of the bed to her friend. She had no idea how, but Beth was able to sleep through the chaos of Operation: Plan Day Two of Jenna's Last Slay. She envied her for a minute, and then pressed the ball of her foot against Beth's rear end. Beth slapped back at her and inched away from Liz, toward the end of the bed.

"How are you sleeping through this?" Liz asked her and sat up. She'd never understand people who felt the need to wake up early on vacation. She remembered a vacation in Disneyworld when she was a little girl, probably seven or eight. Her father had insisted on having a wake-up call every single morning at seven a.m., sharp. Liz had never been an early riser, even has a child, and she distinctly remembered that she had actually cried one of those mornings. She may have said she hated Mickey Mouse or something along those lines. She had been dramatic in those days and took her slumber very seriously. And although there were no tears today, she just wished everyone would be quiet and let her go back to sleep until her body woke up naturally. But it wasn't to be.

"So, what's on our packed agenda for today? Eggs Benedict at some stupid overpriced bistro and more matching ensembles?" Beth asked at a volume only Liz could hear. "Can't we just lay by the pool and not speak for a few hours?" She covered her eyes against the sunlight that was streaming in through the windows.

Beth, having imbibed a bit more than Liz, looked as if the shadow of a headache might be pulsing rhythmically behind her brows. She turned to Liz, "Can you please get me two Advil and something to take them with? I can't possibly get through this morning with this headache. I might slap a bitch."

Liz did as Beth had bid her to do, and brushed her teeth while she was in the bathroom. She looked at herself in the mirror. She had managed to take off all of her makeup before falling into bed last night. It was a late-night habit drilled into her as a faithful subscriber of Teen magazine all of those years ago. Her hair, however, was another story. She wished she hadn't opted to go with curls last night as today, after seven hours with her head resting on a pillow, she resembled the bass player in any '80s hair band. She'd have to wash it and go with the ponytail today.

She returned to the room and handed Beth the pills and a bottle of water. She flopped back onto the bed and laid back on the pillow. She grabbed her phone and checked her emails and texts. Nothing of great import, and she was relieved that Pete hadn't messaged her. He was giving her the space she'd asked for, and it made her feel glad and also guilty. She knew he still held out hope that this was a phase, but she knew, now more than ever, that she was ready to close the book on that part of her life.

Cara popped her head into their room of the suite. "Hey, so we're thinking of going down and seeing what the breakfast options are in the hotel. You guys in?" Liz surveyed her thoughts. She was definitely hungry, and she could certainly use a cup of coffee.

"Yup, sounds good. I just want to hop in the shower real quick."

"OK. We figure like a half hour or so."

Liz nudged Beth. "You want to shower first, or do you want me to go?"

Beth urged her to shower first. Liz figured she was going to try and sneak in another twenty minutes of sleep. She grabbed a romper, underwear, and a camisole and headed to the bathroom. She agreed with Beth. She would like to sit near the pool today and just enjoy some silence. Maybe listen to an audiobook for a while and sip on a frozen concoction. She doubted this would be the plan. Jenna was hell-bent on wedging in every event possible during their epic four-night slay. She rolled her eyes at the word, even though she'd only thought it and hadn't said it aloud.

She stripped off her pajamas and surveyed herself in the hotel mirror. She always noticed that she looked slimmer in hotel-bathroom mirrors. She wondered if these were deceptive mirrors and if there was a motive behind them; if people think that they look good, they will probably feel better about themselves, and possibly, as a result spend a little more recklessly. Seeing as they were staying at a casino this seemed especially plausible. She could also, she thought, use a bit of color. It was April, and as a New Yorker her skin, except for her hands and face, hadn't seen the sun since September.

After some negotiation with the tub faucet, which for some reason always eluded her when she was away from home, she stepped into the shower and let the hot water and steam envelop her. She faced the showerhead and let the hot drops hit her face. It was a little too hot and the water that hit her face felt like, she imagined, being stung by a bee, although she'd never been stung before. She adjusted the water slightly. She washed her hair and then her body, and then stepped out into the bathroom. After toweling herself off, she pulled on her undergarments and romper. The mirror was still a bit foggy, but she wiped away a section with a towel and pulled her hair back into a low ponytail. Then, she made a conscious decision to give her skin a break that day. She skipped applying makeup but did apply her sunscreen and stepped back out into the hotel room.

Beth was already up and dressed. Liz was surprised that she was skipping her morning shower. "You know what? I think after breakfast I'm just going to go down to the pool and languish there." She pulled her tank top strap aside and revealed to Liz that she had her swimsuit beneath. "Come with me. There's no law saying we're obligated to attend every event of this godforsaken bachelorette party. It's our vacation, too." Beth lowered her voice for the last sentence. Although she didn't want to tag along on all of the outings, she also wasn't a bad friend and she didn't want to hurt Jenna's feelings.

"I might. Let me see how I feel after I get some coffee in me."

Beth shrugged. Liz wished she had a little more of the gumption that her friend did, and her penchant for sharing what was on her mind without concern for consequences most of the time.

"Alright guys, let's head down. You all ready?" Cara asked, as she slung her straw tote over her arm. Liz saw that Jenna, Sonia, and the other girls were lined up and ready to go, so they all headed downstairs together to eat.

15.

When Ben was in high school he had dated a girl named Summer. Summer's parents had been your average aging former hippies. They had fully embraced the Peace, Love, and Whatever movement of the '60s and '70s and had been instrumental in molding Summer into what Ben's mom had liked to call a "weird new age girl." He remembered that her room had been festooned with crystals and dream catchers; she'd had golden statuettes of Buddha in her room and had fancied herself a yogi. Ben, despite having been a native Californian himself, had considered himself a pragmatist and had thought that mostly everything Summer believed in so wholeheartedly was silly, nothing more than a veil that conveniently kept Summer, or people in general, from facing the realities of the world. But she had been pretty and quite limber from all of the yoga, so he'd looked the other way with regard to her crystals and her singing bowls.

But there was one thing about Summer that had always stayed with him. She had truly believed that she could make things happen just by sending out some sort of positive vibration into the universe. Manifestation of some sort. For example, Ben recalled on one occasion, probably circa 1997, there had been something that Summer had been coveting in a store—it may have been a shirt, or maybe a CD, the details were a little foggy after twenty-five years. When they had arrived at the mall to, ideally, purchase the item, Summer had stopped and closed her eyes and asked the universe to put the item into the store for her; she'd quite literally thought that God, spirit, the universe, something, would at that very moment place the very thing she had been wanting in her path so that she could purchase it. Perhaps not the most noble thing to ask of a higher being. Ben hadn't really believed in any of this back in high school, and he believed it even less today after a life filled with disappointments and hopes unfulfilled, but it had stuck with him after all these years. Because whatever the trinket had been that day, much to Summer's delight, it had been in the store waiting for her.

Ben hadn't thought about this memory in years, until that very morning. And, again, although he didn't quite believe in Summer's hokey magic, and he wasn't a particularly spiritual person, he took a moment to ask some greater entity at large if he, she, it, whatever, could please be so kind as to place Liz and Beth in their path sometime today. He figured a little positivity couldn't hurt.

He looked at his watch. It was just shy of ten o'clock and they had been staked out in the lobby for nearly an hour, to no avail. His coffee was empty and his bear claw long since gone. He yawned and Joe interjected, "I think I'm going to grab another cup of coffee. There has to be some sort of coffee shop in here, right?" He looked around the lobby. "Do you want? I feel like we might be in for the long haul, here."

"You know what, yeah I do. You know how, right? Two cream, three sugars."

Joe rolled his eyes, "Please. I've been your trusty sidekick for years and you don't think I know how to make your coffee?" Ben laughed, but truth be told, whenever Joe did bring him a coffee, it was often wrong. He had no idea, though, if he should place the blame on Joe's faulty ordering tactics or the collective incompetence of the baristas that had been assigned with the task of making his coffee. It didn't matter, though. Three sugars or no sugars, he just wanted the caffeine in his body today.

He watched as Joe asked an employee a question, presumably about the location of the coffee shop, and then changed course and headed in the direction of the casino. He figured he had a minute or two until Joe returned, but didn't want to take his eyes off of the lobby population, so he ruled out tooling around on his phone too much. He did send Jack a text, asking what he was up to. He realized it was still fairly early and that his twenty-year-old son would likely still be asleep.

He wondered what type of incantation Summer had said inside of her own adolescent mind that made, at least in her mind, the coveted item somehow appear in the store. He knew in his heart that even before Summer had closed her eyes and prayed for the item — was it a shirt? He was pretty sure now that it had been a band tee shirt — that the item was actually in that store, more the work of an efficient merchandising manager and less the work of some beneficent spirit. Even so, he did his best imitation of what he expected her incantation could have been: appear in the lobby, appear in the lobby, please goddammit appear in this lobby.

He wasn't sure what he expected to see when he looked around after his mental exercise. He did know that the only thing he could see was unfamiliar face after unfamiliar face. He rolled his eyes at the memory of Summer and her fake magic. He was annoyed at himself for even giving any of it a split second of half belief.

He heard Joe walking back before he saw him. And then there he was, indeed holding two takeout coffee containers, flanked by Liz and Beth both looking confused, but could he also detect curiosity? Had Joe debriefed them alone? Ben imagined that his mouth was wide open.

"Look who I found!"

"Yeah, he dragged us off the line and wouldn't even let us order a croissant," Beth said, wryly.

"I told you that Ben here would happily buy you breakfast if you'd just come with us for, say, twenty minutes." Joe was almost giddy, but Ben knew that breakfast was merely the crucial first step.

16.

They settled into a booth at Denny's, their second visit to this exact restaurant in less than twelve hours. It wasn't exactly the type of locale Liz imagined would have had a central starring role in her Vegas vacation. She and Beth had planned on grabbing a quick breakfast at the coffee shop in the hotel and then laying around by the pool for a few hours, but when one of the guys from last night, Joe, had approached them as they waited in line for coffee, and he had been almost breathless, like he had just seen a ghost, so breathless that maybe Liz and Beth were the aforementioned ghost, the ladies were intrigued enough to see it through. At least until the end of breakfast.

She ordered a loaded veggie omelet and a side of french fries; she felt ravenous this morning. The waitress brought their beverages, and as she sipped her coffee she looked back and forth from Ben to Joe. "Alright, to what do we owe this emergency breakfast?"

"Do you want to go or should I?" Ben asked Joe. It was, after all, Joe's plan even though it centered around Ben.

Joe tore open two sugar packets and emptied them into his coffee. "I tracked them down. Now you're up."

Liz and Beth looked at each other. Ben couldn't tell if they were friendly and intrigued, like last night, or completely freaked out, or perhaps just indifferent. He took solace in the fact that they were in a public place, so they couldn't feel too threatened.

"So, here's the thing," Ben started. But then he abruptly stopped and looked at his coffee, at a loss for words. What had seemed like a zany plan that "just might work" this morning at six o'clock while sleep-deprived now seemed questionable at best, putting the future of his career and his life in the hands of a stranger, who might very likely stand up and walk out of the restaurant upon hearing what they had to say.

He thought back, for a moment, to their first meeting with Spink. How his wife had maneuvered her body right next to his and had kept her hand on his upper thigh for the length of the meeting. Despite her reputation, he had been so caught off guard, as he didn't fancy himself a chick magnet and he couldn't believe she would be so brazen with her husband mere inches away, that he had been almost mute the entire meeting. He had seen his dreams slip through his fingers like sand once, and he was determined, no matter how convoluted the road might be to get there, that he was going to succeed this time. Or at least give it his best shot.

He continued, "Well, let me start by saying that we know how absurd this all is going to sound." He looked up at them, unable to read their expressions. "I'm just going to plow straight through it I guess." He took a breath. "So, last night we mentioned that we had a meeting tonight to try to hopefully have our screenplay produced. And we still do, but it was supposed to be at a restaurant with just the two of us"—he motioned between himself and Joe—"our agent, and the development executive. But we found out early this morning that the meeting is now going to happen at the executive's house somewhere on the outskirts of the city, a suburb or something." He exhaled sharply. He felt like he was nearly done with a marathon. The homestretch was only a few sentences away.

"Annnd...?" Beth asked, and let the word drag out a bit. The waitress had begun to set down their breakfast, and she set out to make the salt mound for her fries as she had the night before. Liz took a sip of her coffee and listened with rapt attention. She couldn't really see where the story was going. Did they want dates for the evening? That seemed like a simple request that wouldn't involve so much subterfuge, or at the very least this much effort.

"And, well, so the thing is, that we did have a meeting with this very executive previously, and it had an unfavorable outcome, because..." Ben was stalling, searching for a way to put it delicately.

Joe interrupted, "Because the guy's wife is a bit of a whore." Beth almost spit out her juice.

"That's not exactly how I would have phrased it," Ben said.

"I know. You're taking way too long to say any of this and I'm getting bored. Here's the bottom line. The wife is a bit of, oh, how shall I put it? She'll grab another man's ass, or worse, the second her husband's back is turned. Sometimes it doesn't even have to be turned. But we've been told on good authority that if someone—a potential client, like Ben here—has their wife present, that her hands might not do any wandering. So, we need you to come to dinner tonight and reprise your role of wife again." He laid it all on the table. Then he downed half a glass of water in one shot, as if the blanks he'd just filled in had dehydrated him. "If you're game, obviously."

Beth began to chuckle. "Well, that certainly sounds interesting." She turned to Ben, "But what's the big deal? Can't handle a little pinch on the hine from a random woman? Sounds kind of scandalous and forbidden if you ask me."

"Ben here feels like he cannot strike a deal with the husband if the wife's hands happen to be on his inner thigh. He's funny like that."

Ben felt a little embarrassed, because the truth was that he wasn't a prude or even particularly shy. He just did not see what good could come from Spink noticing that his wife had taken a liking to him. "I just don't think it's appropriate to interact with her in that way, especially when we hope that her husband will green-light our script." It came out a little sharper than he had anticipated, but he also didn't appreciate how lightly Joe had been taking this situation.

"So, let me get this straight. You want me to come with you to a dinner, tonight, and pretend to be your wife for a few hours, so that Mrs. Dinner Party Executive Wife keeps her hands to herself, and you can have your meeting without worrying about her, um, flirtations? That's it?" Liz looked from Ben to Joe, and back to Ben again.

"In a nutshell."

She turned to Beth. "What do you think?" On the one hand, it was just a dinner. She could play a role for two hours, of that she was confident. But on the other hand, maybe she was trivializing how difficult it might be to keep up the ruse. Not to mention the fact that she was supposed to be in Las Vegas to support Jenna, no matter how reluctant she was to participate in Last Slay activities.

"I'd do it," Beth said. Liz knew this was the truth. Beth relished the role of risk-taker sometimes. "But you're more wife-ish, obviously." She laughed at her own statement, and turned back toward the guys and said, "Alright, but how do we know you guys aren't sociopathic serial killers? You want to take my friend away to a random house. You seem normal, but I'm slightly uncomfortable with that." It was true. They'd only known these men for a few hours, and if they were honest their entire interaction up to and including this meeting was based on deception.

Ben broke in. "I totally understand, and we assumed that this might be a concern, so Joe here came up with a plan."

"Yes, so, we thought we'd make a video, on your phone, with both of us, detailing the scenario, as well as the address of the dinner party tonight. That should prove to you that we don't plan on abducting your friend. Also, to give you an extra measure of security, you, Beth, can hold on to both of our driver's licenses until we safely return Liz to you this evening," Joe said.

"Alright, that's satisfactory to me. Let's do this," Beth replied, and turned back to her fries.

"Um, shouldn't this be up to me, though?" Liz noted, as Beth had seemingly taken over the negotiations for the adventure. Ben was concerned that she might be slipping away, but her demeanor seemed positive.

Ben turned to her, "We can go over some key points so that our stories match, and I can pretty much promise you that it's going to be some really great food. Our agent said that it's going to be catered by one of Gordon Ramsey's restaurants here on the Strip." He shrugged boyishly. "It could be kind of fun, too. Just one night. Three hours of your life."

Liz wasn't adventurous and she rarely took chances, but she promised herself that maybe, just maybe, this trip would help her break out of her own self-imposed bell jar.

"Alright, let's do it. Just one night." They shook hands over the table and began to invent some bullet points for the evening ahead.

17.

The balance of the breakfast meeting, which turned out to be just shy of two hours, was used as a debriefing of sorts. They wanted to settle on a backstory for their marriage that was simple, and more importantly, easy to remember. While Beth was initially insulted that none of her ideas were being taken seriously—You met on a hike in Machu Pichu! You fell in love during a production of Uncle Vanya while you were both studying abroad in Moscow!—even she conceded that it was unnecessary, and unwise, to complicate the situation with faux facts about which they would be unable to provide additional details if pressed.

In the end, they kept it simple: they had met ten years ago on a dating site. They had married three years later, and lived in Manhattan Beach; this detail agreed with Liz, as she lived in Manhattan and knew it would be easy to recall the name of the California town. No kids, no pets. Ben had felt a little reluctant to pretend he didn't have a child, as if denying Jack's existence during this absurd improv exercise was akin to abandonment. He pushed it aside. It was just one evening of role playing and it was for the greater good.

Liz had made him privy to her job as a paralegal as well. "Alright, that should be easy. There are plenty of law firms in Los Angeles that could employ you, in theory," Ben said.

"You know what? Tonight I don't want to be a paralegal. For one day only I'm going to make use of my college minor," Liz said, smiling.

"Sure, why not. And what was that?" Ben asked, truly interested.

"Interior Design. It's been over ten years since I've actually done anything with it, but I watch enough HGTV so I feel pretty confident that I can fake my way through some pillow axing."

"Pillow axing?" Ben was truly confused, and Joe looked perplexed as well.

"Like, abusing pillows? Now that just sounds mean, Liz," Joe interjected, in a tone that felt like they were old friends.

Liz laughed. "You don't know about pillow axing? Maybe I coined that term."

Beth noted, "Guys don't think about throw pillows with the same frequency as women. What she means by pillow axing, and yes, I do think you're the only person who actually has ever used that phrase by the way, is the act of slicing your hand in the middle of a throw pillow after you place it on the couch."

"For what purpose would one do this?" Ben asked. He and Joe were truly confused, and mildly amused.

"You slap a pillow in the middle, and it makes it look full and fat. Look it up. It's a thing," Beth replied.

Joe whipped out his phone and after a quick search he said, in a mock authoritarian voice, "Actually, ladies, it's called pillow chopping not pillow axing."

"You abuse pillows the way you want, and I will abuse them the way I want," Liz said. They all laughed. The mood was light and Ben thought maybe this plan just might work. He felt like with a little luck, and some very simple planning, he and Liz could pull off a fake marriage for three hours.

After they had finished their breakfast, they stepped outside onto the street. Liz and Beth still hoped to get in a bit of time at the pool before reconvening with the other ladies.

"So, we have a car coming to pick us up at Bellagio at 7:15, so if you could be there early—say a few minutes before seven—that would be great. It would just be odd if it somehow got back to our agent that we were staying at separate hotels."

"You got it. Bellagio, 6:55. Oh, I didn't even ask—what do you think the dress code will be? I know it's dinner at a private home, but you also made it sound kind of swank," Liz said.

Ben wasn't actually sure. It was easy for guys. Dress pants, a button-down, and a blazer could take you through a variety of dress-code options. He looked to Joe for advice, "What do you think?" Joe shrugged and looked at him blankly.

"I mean, I guess business casual? I'm not sure what that means for a female though, to be honest," Joe said.

"Oh? What would Jennifer wear to an occasion like this?" Beth interjected, and Liz thought she sounded a little perturbed.

Joe looked at her point blank and just said, "Fur."

Liz didn't see any good that could come from this line of conversation, so she brought the focus back to the matter at hand. "Alright, I'll be there tonight, slightly before seven, in something nice but not over the top. Sound good? The game plan is to speak little, keep it simple, get the job done. Yes?"

Ben was glad that she sounded so confident. "Yup, perfect. We really can't begin to tell you how much we appreciate this. How much I appreciate it. You are really saving our lives tonight." He smiled at Liz. It was a nice smile and she thought to herself that although Joe was right, Ben was in desperate need of a haircut, there was something there. Something warm and sweet in his eyes. She smiled back at him.

"Alright then. I guess we'll see you guys later." And they parted ways until that evening.

* * *

THE MIDDAY SUN was much more oppressive in Las Vegas than Liz had ever felt it back home in New York, even on the hottest July day. She had second-guessed their decision to sunbath at least a half a dozen times but was able to muscle through the heat by taking periodic dips in the pool. She'd often heard people talk about the weather in places like Las Vegas and suggest that the heat was somehow more bearable because it was a "dry heat." Wet heat, dry heat, they both felt like an afternoon in hell if you asked her. It was nearly time to jump back in the pool. Beside her, Beth had been yammering on about their morning, and what the evening might hold, as well as some other superfluous details about the last two days that she found of particular importance.

"It's the desert. Why would someone wear fur to a dinner party? What kind of woman is she? Who even wears fur anymore unless they live in Siberia and they wear one of those big-ass hats. Gross," Beth complained to Liz as they enjoyed some kind of tropical drink that the waiter had called a "Sweet Desert Bloom."

"Why do you even care? Not only is he obviously not available, but he also lives like three thousand miles away."

Beth snorted.

"Alright, forget about Joe. We have a few things to go over. Are we about done here? I'm beginning to feel like a microwaved potato," Liz said, looking at her arms, which were beginning to show signs of a subtle burn.

"Yeah. I could really use a shower. Let's walk and talk," Beth said as she sat up and started to gather her things and toss them into her tote bag.

"I need to be in the room when you break the news to Jenna that you're not coming out with us tonight," Beth said as they started walking through the pool area and back toward the hotel. "If you want my advice, don't tell her what you're doing. She will be like a bat out of hell if she knows you're picking dinner with some strange guy you just met over an evening of her bullshit, I mean super fun whatever the hell."

"Please, I'm dreading it. I know. But I don't really know what to say. I can't fake sickness, because I'll probably be leaving before you guys. What the hell am I going to say?" Liz was truly at a loss. Ideas ran through her head like a ticker tape. Maybe she received a call today for a job interview via zoom that she just couldn't refuse? But why would it be so late in the day?? She thought about pretending that she was feeling depressed about her recent breakup and mentioning that she just wanted some time alone, but she hated to tempt fate like that. Every plan she thought of seemed to have a gaping hole in the middle.

"What about your aunt Lorraine? She lives around here right. Wasn't she having some health issues?" Beth asked, as they traversed the lobby.

Liz looked at her like she'd lost her mind. "What are you talking about? I don't even have an aunt Lorraine."

Beth stopped walking and rolled her eyes emphatically. "You're kidding, right?"

Liz stared at her for a full thirty seconds before the bell went off in her head. "Ohhh. I guess that might work. God, I feel like I'm turning into such a liar though these past twenty-four hours. It's beginning to feel a little uncomfortable," Liz said, and laughed a little nervously. "But I guess that's as good idea as any."

Beth said, "Of course it is. That's why you keep me around. I have fantastic ideas, and we wear the same shoe size."

"Alright, but why am I getting dressed up to go and visit a sick aunt? Wouldn't I be casual for that sort of visit?" Liz asked. It was a fair point. She wanted to make sure she crossed her t's and dotted her i's.

"Ok let me think," Beth said pensively. She was quiet for a minute and then she stopped in her tracks. She had a eureka moment. "Duh. Just leave the room in shorts and a tank or whatever and stash your change of clothes in a tote. Get to Bellagio a few minutes before you're supposed to actually be there and change in the bathroom. Boom. Done. You're welcome." Beth was very pleased with herself.

It was a simple solution and Liz didn't see why it wouldn't work. She'd have a tote bag with her for the rest of the evening, which wasn't ideal, but perhaps she could arrange to leave it in the car. It was a minor inconvenience.

They approached the suite and stood outside of the door for a minute. "I'm a little afraid. Not just about telling Jenna and whatnot, but like, this all seems so..." she stopped. She didn't really know what it was. She had been so caught up in the drama of last night, and then this morning, that she really hadn't taken a moment to realize that she was actually going to do this. This wasn't something real people did—this was something you watched actors participate in from the comfort of a movie theater with a fountain soda and a huge vat of popcorn.

Beth put her hand on her shoulder, "It seems insane because it is. But you'll have a hell of a story to tell when the evening is over." She smiled at Liz. "Much better than the story I'll have after Slay Night Number Two."

* * *

"OH MY GOD, I didn't even know your mom had a sister! What is wrong with her?" Jenna asked and took Liz's hand in hers, and her genuine concern made Liz feel like the worst friend in the world. "I mean, I probably could have said that better. What is her...um...illness?" Jenna had been surprisingly understanding about Liz's unexpected absence from tonight's festivities. It most definitely made phase one of the evening a little easier, but she felt guilty.

"Actually she's my grandmother's sister, my great-aunt. Yeah, she hasn't been doing well for a while, but it seems like she's taken a turn for the worse as of yesterday."

Beth had been sorting through her makeup on the bed and jumped in, "She had to have her legs amputated." Liz spun around, so confused about why Beth chose to inject this snippet into a conversation that she'd hoped to keep vague. Beth shrugged and went back to her makeup.

Liz had no choice but to continue with "leg amputation" and so she scanned her brain, which had no medical knowledge to speak of, and tried to think of what might have been the root cause of dear old Aunt Lorraine's tragic double leg amputation. She immediately ruled out war hero and motorcycle accident, and was drawing a blank.

"Oh my goodness, that is tragic. Is she diabetic?" Jenna asked.

"Yes!" Liz exclaimed, and Jenna jumped back a little at the enthusiastic response. "Yes," Liz said, more subdued. "She had to have both of her legs removed because she has very severe diabetes. I'm sorry. I guess it has me a little on edge. I haven't seen her, you know, without her legs yet." She shot Beth a look across the room.

"Well, of course you have to go and visit her. It must be so hard having her family on the other side of the country," Jenna said sympathetically.

"Plus, her husband recently left her for his home-care nurse," Beth interjected, unnecessarily. She was enjoying this way too much, Liz thought.

"That poor woman!" Jenna said.

"It was hard on the whole family, but you know, at least we know he's cared for I guess," Liz replied. She was ready for this conversation to be over.

"So what is your plan? Is there anything I can do to help?" Jenna asked.

"I'm just going to go and spend the evening with her. Maybe help tidy up her house or whatever she needs. I'll take an Uber there around six tonight, and I'll be back later this evening," Liz said, and let her shoulders drop. She was glad that this conversation, one which she had been dreading, was coming to a close.

Jenna hugged her. "You're such a good niece. We'll miss you tonight, but still have Friday and Saturday! "

"Thanks, Jen," Liz said, and Jenna left to her side of the suite.

"What the hell?" she said to Beth, who was now lounging on the bed surfing through channels on the television.

"I was helping you. You have three hours of improvisation to get through tonight. You have to be able to think on your feet. You have to be quick," Beth said, and snapped her fingers three times.

Liz knew she was right, but she might have appreciated a heads up before being thrown to the wolves with an impostor diabetic non-ambulatory great-aunt. She sat on the bed next to her. "Ugh, right now I can't wait for this to be over. I think I'm going to stop and grab a bottle of wine to bring. I might need it."

"You should. A good wife would not attend a dinner meeting for her husband empty-handed," Beth said as she popped a piece of gum into her mouth. "Are you wearing that?" she asked, as she pointed to an outfit that Liz was laying out on the bed. It was a simple black shift dress and a pair of wedge sandals. She figured the sandals would work with her "leave the hotel for her aunt's house" outfit, a shorts romper, but would also work with the dress. She chose the black dress because it was wrinkle free and would survive the trip across town folded into a tote bag.

"Yeah, why? No good?" Liz looked at the outfit. It was simple. Classic.

"No, I think it's a great choice actually. Understated."

Liz was relieved to have a second opinion. She wanted to fly under the radar tonight, not stick out like a sore thumb. She still had two hours before she had to leave for the evening.

"I'm pretty stressed," she said.

"Take a hot shower, then lay down on the bed and listen to some meditation music or something. Zone out," Beth suggested.

"You know, your amputation idea was out there, and I can't say I appreciated the crash course, but I will take your advice about zoning out. I'm going to hop in the shower now."

She went into the bathroom, turned the shower on to nearly scalding, closed her eyes and tuned out the world for a while.

18.

Liz arrived at the entrance to Bellagio at a quarter to seven with her costume change in hand, or at least in tote. She had taken an Uber and had made a quick pit stop at a liquor store to pick up a bottle of wine to bring along to the dinner meeting. It was ingrained in her that she should never attend a dinner or a party empty-handed. Although she was attending this particular dinner as a character, and not exactly as herself, she figured the rule still applied. She was most definitely not a wine expert, so with the help of the clerk she chose a bottle of Sauvignon Blanc by a California vineyard named Sunstone, because when it came down to decision time, she just thought the label was pretty and that seemed as good a reason as any to choose a wine.

She took a quick peek around Bellagio's lobby, which was packed with people milling around, likely on their way to dinner, and made sure she didn't spot Ben or Joe. The coast was clear. She snuck into a nearby restroom and began her transformation. She opted for a small brown leather tote, which could easily double as a purse, because after some consideration she didn't want to chance leaving her bag in a town car, and keeping everything with her seemed to complicate matters less. She closed herself into a stall, stripped off her white cotton romper, and rolled it tightly into a cylindrical shape. Then she took the black dress out of her bag, gave it a little shake, and slipped it over her head. She stuffed the romper at the bottom of the tote, and placed the rest of her items—wallet, room key, cell phone, lip balm—on top of the romper.

She stepped out and took a look at herself in the full-length mirror. Understated was the word Beth had used. She agreed. She pulled a simple gold necklace out of the dress and positioned it so that it was now visible. She reapplied her lipstick and snapped off a quick selfie to send to Beth when she was satisfied that she looked good. As a final touch she opened up her wallet and retrieved the engagement ring. She slipped it on her finger. She wondered what Beatrice would have thought of her using her beloved wedding band as a prop. She dismissed the thought. It was 6:50 p.m. and there was no room for sentimentality now. It was nearly showtime.

* * *

FIVE MINUTES LATER Liz stood and waited near the front door of the hotel, tote on her shoulder, bottle of wine in hand.

"Hey!" Liz heard, and then saw Ben waving toward her as he and Joe approached. They both cleaned up well, she thought, in dress pants, button-down shirts, and blazers. She wondered if that was the standard uniform for California writers. They stopped a few feet from her, and it was awkward for a moment. They certainly didn't know each other well enough for a hug or kiss hello, and a handshake seemed too businesslike for this setting, so they settled for a minute of strange small talk.

"A bottle of wine! Look at you being the perfect wife. I bet Ben here didn't even consider bringing a gift tonight. I know I sure as hell didn't," Joe said, and the mood was lightened.

Liz lifted the bottle of wine up. "Yes, my mother taught me well. Also, I thought I might need to drink most of it to get through this evening." They all laughed nervously. There was a lot riding on her performance this evening, and she intended to deliver.

"The car should be here any minute. Brit should already be in the car—that's our agent. Then we'll head over there and the game will be on," Ben said as they waited.

"Wait, your agent? Isn't he going to realize that I'm not, um, your regular wife? Or is he privy to whatever it is we're about to do?" This caveat made her anxious.

"Actually, I make it a point to keep my personal life and my professional life separate, so he's never even met my wife. Ex-wife, I guess. He's never asked, and I've never volunteered," Ben said. "And to be completely transparent, my wife was never really interested in my work anyhow." Liz thought she detected a little bit of scorn behind his voice and knew there must be a world of hurt lurking behind the breakup of that marriage. It wasn't her business, so she certainly wasn't going to inquire. And she didn't have to, because Joe cut in, "There's Brit," and pointed at the agent, exiting a car and striding toward them.

Ben turned to her and looked her in the eyes, "Alright, break a leg, Elizabeth. You look lovely, by the way. I should have said that first. Pardon my manners." She was a little taken aback that he had used her full name and hearing it in combination with the compliment made her blush slightly, but there was no time for reading into it. She stepped through the revolving doors and onto the sidewalk.

* * *

THE CAR RIDE TO THE dinner was short and pleasant. Liz found Brit to be affable and thankfully he was only interested in making pleasant small talk with her; he was more intent on going over a game plan with the guys about how tonight should go. After thanking her for flying in on short notice today, as Ben had informed Brit that she had, he asked how her flight was and if she was enjoying Sin City. She kept her answers short and friendly, and thankfully he moved on to the guys soon enough.

"Alright, so you brought a nice bottle of wine, great move. Never hurts to bring a consumable. I'm thinking let's follow his lead as to when to bring up script of course, but maybe we can force the issue a little bit as soon as we arrive, or at least broach the subject early. Let's get that part out of the way so that you all can relax and enjoy the dinner." He smiled and included Liz in the eye contact he made during this advice. "That way the threat of, you know, she won't be a problem for you anymore Ben, if the deal has already been sealed." He turned to Liz. "I'm sorry to bring that up in your presence, but I'm sure Ben has clued you in about why you had to rush here on such short notice. The woman is incorrigible." Liz just nodded.

The ride lasted no more than twenty minutes, and although Liz didn't feel like she was fully prepped for the performance ahead, she felt like every minute that passed brought her closer to the end of the night. Hopefully her presence helped. She felt like she was growing to like the two men, and she truly did hope that their endeavor was successful. Despite the obvious deception that they were currently engaged in they seemed like genuinely nice people.

The car pulled into a long driveway and parked. Ben stepped out of the car first and offered her his hand to help her out. She took it, knowing that some body contact was going to be part of the charade tonight. She was caught off guard with the site of the home. Liz had expected something extravagant, but she was not prepared for what she saw. It was a sprawling home. It was one story but it appeared as if it went on for a block. The front yard was manicured so meticulously that it almost looked like a resort, and the front doors, which were glass and wrought iron, shone with a gold glow from inside of the house. It was positively enchanting, she thought to herself. She turned to Ben and mouthed, "Wow," and he nodded at her.

"This is how the other half lives, Cinderella," he said, and laughed. "My current apartment could fit right in there," he said, and pointed to an attached three-car garage.

"Well now I wish I'd spent more than forty dollars on this bottle of wine," she said.

"Don't worry about it. It's perfect. I have a good feeling about tonight and I'm guessing that it will all come down to this excellent bottle of wine right here," he said, and smiled at her. It was boyish, and it made her smile back. It was a clear night and it had cooled down substantially, but she felt a little flush color her cheeks.

She hooked her arm into the crook of his. "Alright, husband. Let's close this deal." And they followed Joe and Brit to the front door.

19.

Liz had never known what the word palatial really meant until she stepped into the home of Development Executive Adam Spink. It was simply breathtaking. The double front doors opened to a grand foyer that was full of warm light, with a large tile medallion on the floor. There were large arched openings in three directions and she could see a huge great room to the left, a large dining room to the right, and in front of her she could see a massive kitchen that was flanked with large windows and a set of French doors; through the doors she could see an expansive yard and swimming pool. She tried not to look awestruck, but it was easily the most gorgeous home she'd ever seen in person.

They were invited in by a woman—Liz assumed she was a maid or housekeeper—to sit down in the great room, and minutes later Adam Spink joined them. Liz noticed that his infamous wife was not by his side. They stood up and Adam took the lead with regard to salutations.

"Thank you all for coming, and we're sorry about the last-minute change," Spink said, as he shook hands with Brit first, and then Ben and Joe. "Guys, I think we're going to do great things together. But we'll talk about that before dinner."

He turned to Liz and gave a warm smile as he stretched out his hand. Ben jumped in, "Adam, this is my wife, Elizabeth."

Spink gave Liz a firm handshake. "It's a pleasure, Elizabeth. We're so glad you could join us. I'm sure you're well acquainted with your husband's screenplay," and then turned to Joe and added, "I'm sorry, your husband and Joe's screenplay, and I can tell you that we all really enjoyed it."

Liz smiled and nodded but froze inside. She wasn't sure how they overlooked such an obvious detail; of all of the points they had gone over, it never occurred to any of them that maybe Ben's "wife" should have knowledge of the very movie they were trying to pitch tonight. She didn't even know the name of the screenplay. Keep it vague, she told herself. "Yes, it's fantastic. Most definitely a story that the world needs to see on the big screen," she said, and looked at Ben. He smiled and looked pleased with her response. She hoped she wasn't going to be called on to elaborate further.

"Honey, there you are, "Adam said, and stood up as the infamous Vivian entered the room. "You remember Ben and Joe, and Brit, from our last meeting? Back in LA?"

Vivian entered the room, wine glass in hand, and although Liz came into that evening with some preconceived notions about her behavior, she never imagined that Vivian would be so attractive. She was impeccably dressed, perhaps an inch or two shy of six feet tall, and had wavy blond hair that looked almost back-lit by the light of the foyer. She was almost as awe inspiring as the house, Liz thought. She could have been a model, and maybe she had been in her youth. Liz placed her as probably mid to late forties, but she based that more on the assumption that she was about the same age as her husband and not necessarily on her physical appearance. Her skin was smooth, likely the work of a high-end plastic surgeon or aesthetician. Or both.

"Of course I do. How are you boys doing?" she said, and Liz could hear both the wine and the flirtation in her voice.

"And this is Ben's wife, Elizabeth," Adam said, and gestured next to Ben, where Liz was sitting.

Liz stood up and extended her hand toward Vivian, who looked her up and down as she took it. "Your home is lovely, thank you for having us. We brought this for tonight," Liz said, and handed the bottle of wine to Vivian.

"Thank you. Nice to meet you, Elizabeth," she said, but it was a flat and disinterested response. She handed the bottle of wine off to the housekeeper without even a glance at the label. Liz could see instantly that her mere presence was an irritant for the woman, and she realized that Ben hadn't been exaggerating. She was obviously annoyed that one of her potential targets was off-limits tonight. Personally, Liz didn't enjoy when someone thought that another woman's husband was up for grabs. She was going to play her part like a pro tonight and mark her territory like a cat. She held Vivian's eye contact for another second or two as she placed her hand on Ben's knee. She thought that she may have felt Ben tense for a fraction of a second when she staked her claim on his leg, but then he must have realized that it was part of the performance and responded by putting his arm along the back of the couch behind Liz. Vivian, temporarily at bay, settled into a chair nearby to her husband.

Adam stood up, "Why don't we all retire to the dining room? I know that Carmen has made quite a spread of appetizers, and we can get the business talk over with early so that we can all enjoy a pleasant evening. Let's open that bottle of wine and enjoy some empanadas. I promise they're the best you've had." He was smiling as he said it. Liz had no idea how these things worked, but she imagined if they were going to talk business and then enjoy a "pleasant" evening, then the news about the screenplay must be positive. She couldn't imagine him saying, "Hey, your screenplay sucked, but let's all have some steaks together now!" That just seemed like the work of an anti-social personality. Ben and Joe must have felt this also, because they were both all smiles as they stood up and walked into the dining room to commence, and conclude, the business portion of the evening.

* * *

SPINK HAD BEEN RIGHT. Carmen certainly put out a delicious spread of appetizers, and, indeed, the empanadas were the best she'd ever tasted, far better than the ones she'd often get from the food truck that she and Beth frequented after happy hour on Fridays. They stood for a while around the dining table, which had been simply laden with food, easily enough for thirty or forty people, and enjoyed the wine and the company. After about twenty minutes, Spink made the transition from small talk to business.

"Guys, I'm not going to really beat around the bush, here. I read the script, as did my team, and we all saw tremendous potential there. Really excellent. So, we've decided to move ahead and green-light the project." He was all smiles as he said this. Liz had no idea what the script had been about, but she felt genuinely elated that this was happening for her new friends and that she could be a small part of the journey. "Next step will be setting up a Post-Acquisition meeting, but Brit, you can handle that. I'm sure you guys have legal representation and they'll want to attend that meeting, too. Pretty standard," he said. "So, I'd like to make it official with a handshake." He stood up and shook the hands of Ben, Joe, and Brit. The energy in the room was palpable and Liz was so caught up in the moment that she gave Ben a big hug. He accepted it eagerly and whispered into her ear, "Thank you so much for this. You have no idea how great it is to have you here." She felt herself blush from her cheeks and all the way down her neck. She was sure that he was just happy that he still had her as a pseudobodyguard, but she almost thought she felt a hint of something else in his tone, in the way he whispered into her ear. It was so personal, so close. Almost intimate. His hair smelled like a mixture of almonds and soap. She brushed these thoughts away, chalking it up to being caught up in the facade of the evening, and maybe because she was a little vulnerable from her recent broken engagement.

They pulled apart and Liz thought that she may have seen both Joe and Vivian eyeing their short embrace. Again, she pushed this thought away. Paranoia. There was still an entire evening to get through, and they hadn't even completed Act I yet. She polished off the wine that was left in her glass and sat in one of the chairs adjacent to the table. She patted the seat of the chair next to her and beckoned Ben to sit.

"You know what I realized before, and by 'before' I mean approximately a half hour ago? That you never even told me the name of your screenplay," she said quietly, so that only he could hear her. He placed a hand over his mouth, dumbfounded.

"How did we not think of that? Jeez, how many other holes do we have in our plan that might surface tonight?" he said, but she could tell that he didn't seem worried. Now that the business was out of the way, and he was seemingly safe from Vivian, he was relaxed. Like a different person, almost, from the guy she'd known for the past twenty-four hours. And the feeling was infections. She smiled widely. She felt a lightness that she hadn't recalled feeling in a very long time.

"Was my hand on your knee a good touch? I felt like I had to stake my claim," she said, with a devilish smirk.

"Ha, it was unexpected at first, but it totally worked. She hasn't even looked my way," he said.

"Can I ask you a question? Why isn't she all over Joe? Is it because she knows about his girlfriend? Why didn't she come along also?"

Ben looked at her, clearly perplexed, "What girlfriend? I can't remember the last time Joe had more than two dates with a girl. I'm talking years."

Liz was confused. "What about Jennifer?" she asked. "He brought her up a million times yesterday and kept looking at photos of her on his phone. It looked like puppy love to me."

Ben almost spit out his drink. "Jennifer isn't his girlfriend," he said, barely able to contain his laughter.

"I don't get it then. Who is she?"

"Jennifer is his cat," Ben said, and started to laugh so hard at the notion that the two women thought that Joe was obsessed with a female human, when in actuality the source of his fixation was a ten-pound feline. Joe walked over to see what the uproar was about.

"Hey, what's the big joke over here?" Joe asked.

"Jennifer is your cat?" Liz said to him, still confused.

"Of course she is, take a look at this little beauty." He whipped out his phone and revealed a photo of Jennifer the cat sound asleep on a couch. He scrolled and there she was on his lap, on the keyboard of his computer, laying on a window ledge in the sun. He must have had a hundred pictures of Jennifer on his phone. There wasn't a hint of shame or embarrassment in his voice. He simply loved his cat and didn't care if the world knew it.

"Oh man, it's your cat. We thought...you know what, never mind. Good for you and Jennifer. I have a cat, too," she said, and could not wait to deliver this news to Beth tomorrow in person. She raised her now empty glass in a toast to Joe and Jennifer. Joe clinked her glass.

Spink refilled all of their glasses and ushered them back into the great room so that Carmen could clear out the appetizers and set the table for dinner. Liz had eaten her fill of empanadas, mini-quiches and so many other delicious appetizers that she couldn't imagine fitting more food into her body right now, but she knew that the dinner had been catered by Gordon Ramsey Steak, so she would just have to persevere. Thankfully she'd chosen a loose dress.

The atmosphere was incredibly convivial, and even Vivian seemed to have softened to Liz's presence with the seemingly endless flow of wine into all of their glasses. The two were seated next to each other on the couch while the four men chatted, likely about the screenplay, and she began to ask Liz some friendly questions.

"Ben is so lovely. How did you two meet?"

Liz was relieved to have a well-rehearsed answer for the question and launched into a diatribe about their initial meeting on a dating app, peppering in some interesting details because she was feeling creative, and Vivian seemed invested in the story. Liz returned the favor and inquired about how the Spinks came to meet, and Vivian said, wistfully, "Oh, it's been so many years now, it almost doesn't matter anymore." Liz thought it was an odd comment. Vivian continued, "But we met in college. Adam was so self-assured even at that young age, and I was just drawn to him, like a magnet. He just knew who he was. And I knew I had to be his. Or he had to be mine. I'm not sure which it was, actually. But those early days, when we could barely afford a pizza and the biggest hurdle we had to overcome was convincing my dad that a film major could ever amount to something...they were sweet days." She smiled weakly as she said this, and her eyes looked as if she'd gone elsewhere for a moment. There was something sad about what Vivian was saying and Liz couldn't quite put her finger on it. She wondered if years of money and power had diluted the feelings of the relationship that Liz imagined had been sweet and powerful all of those years ago, and the ghost of which seemed to hover right behind Vivian's eyes as she spoke with Liz.

"That's very sweet, that you two have such a history," Liz said. This woman, speaking so tenderly about a memory, didn't seem to be the same woman known about town for misbehaving hands.

Vivian shrugged and tipped back what was left in her wine glass. She leaned in close and said something so cutting, and so personal, that Liz almost wished she could disappear. "Elizabeth, at my age I care for the memory more than I care for the man." Liz had no idea how to respond to this bombshell, and she had less of an idea as to why this stranger would have shared it with her. She had never been so thankful to be interrupted. Carmen had entered the room and began to guide them back into the dining room for dinner.

Ben joined her and said playfully, "Was Vivian keeping her hands to herself or do I have to step in and defend my wife?"

Liz looked up at him and said simply, "That woman is broken." He looked confused. She didn't want to dampen the mood so she waved her hand in the air and said, "You know what? Forget what I said. I'll fill you in on the ride home later. Let's go eat some steak." She took him by the hand and they walked into the dining room and to anyone who didn't know better they were the picture of husband and wife.

20.

Dinner had been outstanding, and Ben couldn't recall when he'd enjoyed a night out more. He realized fully that the general mood of the evening had been heavily colored by the sealing of the screenplay deal, but the conversation among all of them tonight had been easy and fun. He found that spending time with Liz had felt incredibly organic and natural, and it was almost as if they'd known each other for years. He even wondered if he, and all of Los Angeles, had misjudged Vivian, as she seemed to be getting on swimmingly with Liz.

It was as if somehow Liz, or a combination of Liz and alcohol, had coaxed an entirely different person out of Vivian's body, like an alien had come down and plucked the Vivian known about town out of the evening's festivities and substituted in a much more likable doppelganger. He wasn't sure how it was happening, or how it happened so quickly, but her preferred interest in his "wife" over himself greatly set him at ease. One less thing to worry about, and it seemed, from a distance at least, that Liz was enjoying her company.

As Carmen cleared the plates from the table, he took a minute to step outside into the backyard to get some air with Joe. They hadn't really had a moment alone to reflect on tonight's victory.

They walked out the large back doors and the air outside was cool. It was a clear night and if it wasn't for the light pollution from the nearby Strip they probably would have been able to see a million stars above. Even so, they were able to see quite a few.

"Well, this could not have gone better," Joe said and shook his friend's hand. Ben could hear the alcohol in his voice and imagined he sounded similar. The wine had been free-flowing all night, and while neither man was drunk, they were both certainly loose. "Did you message Jack? Let him know how it went?"

"Of course! I slipped into the bathroom before and gave him a quick call, actually. He was ecstatic," Ben replied.

"Did he say anything else? News from the home front?" Joe ventured.

"He did not, and you know what? I didn't even ask. Fuck her. I'm not even going to fight her. I'll sign the papers as soon as I get home, because you know there is no way she'll be getting a piece of this." He twirled his finger around in the air, as if the atmosphere in which they were currently occupied somehow represented the success of the screenplay. Ben had contempt in his voice. There was no way he was going to share the profits of this deal with a spiteful and vindictive ex-wife; this movie was his heart, and she'd already done her best to crush his soul. She couldn't have this, too.

"Of course not. And it looks like you have something new cooking anyway," Joe said, and glanced at Ben like a gossipy teenager. Ben looked at him confused.

"What do you mean? What exactly do I have cooking other than this screenplay?" There was no guile in what he was saying. He didn't know what Joe was talking about.

"Come on."

Ben stared at him blankly.

"I see you two 'playing the part' tonight but, please. You're telling me that there isn't something else there?" Joe inquired, eyebrows raised. Ben looked shocked at his assumption.

"What do you mean? You know that we're just playing a role for the night."

"Ben, I see you two looking at each other, whispering to each other. Jesus if I didn't know better I'd think you were married. I can't speak for her, but I know that you're really not that great of an actor," Joe shot back. He saw the look of bewilderment on his friend's face and continued, "Oh don't look at me like that. You're allowed to be interested in someone. I'm not telling you to go in there and propose."

Ben was at a loss for words. Hadn't he felt a little rush when Liz had placed her hand on his knee earlier? Or when she leaned in close to his ear so that other present company couldn't hear what she was saying? He may have, but he certainly didn't think that his behavior tonight belied that. The last thing that he wanted Liz to think was that he had lured her to dinner under false pretenses. The situation was so odd and confusing that he actually wasn't sure which parts of Liz were actually her and which parts belonged to the character she was playing. He imagined that she probably felt similarly.

"I..." Ben started. But he didn't know where to go from there. He was having a great time, and he was eternally grateful that Liz had risen to the occasion of tonight with such expertise, but he hadn't seriously considered the idea that he might be attracted to her; and he definitely hadn't considered that she might like him as anything other than a new friend. She was attractive, so it wasn't that he wouldn't have been interested under the right circumstances. He had been so focused on the endgame of the screenplay that he hadn't given thought to anything else.

"That's what I thought," Joe said. Ben didn't have an answer for him.

Joe sighed. "Ask her to lunch or something. You can't end this tonight. I mean, the worst that can happen is that she'll say no, and then you'll be back where you started." Ben had no idea why Joe was suddenly so invested in his personal life, and it was not a subject he'd have ample time to ponder, because as Joe said this the doors opened, and Spink walked out to join them, drink in hand.

"I know it's frowned upon but sometimes I just have to have one when I'm enjoying a drink," Spink said to them as he lit up a cigarette. He gestured toward the two men with the pack, the universal sign for, Care to join me? Both men waved him off. "I hope you're both having a nice night. I'm really so excited to move forward with the project, and it's nice to be able to enjoy a few drinks and some food. Look at the girls inside." He elbowed Ben and motioned to the dining table inside where Liz and Vivian were chatting away like old friends. "You know, I don't want to get too personal, but my wife isn't the easiest to live with. She's difficult. Has very few friends, truly. Has always been that way. But now I see she and your wife are really getting on. It's good."

He exhaled and blew a plume of smoke out of his mouth. "And lately, well, let's just say we're in a bad space right now because of some, err, transgressions." He paused. Ben wasn't sure where he was going with this, and stole a quick glance to Joe, who looked equally confused. He continued, "I won't bore you with the details, but I feel like I should do something to make her happy. Shouldn't I?" He looked to both guys for approval. They nodded and mumbled accordingly. "I'm glad you agree, because I am going to need a big favor from you both."

The hair on the back of Ben's neck stood up. He had the distinct feeling that whatever favor was about to be asked of him, it was one that he could not refuse and was apt to make him terribly uncomfortable. He had been under the pretense for the past few hours that Spink thought of him, perhaps, like an equal, but the last two minutes showed him that there was, indeed, a hierarchy, and he and Joe were still very much at the bottom. "Alright..." Ben said, slowly.

"Well, Vivian has really taken a liking to Elizabeth, as I mentioned. And she doesn't make friends very easily these days. She has in her head that she would like for you all to stay here the weekend. Maybe they can do some spa shit or something, we can golf. We have plenty of room here at the house for you all to stay; all of the bedrooms are suites probably larger than your hotel rooms." He took another drag on the cigarette and exhaled after a second. He placed a heavy hand on Ben's shoulder. It wasn't a suggestion, it was a demand. Ben knew that to be true. "Vivian doesn't handle the word 'no' very well, so it would really be great if you guys could stay. It would be a personal favor for me, as well."

He knew that it had been too easy tonight. They didn't even have to work for it, and now here was fate coming down on him like an anvil, because he knew that as lucky as he had been to convince a complete stranger to come and pretend to be his wife for one night, he also knew in his gut that there was no chance that he could convince that same stranger to abandon her friends and spend a whole weekend playing a role. If the roles were reversed he knew that he wouldn't. He also had the sense, as Spink let his heavy grip sit atop Ben's shoulder for a bit longer than he probably had to, that the fate of the screenplay hung on his response. He looked at Joe, and saw in his eyes that he registered Ben's inner turmoil.

"Let me talk to my wife. I know she has some activities planned for us..." Ben said slowly.

"Cancel them! Trust me. I'll be great," he said, as he released Ben's shoulder, put out his cigarette in his now empty glass, and started back inside. "I'm gonna go back in now and refill." And he took his leave of the two men.

Joe simply turned to Ben and said, "Fuck."

* * *

BEN AND JOE OPENED the doors and stepped back into the house. "Wow, I wasn't sure if you were coming back," Liz said playfully. "Come sit down. Vivian and I were just talking about how much we both really enjoy the zoo." Vivian burst into peals of laughter when Liz mentioned the zoo, and Ben could see that both women were hammered.

"I just love parrots," Vivian attempted to say, but it came out more like "I juss love pars." Ben had no idea how they had gotten on the subject of zoology, but what Spink had said was true—the two ladies were getting on like old friends. It was a side of Vivian that Ben had never heard about—Serial Cheater? Yes. Gold digger? He'd heard that. Stone-cold bitch? He'd heard that, too. Silly drunk who loved to talk about birds and monkeys? Ben felt like he was in the Twilight Zone. Apparently, Vivian found Liz to be simply delightful. "Liz, Liz," Vivian slurred and waved her hand to get Liz's attention, despite the fact that the other woman was seated inches from her, "let's go to the zoo tomorrow."

Liz burst into hysterics. "I don't even think there is a zoo in Las Vegas. Ben, is there a zooooo in Las Vegassss? Look it up!" She let the s's on the end of Vegas drag out a full two seconds, and Ben and Joe exchanged a confused glance. Had the two women already talked about spending the weekend? What the hell had happened in here tonight that had caused these two seemingly polar opposites to become best friends? He guessed if Vivian was planning a trip to the zoo that anything was possible.

"I'm pretty sure there isn't a zoo in Las Vegas, but I'll check it out. Can you come with me outside for a sec? I have to ask you something."

Liz stood up and stumbled a little bit. Ben steadied her and walked her to the door. He chastised himself for not paying attention to how much she had been drinking. Not only was it dangerous for their story, but he just felt like it was irresponsible to let her get so out of control. How could he return her to Beth in good conscience in this condition? He made a mental note to make sure she didn't have anything else tonight. He was disappointed in himself that he'd been so centered upon his goal that he hadn't considered what Liz had been doing.

"Oh, it's chilly out here," Liz said, and Ben immediately took off his blazer and put it over her shoulders. She thanked him. As if reading his mind she interjected, "Don't worry, I'm not as drunk as I appear. I'm just reading the room in there and going with the flow."

"Wow, then you are Oscar worthy because I absolutely thought you were trashed and I was starting to feel like an enabler for throwing you to the wolves." He gestured to a patio set that overlooked the swimming pool and said, "Let's sit for a minute." He wasn't quite sure how he was going to broach the subject of staying here for the weekend.

"OK, what's so important that we had to leave that parrot party in there," she said, and looked up at him. She looked a little more disheveled than she had earlier today—her hair was a little out of place, and some of her eye shadow had migrated beneath her eyes, but he thought she looked lovely in the moonlight. He pushed that feeling aside, though. Damn Joe for putting these thoughts into his head, he thought. Like it or not, there was still more business to be done.

"You're having an okay time tonight? Seems like you and Vivian are getting along?" he asked.

"Yeah, this was totally fun. And she's actually really nice once you crack through the nutshell," she said. Ben wasn't quite sure what she meant, but gleaned it was generally positive, and made a mental note that although she said she was not drunk, her tone and speed of speech let him know she was well on her way.

"OK, great, because I really appreciated that you came here tonight. More than you know."

"Of course! I was happy to help. It was an adventure," she smiled.

"Well, I'm glad to hear that because I have another proposition for you," he said, and tried to sound as light and charming as he could possibly muster.

She looked confused. He was concerned that she thought he was hitting on her, and he didn't want her to feel like he used her for some personal gain—other than the obvious personal gain about which she already knew.

"OK, let me just spit it out. Vivian really likes you and apparently she hates all other women. She wants you to stay the weekend—us, to stay the weekend. Apparently she'd go to a spa with you, Joe and I would do some shit with Spink. Believe me, I know that this is an insane ask, but he also made it clear without saying so that likely the future of our screenplay heavily depends on this weekend. So, I'm here pretty much begging you to stay. Just until Saturday night." He let it all fly out in one breath and stopped there. He didn't want to pile it on thicker than that; he didn't intend to place the burden of his future onto her back, because that wasn't fair.

She was silent, and she looked away, as if something in the distance suddenly commanded her full and undivided attention. He had no idea how to read her. Honestly, he couldn't imagine that she'd be game, but he also selfishly hoped that maybe the wine would tilt the scales in his favor. He brushed that thought away as soon as it surfaced.

She looked up at him for a long moment and he felt his cheeks flush and his heart race as he returned her unrelenting and completely unreadable stare.

And then she broke into a smile and said, "Alright."

21.

Liz surprised herself when she made the impulsive decision to stay for the weekend and extend her tenure as Ben's fake wife, but then she remembered her own words to Beth in her bedroom when they had been planning for the trip—she just needed to prove to herself that she wasn't boring. That there was more to her than routine and predictability. The wine she'd shared tonight definitely loosened her inhibitions, but she couldn't blame this on the alcohol. The truth was this trip had been exactly what she needed to shake up her increasingly mundane life. She hadn't done a single thing in the last twenty-four hours that the Liz of "last week" would have and it was exhilarating. She had never felt so free.

Ben looked almost speechless at her response, and she understood that he'd expected it to be a hard sell. She liked him, though, and being with him had been fun and easy. Part of her was relieved that it wasn't all ending tonight, because she might like to spend some time with him. He was someone that she would like to know. She liked Vivian, too, and sensed that the woman had been starved for genuine companionship. So, she had thought, why not?

She'd spent her entire adult life—no, her entire life—doing what was correct and expected, rarely taking a chance and never once flying without a net. But when she broke her engagement she felt like the floodgates had opened, and there was no turning back.

"I know you think I've agreed because you think that I'm drunk, and that is partially true, but I just feel like these boundary-testing events have been falling right in my lap, and I have to take them while they're available." She spoke slowly. "And I just like you, so that helps." She smiled. Ben wondered what she meant. He'd liked a lot of things in his lifetime: ice cream, hamburgers, a good baseball game — and he wondered if this was the feeling she spoke of. He wondered why he even cared. Joe's words had gotten into his head, and he swatted them away like a fly.

"Alright, help me up." Ben put out his hand and pulled her out of the chair. She fell forward onto him, and for a split second he held her steady in his arms, and then pulled back. It was a complication that he didn't need right now. "Let me give Beth a call and clue her in. But I'll also have to go back to the hotel tonight and pack a bag. You will also, right?" She looked up at him.

"Yeah, I guess we should get moving on that. Let's grab Joe and we'll make a quick trip back to the hotels," Ben said. He was sure Joe was going to have some sort of "told you so" look on his face, as if Liz's agreement to reprise her role for a few more days was proof that fate was somehow conspiring to get them together. For all he knew it was, but he'd given up on romanticizing his life years ago.

* * *

"WHAT? IT'S REALLY loud in here. Let me walk outside," Beth said.

"Alright, I'm outside. My ears are still ringing, but at least I can hear myself think. Start over. How did it go?" she asked.

"Well, it's a lot. Way more than a phone call. But, bottom line, it worked, and they sold the movie," Liz said.

"Oh, that's awesome. Good for them. And now you're back at the hotel? Come by here. It doesn't seem like we're leaving anytime soon. Jenna is tanked right now and it's pretty amusing to watch."

"Actually, wow. Yeah, it's a lot. So, I am running back to the hotel for a few, but, hm. I wish I could tell you this in person, because I know it sounds crazy," Liz said.

"Wait, are you staying the night with this guy? Did it take that turn?" Beth sounded like a combination of surprised and pleased.

"No. Well, no. Not exactly. Look, I will tell you more tomorrow. I'm running to get some of my things now. I just need you to cover for me, about Aunt Louise or whatever."

"Liz, how could you forget dear Aunt Lorraine's name? And on her death bed!" Beth retorted.

"Lorraine. Like, I promise that I will fill you in tomorrow morning. But make up something tonight. She took a turn or something."

"Well, Elizabeth, this is so out of character and I, for one, am shocked. And pleased," Beth said, "Of course. Auntie had a setback and you have to stay the night..."

Liz interrupted, "The weekend. I have to stay the weekend."

Beth was silent on the other line for a minute. "Wow, this is a story, isn't it?"

"Yeah," Liz said, and then she didn't know what else to say. "Alright. I promise tomorrow I will give you all of the details."

"You better. You're out there doing some crazy shit and I'm sitting here watching Sonia pump in the ladies room while also attempting to stop Jenna from hoisting herself up onto the bar. I got you, though. You know I do. Call me tomorrow, dammit."

* * *

THE CAR BROUGHT LIZ to her hotel and she stepped out onto the pavement. "I'll need about fifteen, twenty minutes to throw some stuff together. Are you going to wait here or will you go and get your stuff and then come back for me?" Liz posed the question to both Ben and Joe; Brit wasn't obligated to stay for the weekend as he had other clients back in California to which he had to attend, so he had taken a separate car back to his hotel earlier in the evening.

"We'll wait here and then head to our hotel afterward," Ben answered.

"Alright, I'll be super quick," and she speed walked into the hotel, across the lobby, and toward the elevators. She was nervous and excited; she had no idea what the weekend was going to bring, but the very idea that their plan was crazy and adventurous and maybe even a little reckless was exactly the reason why it appealed to her so much.

She opened the door to the suite and used the bathroom quickly; she took a glance at herself in the mirror and was horrified to see that her makeup was practically melting off under her eyes. She quickly washed it off and applied some concealer. Then she bagged up her toiletries and some of her makeup and threw them into her duffel bag. She had no idea what the weekend held for her, so she stuffed a variety of clothes into the bag—pajamas, lounge wear, a few swimsuits, two sundresses, a pair of flip flops and a few other items. She looked at herself in the mirror again and thought that maybe, seeing as it was already fairly late, she should probably change out of her dress and into something that she could also sleep in. She grabbed a pair of lounge pants and pulled them on, and topped it with a loose-fitting tank top. She pulled the flip flops out of the duffel, put them on, and placed her wedge sandals into the duffel. Then she bid adieu to the suite and proceeded back down to the lobby.

They drove to Bellagio, and Liz waited in the car while the guys went up and grabbed a few items for the weekend; they were much more efficient than her, and they were back on the road in under ten minutes. It was already nearing midnight and between the excitement of the day and the wine, Liz was pretty exhausted, and Ben and Joe looked like they were in the same boat. She hoped that Vivian didn't expect more socializing tonight; she pushed that thought aside and assumed that, after the quantity of wine that Vivian had consumed, she had probably passed out as soon as they'd left to pack bags. At least Liz hoped so.

When they arrived back at the Spink residence, Carmen greeted them at the door. It turned out that both the master and mistress of the house had retired for the evening, and Carmen showed Joe to his room, and then Ben and Liz to theirs. She had been a bit nervous about the sleeping arrangements, but was relieved to see a large bed on one side of the room, and the other side of the room boasted a sitting area that had not one, but two full-size couches. They could negotiate who would sleep in the bed, but Liz was so tired that she didn't much care if she had to flop on the couch for the night.

Ben pulled the door closed behind them. Liz looked around the room. It was much larger than the suite at the hotel, and it was nearly the size of her apartment back home. She looked at Ben and said, "Wow, this is pretty swank, huh?" She took a walk to the far end of the room where there was a large en suite bathroom with a stand-up shower, double sinks, and a freestanding claw foot tub. It was decadent, complete with burgundy and gold-trimmed towels, a massive, bejeweled mirror that hung over the sinks, and brass faucets in the shape of some type of exotic bird. Even the knobs on the cabinet under the sink were sparkling crystal frogs. Not exactly Liz's taste, but it all oozed money and gaudy opulence.

She stepped back into the bedroom and Ben was already sitting on one of the couches. "You take the bed. I'm good on one of the couches."

"Are you sure? I really don't mind taking a couch, either" she said.

"Nah, I'll take it. You're doing me a huge favor and it's the least I could do. We can pretend we've just had our first fight and I've been relegated to the couch." He smiled, but he looked exhausted. She laughed lightly, but she was also exhausted and was aching to wash her face and pass out in the king-size bed. She excused herself to the bathroom to make her final nighttime preparations, and then slipped under the covers.

"So, what exactly do you think tomorrow is going to bring? I'm not going to be flying solo with Vivian all day, right?" she asked.

"I have no idea. He mentioned golf, which I don't even play, but you know. I guess I will. I thought you two were instant best friends or something. At least that's how it looked," he said.

"She's fine, really. I got the sense that she was just kind of, I don't know...lonely. And I said the right things to fill that void. I've always been good at that, making friends quickly. And so we forged an instant friendship I guess. For the night. I didn't really expect it to go any further. But I also feel a little bit weird spending lots of time with her because it's like, my relationship with her is based on a total lie, and I feel a little bad about that. But I can play the part, be that friend for a day or two. I just hope she doesn't want to meet me for lunch when we 'get back' to Los Angeles," she said, and although she said it lightly, it was a very real complication that they hadn't planned for. What if, when they each returned home, someone inquired as to why Ben's wife had suddenly disappeared?

"I hadn't really thought about that. I'm going to try and not stay away long, because I don't want you to have to be here alone carrying the load. I'll talk to Joe in the morning and we'll see what we can do to make sure you're not by yourself for too long."

"Alright. I'm going to close my eyes now. I need to be on my A game tomorrow," she said.

* * *

AS THEY SAID THEIR goodnights, Ben couldn't help but notice that Liz sounded so unafraid and confident, as if she partook in this sort of strange deception on the regular, and he wished he knew how to turn that on. He was still on pins and needles about their story holding up; one night was a challenge, and right now, as exhaustion began to set in, a whole weekend seemed almost insurmountable.

Then Liz chimed in with, "Good night, fake husband. Happy one-day anniversary," and he smiled in spite of himself. And as he fell asleep, he thought to himself that Joe was right. She was a person he'd like to get to know, but almost before he could complete the thought, he had drifted off to sleep on the couch.

* * *

SLEEP HAD TAKEN Liz so quickly and so completely that when she woke up in the middle of the night to the sound of her phone vibrating, she was startled, and couldn't even remember where she was. It took her a full forty-five seconds to shake off her brain fog and recall where she was: Las Vegas, bedroom suite in the gigantic home of some sort of Hollywood executive, random man to whom she was pretending to be married asleep on the couch on the other side of the room. She rolled over and took a look at her phone, face down on the nightstand but still able to illuminate the darkened room slightly. She had a handful of texts that had come in over the last few hours, but only the very last one had woken her. There were about five from Beth, with increasingly poor spelling; presumably her attention to detail and ability to choose the correct letters when texting had decreased exponentially as the evening progressed and her level of intoxication grew.

Then the final text, the one that had awoken her, had come from Pete. The timestamp was 3:23 a.m. She wondered what time that was back on the east coast. Her brain couldn't do the math at that hour. 5:23? 6:23? The text simply said the following: Hey, did I leave my box of Magic the Gathering cards at your apartment?

She stared at the text for a moment. It embodied everything she felt about her relationship, about why she had finally ended it and only served to remind her that she had made the right move. Not only was he up in the middle of the night, probably on one of his eighteen-hour video game binges, but he felt that it was fine to bother her in the middle of the night—when she very well could have been asleep—because he couldn't seem to locate one of his toys.

She stood up to use the bathroom. It was chilly in the room, a fact she hadn't noticed while under the plush comforter on the bed. She tiptoed toward the bathroom, careful not to wake Ben. She saw him curled up on the couch, with his back toward her, the fleece blanket he'd covered himself with earlier had fallen to the floor. Liz, quiet as a mouse, walked over, picked it up, and covered him. Then she quickly went to the bathroom, walked back to bed, and was asleep again almost immediately.

* * *

BEN HAD BEEN AWOKEN by the sound of the phone also, but had remained still, feigning sleep. He forced himself to remain still as he heard Liz carefully approach the couch; he had no idea why she would have walked over. Then, he felt her pick up the blanket and cover him, carefully and slowly. The tenderness of the action touched him, as he'd spent his life with a woman who didn't seem to care about his very existence, let alone whether or not he might be chilly at night. It was all he could do not to turn over, open his eyes, thank her for just...caring. But instead, he kept still and after a time, sleep took him as well.

22.

When Liz awoke, she could hear that Ben was already in the shower. He had left the curtains drawn, for which she was grateful. She wasn't one of those people who hopped out of bed the second her eyes opened, and bright light entering in through an open window was something she considered to be a full-on assault on her senses. She liked to ease into the day. She rolled onto her side and grabbed for her phone. There hadn't been any new messages since the one that had woken her in the middle of the night. She saw that it was a little after nine o'clock, and figured, given the state of Beth's texts last night, that she probably wasn't awake yet. She sent her a text anyway and let her know that she would touch base with her as soon as she could to fill her in on all of the blanks. There were so many blanks. It was going to be a hell of a phone call.

She heard the shower turn off, and after about five minutes Ben emerged, dressed in shorts and a yellow polo shirt, likely because there was a game of golf in his future. She thought to herself that the polo shirt just didn't suit him. He didn't strike her as the country-club golf-playing type of guy. She let her mind wander for a moment and imagined that he was more of a "let's get Chinese and rent a movie" type of guy, but in actuality she knew nothing about him, and realized that she was probably projecting attributes onto him that she would prefer in a man. He might be none of those things. He smiled at her, and said, "Good morning. How was the bed?"

"Actually, it's quite possibly the most fantastic bed I've ever slept in," she replied. It was true. It was like the mattress sensed exactly what she needed for the ideal night's sleep—mostly firm, with a little bit of memory foam—it was like a hug for her entire body. She made a mental note to take a look at the brand later, because it might be worth the investment when she got home to New York, even if the price tag was steep. "Golf today I presume?" she asked and gestured toward his polo shirt.

He nodded. "Well, the good news is that apparently we're only playing nine holes. The bad news is, I don't play golf, and I feel like a dick in this polo shirt, which I had to borrow from Joe. I don't even know how long nine holes would take. That's how golf-ignorant I am."

"Maybe an hour and a half," she said, and he looked at her skeptically. "My dad is a huge golfer," she said, and he nodded.

"Alright, so not too much humiliation. With any luck by lunchtime, I will no longer look like a douchebag frat boy from Stanford." She laughed and thought maybe her assessment of him was correct.

"And what else? What is on my agenda for today? Do we know that information?" she asked, with very slight trepidation.

"Joe was out and about early today, probably strolling around outside, calling his parents to check on Jennifer, and was roped into having an early morning coffee with Spink. He got a rundown of the day's activities." She thought she noticed a twinge of disgust when he landed on Spink's name, and she was positive she saw an eye roll when he spoke the word activities. "So, actually, I do know, and I'm a little bit jealous," he said, with a hint of tease in his voice.

"Oh really. OK, do tell."

"Well, I heard that after breakfast Vivian has some people coming by to give you guys facials and pedicures in the cabana out by her pool," he said. Liz's mouth dropped open. "I don't know what you did, but that woman loves you."

"Really? Wow. Now I feel better about my decision to marry you," she said, and immediately regretted how familiar it felt to say that, even in jest. Too much. That line was too much, she thought. But a facial and a pedicure overlooking a lovely private pool? She almost felt guilty that Ben would have to spend the day on a golf course with the hot sun glaring down at him in that egg yolk-colored polo.

"Yeah, you are absolutely getting the better end of the deal," he said, smiling. "And then I had the idea that you might want to meet up with Beth today, maybe fill her in, so when I stepped out into the kitchen earlier for some coffee I told Spink that we had lunch plans with an old family friend who lives in the area that simply couldn't be changed. The three of us can escape for a bit and maybe go back to crappy Denny's, because that's kind of our place now."

Liz loved this idea. She appreciated that Ben really tried to take into account her comfortability level, and how she might want to touch base with her friend today. She imagined that her facial expression as he mentioned this part of the plan belied her pleasure, and she thought that he seemed pleased with himself.

"Yes! That would be awesome. I can see from the batch of practically illegible texts that she sent me last night that she's desperate to find out the situation," she said. It would be so much easier to explain the whole plan to Beth with Ben present, and she also looked forward to a break in the action — an hour or two where she could just be regular Liz.

She also couldn't deny that she felt a little flutter when he mentioned that Denny's was their place. She'd never actually had a place with anyone before, unless of course you counted Wendy's, which she did not. Liz didn't want to read into how she felt, because this was absolutely the wrong place and wrong time to even begin to develop feelings for Ben. Both were fresh off of breakups—she didn't know the details of his, but she knew that she, herself, would probably benefit from a little bit of solo time after eight long years with a bona fide child. And even if she did want to pursue it, Ben lived on the complete opposite side of the country. What point was there in even exploring these feelings? She didn't see any. She also wasn't sure if she could help it, but she was going to try.

"Will Joe be joining us?" she asked. Liz really wanted to deliver the Jennifer news to Beth, but she knew that she couldn't do it with Joe present.

"He will be. Is that okay?" he asked.

"Of course! I would hate to leave him stranded here all alone," she said, but she realized she felt slightly disappointed, and she wasn't 100 percent sure why she felt this way. True, she would have liked to have had an afternoon with Beth to really dish the dirt without censoring herself, but she also knew that a small part of it was that maybe, just maybe, she wanted a little bit of alone time with Ben. She knew that she was only seeing one side of him, a persona that he was creating for the purpose of this weekend, but she sensed that there was a more quiet and maybe even sweet side to him. Or maybe there wasn't; she couldn't be sure. She made a mental list of the things she did know about him: he'd rescued her, a complete stranger, when he'd seen a questionable guy pushing himself on her at a bar; he'd been so sweet and attentive, opening doors and acting generally chivalrous, but that could be part of the act, she reasoned. She was so confused.

"Hey, did you hear me?" he asked. Truth be told, she didn't hear him. She shook her head from side to side.

"I'm sorry. I was zoning out there for a sec, what did you say?" She felt stupid that she had allowed herself to descend into a pointless reverie.

* * *

Ben wondered where she had gone for that moment; he had watched her face change from happy to, something else—bewildered, introspective maybe—like a summertime squall touching down unexpectedly on a beautiful July afternoon. And then, it was gone, and she was back to smiles. He was going to repeat his question, but he also wanted to know what was going on behind those eyes. He wanted to know this more than anything he'd wanted in a while. In fact, he couldn't remember the last time he'd been so fascinated by another human being, other than his own son.

There was a moment, before either started to fill in the missing pieces of the conversation, before either of them had even begun to think about what they wanted to say next; it was even before either one of them realized that there might be anything different or special about that very moment, that there was silence, save for the sound of the breeze beating the shade against the now open window. Their eyes locked, and neither could look away or speak or move. The moment lasted perhaps three seconds, not much more than that. Ben could see the color coming to Liz's cheeks, and then her neck, as if she were flustered, and then she touched her hand to her cheek. She looked down at her feet. She must have felt that she had to break the glass. Maybe, like Ben, she was afraid of how she knew she was beginning to feel; afraid that it was based on a facade, a farce, but perhaps even more afraid that it might be based on something real. He pushed it away. Maybe she was doing the same, he thought.

This motion seemed to break the trance for Ben, and he cleared his throat and said, "I said that our tee time is ten, so I should be back by noon. Maybe tell Beth to meet us at one p.m.?" He had the overwhelming urge not to leave on the golf outing. Not because he wanted to do something dramatic like sweep her off her feet or confess his feelings; he just wanted to say here awhile, maybe sit on the couch, find out Liz's favorite color or food or her cat's name. She had mentioned she had one, hadn't she? He thought so. Without realizing it, he had been absorbing every word she'd been saying.

"Yes, that works. One o'clock. I'm going to hop in the shower now and get ready for my morning of beauty. I'll see you back here in a few hours," she said, forcing a smile. Without knowing how he felt at all, she also felt like she wished she could stay there, in that moment, just a little while longer.

"Catch you later," Ben said.

Neither said anything else, and yet the room felt palpable with all the words left unsaid.

23.

Liz showered and dressed. She wasn't sure what one wore for random spa services by a private pool, so she pulled on a swimsuit and topped it with a plain cottony romper. She slipped into her flip flops and grabbed her sunglasses and hoped that there would be some coffee this morning. She felt a little weird being here alone without Ben or Joe, but she had felt a genuine rapport with Vivian last night and hoped it carried over into this morning, even if there wasn't any wine involved.

She walked out of the room and figured she'd head toward the kitchen. No one, save for Ben, had given her any direct information about what she was supposed to do today, but she assumed Vivian, or at least Carmen, would be around to greet her.

The latter happened to be milling around the kitchen, and smiled at her when she entered the room. "Good morning, Elizabeth. Mrs. Spink is out by the pool, through those doors. Can I get you a cup of coffee first? Perhaps a pastry?" She gestured to a plate of assorted pastries, croissants, and muffins on the kitchen island.

"Thanks so much Carmen. I would love a cup of coffee." She smiled. "I think after all of your empanadas last night maybe I should skip breakfast this morning," Liz said, and patted her stomach. Carmen chuckled at the comment and looked pleased. She poured coffee into a large mug and motioned to another tray on the island.

"The white pitcher is cream, and the blue pitcher is almond milk. Sweeteners are in the basket." Liz dropped two sugars into her coffee and followed it with regular cream. She was impressed by the spread—even the coffee creamers were sitting atop a bed of crushed ice. She wondered if Carmen put out this kind of breakfast buffet for the Spinks every morning, or if this was something special that only happened when they had overnight guests.

She thanked Carmen again, stepped outside with her coffee, and headed toward the pool. Vivian was sitting cross-legged on a padded lounge chair beneath a cabana and waved at her. Liz could see she was wearing a knit kimono-style cover-up over a one-piece solid black swimsuit, and she was relieved that she had guessed right with regard to her wardrobe today. She wondered how her impression of Vivian could be so grossly different than what, apparently, everyone in the state of California had thought about her. Aside from her initial coolness, Vivian had been so eager to open up to her; it was like the woman was starved for attention and just wanted to talk about anything, even if that topic strayed to zoo animals.

Liz sat down on the lounge adjacent to Vivian's and took a sip of her coffee. It was strong and good. "Good morning! So, I heard from a little birdie that we have some exciting things planned for this morning," Liz said, and her excitement was genuine.

"Oh, boo! I wanted to surprise you! I guess Adam spilled the beans to the guys. I told him not to, but naturally he probably wasn't even listening when I was speaking to him," she said, and although her tone was affable, her eyes grew icy at the mention of her husband's name. There were certainly some issues there, Liz thought. Maybe they'd get into it. She knew a thing or two about one-sided relationships.

"I was surprised! And excited! Would you believe I've never actually had a facial before?" Liz said.

"Oh, you'll love it. I have people from my regular spa coming and they are the best," Vivian said. There was a bit of awkward silence after this, and Liz wasn't sure how to fill the void for a moment. She was typically very good at becoming fast friends with strangers, but she wasn't sure where she should take this conversation. It was too early in the morning to get into deep topics, she decided, and so she rifled through her head like a Rolodex and settled upon talking about the house. It was innocuous enough, she figured.

"This yard is amazing. The whole property really. How often are you guys here? I know Ben said you're typically back in Los Angeles," Liz said, hoping this line of conversation would carry them into the arrival of the facialist and pedicurist, but she had no idea what time they were slated to arrive.

Vivian sighed wistfully. "It is beautiful, this property. I wish we could be here more often, but most of Adam's business is back in California, so we don't get here much anymore. Nevada feels like more of a home to me than California ever will." There was something in her voice that Liz placed midway between melancholy and distaste.

"Are you from California originally?" Liz asked.

"No, actually. I grew up near here. Well, not in this area exactly. I grew up in Sunrise," she said. Liz wasn't from the area and had no idea what Sunrise might be like with relation to this area. From what she'd seen, and it had been limited to the two drives she'd taken to and from the hotel, most of the suburbs of Las Vegas seemed neat and clean, with large houses and austere properties covered in rocks. It wasn't her preferred aesthetic, but she understood why people liked it. The upkeep must be easy.

Liz wasn't sure where to go from there with the conversation, and Vivian hadn't offered up any other information. "Well, it must feel good to go back to your roots, sort of," Liz offered. She was not prepared for what happened immediately after she uttered these words.

Vivian pushed the heels of her hands against her eyes, as if she was frustrated or had a bad headache, but when she pulled them away, Liz could see that her eyes were red and overflowing with tears. "What is it? What did I say?" Liz asked, alarmed, and rushed to sit next to her on the lounge. Vivian just shook her head. Liz didn't know what to think. Not two minutes ago Vivian had seemed fine.

"It's not you. You didn't say anything. It's just..." But then she stopped. Liz knew from experience that sometimes when someone is upset it's best to let them unleash on their terms. People tend not to want prodding or advice when they're at their most vulnerable. She just sat in silent support and waited for Vivian to make the next move. She put her hand on Vivian's shoulder for support because she felt compelled to do something.

Vivian took a deep breath and gathered herself. "I'm not sure why I'm telling you this, and maybe it's not fair to burden you with this because we've only just met," she started. "But, after seeing you and Ben last night, and how sweet and attentive he is to you. I don't know, all of these feelings that have been simmering right beneath the surface for, like, ever... I guess they just couldn't be contained anymore." She looked at Liz, but Liz still wasn't quite sure where Vivian was going with this line of conversation, and she felt horrible that her theatrical marriage could have made another person feel this badly.

"I'm so sorry that something I did made you this upset..." Liz started, but Vivian stopped her and put her hand on Liz's upper arm.

"No. You did nothing. And you have nothing to apologize for. Adam and I have been going through the motions for years now. Do you know that we don't even share a bedroom anymore? Not for years." Liz was dumbfounded that this information was being dropped upon her this morning. It was not how she expected the day to commence. It wasn't even ten o'clock. "And I know what people think about me. Call me some kind of whore, assume that I'm sleeping around because I've admittedly been a bit too free with my hands sometimes. But let me tell you something. I have never once, not once, been unfaithful to my husband. Not that he can say the same." Liz's eyes widened and she took a gulp of her coffee. "He doesn't even hide it anymore. I can't even keep count—young actresses, old actresses, assistants. It's like he'll put his dick in anyone that isn't me." Liz almost choked on her coffee.

"Vivian, I'm... I don't even know what to say. That's just horrible," Liz said, because what else could she say? No one deserved to be treated like that. And she felt awful that even she had initially fallen prey to assumptions about Vivian's reputation.

Vivian shook her head side to side, like an angry little girl about to have a tantrum, and then took a deep breath to collect herself. "I need to get this out. It's been inside of me for years now. So, yup. That's me. Vivian Spink. My husband will fuck anything that moves, and so, to get his goddamn attention, or maybe to be a spiteful bitch, I don't even know at this point, I will blatantly hit on any man that happens to be in our mutual presence. And does he care? Does my husband give a shit?" She paused, as if Liz had the answer. She did not.

"Nope. I could be on the lap of someone he is about to purchase a screenplay from and it's almost like I'm invisible. It's like I'm just another acquisition to him. He lured me, he bought me"—as she said this part, she gestured all around her to the sprawling manor"—and then he threw me on the back burner for someday, or maybe for never like one of his motherfucking screenplay projects." Liz exhaled sharply. She looked at her mug. It was empty. She wished she had more coffee, or something stronger.

"But, Liz, you were the straw that broke the camel's back. You want to know the moment I decided this?" Liz gulped. She didn't really want to be the cause of this outburst, and she also didn't necessarily need to know specifics.

"I saw Ben help you out the door last night because you were a little wobbly from the wine, and then put his jacket over your shoulders. I guess it was chilly outside. That is what a husband does. Not fuck every blonde bitch that strolls through his office and then expect to pay for your silent obedience with houses, luxury, or whatnot." She stopped for a second and looked around the yard before continuing. "Here's a story about my husband." She spit out the word with contempt. "No secret that I had too much to drink last night, and I tripped in the hall on the way to bed. Broke the heel clean off of my shoe. Would you fucking believe he saw me fall and twist my ankle because of the broken shoe, and the son of a bitch stepped right over me to go into his bedroom? Right over me. Didn't even offer me his hand." She was reaching that point of anger when for some women, tears began to make a forcible escape despite someone's best efforts to keep them in line. "You know, I don't come from money. I didn't grow up with this. So I blame myself, too. I got used to all of this, his compensation for my silence. But no more. When we go back to California next week I'm filing for divorce. And then I'm going to sure as shit get my half of all of it." As she said the last part, she twirled her finger in the air, as if staking her claim on all the eye could see.

Liz was speechless. She felt like it was probably not a good thing that her mere presence might bring about the end of a marriage. At the same time, she felt for Vivian. This was a broken person who had become so accustomed to being some sort of a kept woman that she was almost willing to sacrifice her dignity. Almost.

"Wow. Well, all I can say is, you have to put yourself first. I don't know much about your situation, and it's really not my business to weigh in, so that's all I'll offer. Take care of yourself first," she said. Vivian smiled at her, and tears came again. Liz thought she looked like a lonely little girl who was lost in the mall and couldn't find her parents.

"I know that was a lot, and I know that we're practically strangers, but I need you to know that you being here this weekend... I feel like fate brought you here because it was time for me to stop being a doormat, no, not a doormat, a whore," she said weakly. Liz hugged her. She was just compelled to, and Vivian accepted it warmly. Liz had no idea how they could possibly segue from this life-altering conversation to spa treatments, but Vivian bridged that gap for her.

"Well, that was a weight that had been sitting on my chest for fifteen years," she said and smiled meekly. Liz guessed that although the outpouring was cathartic, she probably also felt a little embarrassed that she'd made a near stranger privy to such personal information. Then she sighed and said, "You know, I feel like I need to shut the world out now and let a stranger massage my face. You don't mind if I put in my earbuds for the facial do you? I just need to tune out for an hour," Vivian said. Liz nodded.

"Of course. I can get behind tuning the world out, myself," she said, and browsed for some meditation music as the ladies from the spa began to set up their tools.

24.

By the time the men had returned from their golf outing, the ladies had already completed their treatments. Vivian remained out by the pool. Liz had sensed that the woman needed a little bit of alone time to process all of the emotions that she'd just let loose into the world. She had offered to sit with her for a while if she wanted to unpack any other emotional baggage. Vivian had thanked her and told her that she'd appreciated everything she'd done so far, but that she just wanted to nap in the sun for a while. Liz felt like she could use some downtime also and was happy to vacate the pool area for a bit.

She had gone back into the bedroom suite and taken another shower; she felt sticky from sitting outside for two hours, and she'd also had no idea that a facial was going to involve a very oily scalp massage. It was lovely and relaxing, but she felt like she couldn't face the world again until she'd washed her hair a time or two, or three.

She'd learned that after her luncheon with the mysterious and very fake family friend, she and the guys would return to Campus Spink where they were planning on ordering takeout for dinner, TBA, and having some sort of game night in the great room. Liz had never had a competitive spirit, and she wasn't a person who enjoyed playing most games, and this included any kind of organized sport, video game, and nearly all board games. It just wasn't her thing, but she realized that tonight she had no choice in the matter. For one, she was committed to this weekend hook, line, and sinker, and so she was going to go with the flow and do what needed to be done; additionally, she thought Vivian had enough to think about today, and if the woman wanted a carefree evening full of wine and Pictionary, then she wasn't going to stand in her way. Although from the way Vivian had described her husband, she was shocked that Adam Spink was even open to indulging her whim. She would have guessed that he'd want to stay as far away from the house as possible, but she was no psychologist and didn't know why people did the things they did.

She'd changed into a sundress and flat sandals for their lunch with Beth and she was waiting on the bed scrolling through her phone absently when Ben returned from golf. She was relieved to chat with someone other than Vivian after the morning she'd had with her, but part of her just wished that they could drop the whole facade. It was getting tiring, and she felt awful that this woman had confided some pretty personal stuff under the pretense that Liz was a person that she was not. It made her feel fake, and she hated to feel that way. She also had begun to acknowledge that she had developed an interest in Ben, and she wished they could just have a conversation that didn't center upon this lie they'd created together. Thinking about it made her sigh aloud.

She looked up, "So how was golf?" she asked.

"It sucked. I hope to never play again," he said, smiling, but he looked exhausted. She imagined that nearly two hours walking around in the desert sun could certainly suck the life out of anyone. "How was your morning? Relaxing?" he asked, smiling down at her.

"Well, it was. For a little while," she answered. He looked perplexed at her reply.

"Oh?" he asked.

"I don't even know where to begin. I'll give you the Cliffs Notes version in the car on the way to lunch," she said. She didn't feel much like talking at that moment, but she knew, given Vivian's reputation, that Ben probably assumed the worst and she would have to fill him in the details sooner rather than later. She genuinely felt bad for Vivian and felt an odd loyalty toward her new friend.

"Alright, let me take a rinse in the shower and then we'll get going," he said. He looked at his watch. "Wow, it's already twenty after twelve. I'll be quick."

* * *

FIFTEEN MINUTES LATER Liz, Ben, and Joe were in the back of a town car, driven by Spink's personal driver, on their way to Denny's. Liz laughed inwardly at the image: they were being driven by a chauffeur to a Denny's. It seemed like such an obvious mismatch. Liz had decided to hold off on filling Ben in about her morning until they got to the restaurant; maybe she was paranoid, but she wasn't quite sure that she wanted the Spinks' driver to hear the nitty gritty details about their defunct marriage.

They arrived at the restaurant and thanked the driver. Ben chatted with him for a moment; Liz couldn't hear the conversation, but it ended with him and Ben shaking hands. Ben walked back to join them and said, "He'll be back to pick us up in three hours." Liz nodded. That would give her some time with Beth, and she also thought maybe she'd stop at the hotel and pick up the handful of items that she'd left in the room. It didn't seem like she'd be spending much time with the Jenna's Last Slay crew, so she may as well keep everything at the Spinks' house.

Liz could see through the window that Beth was already sitting down inside of the restaurant when they walked up. She looked like she'd had a rough morning, and Liz felt a pang of guilt that she was barely spending any time with her best friend on this trip. Beth waved them over to a booth near a window, and the trio walked over and joined her. She was already nursing both a cup of coffee and a large glass of water. Liz was no stranger to the double-edged sword of the hangover—dehydration and exhaustion—and understood fully why Beth required both beverages.

"Hey," Beth said, and was unable to suppress a huge yawn.

"Long night?" Joe asked her, smiling.

"Oh, you have no idea," Beth said. "Unfortunately, I needed to drink myself into a stupor in order to distract myself from the fact that the group of ladies that I am here with are just, well, I guess lame is the word I'm looking for." She turned to Liz. "It's like Jenna has no idea that she's thirty-five years old and looks thirty-five years old, and she was pathetically trying to get these guys, I don't know, maybe like twenty-two years old, to buy her a shot. It was hard to watch. Like, I felt bad for her and also just annoyed that she completely lacks self-awareness." She turned to the guys and said, "And you two took away my only sanity, so now here I am, hungover like a dumb adolescent, double fisting coffee and shitty tap water." She exhaled hard, and softened a little, "I'm sorry. I'm just tired. Tantrum over. Oh, and before I forget, take your driver's licenses back. I'm pretty sure you guys are safe, and I hate holding them hostage." She placed them onto the table.

Liz felt awful, because she wished that she could tell Beth that she, too, was not having the vacation she had hoped, but truth be told, minus the guilt and anxiety tied up in keeping up the facade all weekend, she was most definitely having a trip to remember. She wished she could have taken Beth along for the ride. It was certainly a story.

"I'm sorry. I know this isn't what we planned for at all," Liz said. Beth shook her head.

"No, you don't have to be sorry. First of all, I was totally on board for this. Second, I need you to fill me in with some good dirt so that I can feel better about the stupid-ass night I had. Third, I'm going to need food," she said, and Liz could hear that if Beth was truly annoyed in any capacity before they arrived, it had dissipated completely. That was Beth. She didn't have it in her to be a bad friend.

The waitress came by, and they placed their drink order. Liz sighed. There was so much to tell, but she also hadn't filled Ben and Joe in on the Vivian breakdown from earlier today. She didn't really know where to begin.

"I'll go," Joe interjected. "I'm a writer, after all. I can tell the story with flair." Joe always seemed to be in a fantastic mood, Liz noticed. Maybe single life with a cat was the secret to a carefree life.

"The floor is yours," Beth said.

"Alright. Let's see. These two put on an Oscar-worthy performance as husband and wife, we sold the movie, everyone had a shitload of wine and empanadas, and then this morning we nearly died of heat exhaustion on a golf course while your girl here got a facial by a pool. I think that sums it up," Joe said, and took a sip of the soda the waitress had put in front of him moments prior.

"Wow. Those are impressive storytelling skills. It's almost like I was right there with you," Beth said dryly. She turned to Liz. "I'm going to need more than that. I carried a bag of breast milk in my purse last night." Joe nearly spit out his soda.

"Joe summed it up, I guess." She gave Beth a look that she hoped her friend could interpret; she mentally tried to tell her, "I will give you details later when it's just the two of us." Beth nodded, seemingly having received the message.

Ben interjected, "What about the other thing? That you didn't want to mention in the car?"

Beth looked confused; she knew nothing about Vivian, and Liz didn't necessarily want to let on to Beth that she'd made a new friend. Not that Beth was the type who would be jealous if Liz had another friend, but Liz felt like she was slighting Beth on this trip by spending time with another woman. She realized it was silly, but it was a feeling she couldn't shake.

Liz started, "Alright, so Vivian, Spink's wife, seemed to need to unload on someone, and I happened to be the lucky party present. You know how strangers like to tell me their problems for some reason," she directed at Beth, who nodded. Beth then recounted the time the two of them had been bathing suit shopping at Macy's in New York City. Liz had complimented the dress of another woman in the fitting room, and the woman had, unprompted, opened up about how the dress was for the wedding of an ex-boyfriend; she had still been in love with him, and she hadn't been sure if she should attend the wedding, but had decided she needed the closure. Beth had watched in awe as a seemingly insignificant moment had gone from a simple compliment to a heart to heart, and ended with Liz and the stranger, whose name they had never learned, embracing in the fitting room in front of the three-way mirror.

"Anyhow, I guess she saw us, and thought we were such a lovely married couple," Liz directed at Ben, and blushed slightly as she said it, in spite of herself, "and it made all of her, um, marriage issues bubble to the surface. She said that Adam is a serial cheater, and that the only reason she acts so handsy is because she's desperate for his attention, and to make a long story short, she's going to divorce him and take half of his money, like, next week. Oh, and she's never cheated on him, not once." Ben and Joe listened with wide eyes. "Apparently he's a huge dick and openly cheats, and she's tired of being made a fool of in exchange for living the high life, I guess."

"Wow, you got all that from her this morning?" Ben asked.

"Yup, all before ten o'clock this morning."

"So, are we not doing the whole dinner thing tonight? Or is that still on?" Joe asked.

"I mean, I don't know, but my guess is that she wants to blindside him with this next week, and so she'll probably lay low for the rest of this weekend so that he doesn't suspect that she's up to anything," Liz answered.

"Wow, your weekend sounds like more stress and less fun than I envisioned when I signed you up for this," Beth said. Liz wasn't sure about that. She had enjoyed last night for the most part, and it was nice to get some spa treatments for sure. She also liked spending time with Ben, and Joe, too, but Vivian had taken up so much of her time and energy that she felt a little more disconnected today than she had last night, or even this morning. She sighed. The waitress came and they placed their lunch orders; Liz didn't feel particularly hungry anymore, so she ordered a grilled cheese. She felt herself falling into such a funk, and she couldn't quite put her finger on why. Maybe Vivian's emotional state had worn off on her, or at least affected her overall demeanor today, but the thrill she'd felt just last night had evaporated, and she found herself feeling a little sad today.

When the waitress brought their food, Liz urged Beth to give them the details of her evening. She listened with her full attention as Beth regaled them with the cringe-worthy antics of her friends last night, and although it put a smile on her face, and helped pass the time, she couldn't help but begin to think that her melancholy was fueled by reasons that she didn't have control over, and the thought made her retreat into her head a little bit further as she picked at her grilled cheese.

* * *

AFTER THEY'D EATEN lunch, they had agreed to part ways for the remainder of their time on the Strip and Liz was grateful for an hour or so alone with Beth. She needed to decompress and turn off for a little bit. They walked back toward their hotel so that Liz could collect the remainder of her items from the suite. The other ladies were spending the afternoon by the hotel pool, and Liz and Beth had the suite to themselves. They settled on the bed and Liz opened up a bottle of water.

"So, tell me the real story. Because I can see all over your face that something else is going on," Beth said. Liz hoped she wasn't so transparent, and it was just because Beth knew her so well, often better than she knew herself, that she saw through her mood.

"I'm not sure what there is to tell, really," she said, but she knew that there was no truth to the statement. There was much to tell, she just didn't want to address the issue aloud. That might make it real.

Beth arched an eyebrow.

"Alright, I guess there's a lot to tell."

"Yeah, of course there is. It's all over your face. But I don't see the problem. You're allowed to like him. You're not married. You're not a nun. He's a good-looking guy, seems nice and all. So honestly, I don't understand why you're so blah. Seems like he could be a prospective suitor for the lovely Elizabeth," she said, slipping into a horrible old-English-type accent for the last few words for reasons unknown.

"No. See, there is where you are wrong. It is literally all problems from where I sit. First of all, let's address the fact that he lives in California. Why would I want to get involved with someone so far away? You know I have zero intention of moving," Liz said.

"No, I'd kill you first, of course," Beth interjected.

Liz smiled. Beth knew how to bring levity to a situation, always. "So, there's that part. And, yes, I am starting to like him. I'm not going to be dramatic, but just being in the room with him, I like it. It feels good to be with him. He puts his hand on my back, and I just feel like, oh, I don't even know." She paused. "I feel like it's the first time I've dated an actual adult." She stopped after she'd realized what'd she said. "You know what I mean, I didn't mean that we're dating." She inhaled and exhaled deeply. She realized that she probably sounded like a stupid teenager. Beth looked at her, without judgment, so she continued, "And that isn't the problem, either. The biggest problem is that I don't know if the person that he is presenting is even who he actually is. Is he acting attentive and nice because that is what he thinks he has to do to keep up the facade? Or is he actually that person? So, here I am, unsure if I'm falling hard and fast in 'like' with a guy or with a character he's created for the weekend. And I'm just so confused," she concluded, and ran her hands through her hair as she often did when she was frustrated.

Beth looked at her deadpan and said, "So why don't you just ask him?"

Liz smirked, "And say what, exactly? Hey, I kind of like you, and have no intention of even pursuing it, but I'm just kind of curious if you're actually as great as I think you are, or if you're secretly actually a jerk and you're just putting on a show for the weekend? Like, why?"

"Alright, then don't. All I'm going to say is this: at lunch, you looked sad. Like, not about to cry your eyes out, but just...sad, yeah I can't think of another word for it."

"Maybe," Liz said. She had felt off.

"And do you know why?" Beth asked. Liz shrugged. She wasn't sure.

"I guess it's just more stress than I'd bargained for this weekend, and it's getting to me," she offered.

"Nope, that's not it," Beth replied, confident.

"Oh? You know how I feel?" Liz answered more indignantly than she'd anticipated. If she didn't understand how she felt, or what was causing said feelings, how could Beth possibly know? Especially given the fact that she hadn't been a direct participant in last night's or this morning's activities.

"I do," Beth said. Liz waited for elaboration.

"You're sad that the weekend will be over in twenty-four hours, and you'll never see him again, and the thought of that is hitting you like a brick." Her words hung in the air like thick smoke, their presence smothering all of Liz's other thoughts and conjectures and assumptions. There it was. Beth was right.

She couldn't put into words how she felt about Ben yet, because the feelings were just too young, too new, too raw and unknown; but she knew that the idea of Sunday's arrival and his departure from her life, forever, was almost more than she could bear to think about.

25.

If Liz had hoped that her afternoon with Beth would help give her some mental clarity, she was sorely mistaken. Admitting her feelings and fears aloud didn't make her more comfortable with them. In fact, it only made her retreat into her own head further and it made the car ride back to the Spink residence a little tense. Ben and Joe both seemed chatty and in high spirits, while Liz stared out the window. She realized that she was ruining her own good time, and she mentally scolded herself. She should enjoy the rest of the weekend, treat it like a wild story that she'd tell people at parties when she got back. People had flings all the time on vacation, not that this was a fling exactly. But they enjoyed the time, and then went home filled with memories and experiences, never regretting or even giving a second thought to what they may have left behind.

"Liz, what do you think?" Joe asked. Liz had no idea what they had been talking about. She had been too deep in her own thoughts.

"I'm sorry. I was off in space for a second," Liz said, and forced herself to smile. "Tell me again what we're talking about?"

Joe eyed her rather suspiciously, "I said that if we're all getting takeout tonight, I'm going to suggest sushi. Are you good with that?"

Liz made a face. "No, I don't do sushi."

Joe seemed surprised. "Really? But you're in your mid-thirties and live in Manhattan. I thought it was required."

"I had no idea you were an expert on Manhattan," she shot back at him, amiably.

"I am an expert. My brother lives on the Upper East Side and I've been there twice in twelve years. Total expert," he retorted.

"Well, first of all I don't really like seafood to begin with. And second, part of me feels like only a sociopath would eat a raw animal. It seems savage if you ask me," she said, with a playful tone, but she meant every word. Joe broke into a smile.

He elbowed Ben, and jokingly said, "Wow, like husband like wife. Alright, so if everyone else is down with sushi, then you two can order a pizza or something, because I have the need, the need for a spicy tuna roll." Liz didn't understand Joe's mixed reference to fish and Top Gun, but she wasn't interested enough to inquire further.

"Ugh, raw fish and mayo. No thank you." She turned to Ben, "Not a sushi guy?"

"Nope. Can't even imagine biting into a raw fish. Why not just hit up a pet store and swallow a goldfish? Save yourself a few bucks," he said, and she laughed.

* * *

ALTHOUGH THE SUBJECT, sushi, wasn't one that Ben was eager to chat about, he was relieved to see Liz laugh when he'd given his commentary on the matter. She'd been incredibly reticent today and he was afraid that she may have checked out. It was good to see her smile again. Maybe they would have some time before dinner to chat and he could find out how she was feeling about all of this, why she'd been so quiet during lunch, and now the car ride back.

As they pulled into the driveway, Ben looked at his watch. It was approaching four o'clock. He hated that they were being held hostage for the weekend. He was not a person who preferred to have a set agenda, especially on vacation. He much preferred to see where the day took him. A planned evening of food, which he enjoyed, and board games, which he could get into in the right context, was something that he probably would have been more comfortable with if it hadn't been forced upon him—if it had been his choice.

The car stopped and he opened the door to get out. Then, he helped Liz out of the car by taking her by the hand. He held on to it for a few seconds longer than he had to, until Joe also exited the car, and found that he didn't want to let go. He wondered what would happen if he didn't, if he took her hand in his like he wanted to. Maybe she'd wriggle free, but maybe she wouldn't. He couldn't risk it. Ben had spent his life with a woman for whom he'd had many feelings throughout the years, from lust, to friendship, to indifference, and finally to disgust, but he had never felt like this with her, not even in those early college days. Ben wasn't naive enough to believe in things like love at first sight, but he certainly believed in chemistry, attraction, and compatibility. Liz ticked all of those boxes for him. He hated to admit that Joe had been right about the connection. He certainly wouldn't tell him so.

* * *

CARMEN GREETED THEM at the door and ushered them into the kitchen where they found Vivian and Adam seated at opposite ends of the large kitchen island; Adam was in the middle of what seemed to be a business call; Vivian was tooling around on her phone. She looked up when Liz entered the room and smiled. It was like she was a young girl who had been waiting all day for her playmate to arrive.

"You're back! How was lunch?" she asked.

"It was a nice time. It was good to catch up," Liz said, because it wasn't a lie. It was good to catch up with Beth.

Adam chimed in, having just ended his phone call. "Well, I hope you didn't eat too much, because we're going to order a whole bunch of sushi for tonight. Joe mentioned it last night and I haven't stopped thinking about it since." Liz thought he seemed so perky and friendly and didn't see why he should be; a serial cheater who had a wife that hated him, as far as she was concerned, he had no right to feel as relaxed as he did. She fully recognized that her image of him was colored by Vivian's diatribe that morning but didn't care. She didn't like the guy.

"Oh, did he? Well, as Joe likely knows, my wife and I here"—and at this point Ben put his arm over Liz's shoulder to drive the point home—"actually both don't eat sushi." Liz was surprised by this move but responded by putting her arm loosely around his waist. It seemed fitting, but she thought she felt him tense a bit when she made the move and wondered if she shouldn't have been so bold.

"It's true," she said. "Bad experience in Tokyo years ago," she added, and instantly wished she'd kept it simple. Adam's eyes opened wide as she mentioned Tokyo.

"OK, well, no good reason why we can't order a pizza also. That works, right? No bad pizza in Japan I presume," he said lightly, but Liz didn't like his sarcasm. She smiled anyway, because she realized, much as Ben had realized he wasn't able to refuse the weekend invite yesterday, that Adam Spink wasn't a man accustomed to contradiction. Liz wasn't going to be the one to test those waters; she took solace in knowing that Vivian was going to give him the business next week.

"Pizza would be great," she said, smiling back at him. "You're good with pizza, right sweetheart?" she looked up at Ben.

Ben nodded. "Of course. Carbs and cheese. What's not to like?"

Liz wondered how good pizza could possibly be in the middle of the desert, although she thought the same could be said for sushi; how fresh could the fish be, she wondered, when the nearest ocean was three hundred miles away. Pizza was most definitely the lesser of the two evils.

Vivian chimed in, "I'm going to have Carmen order both and have it arrive, let's say, 5:30? I think I'm going to swim a few laps and then change into something comfy."

Then they decided to retire to their respective quarters and reconvene in the dining room in an hour and a half for an evening of food and revelry. Liz could think of nothing that she wanted to do less.

* * *

LIZ AND BEN RETURNED to their room to wait out the minutes until dinner and Ben immediately flopped down onto one of the couches. She silently sympathized. She also felt exhausted, mostly mentally, but the desert sun had certainly been sucking the life out of her body. It was only April. She couldn't imagine what it felt like to be in this city in July. Ben popped on the television and began flipping through the channels, looking for something entertaining to kill the time.

"I'm just going to wash my face. I'll be right back," she said, and escaped into the bathroom. She leaned hard against the bathroom vanity, allowing all of her body weight to fall onto the palms of her hands, which gripped the edge of the granite countertop. Then she looked up at herself in the mirror. She looked remarkably the same as she had when she'd given herself a once-over in the mirror of her bedroom only last week, and yet, she felt like a world of events had happened since then and changed everything. She had thought that ending her engagement—which was absolutely the correct move, of that she was still sure—and escaping on a trip with friends would help to clear her head, but the truth was that fate had taken her down a curving road that left her more confused and conflicted than she had felt last week.

She let the water run until it was warm and splashed it over her face. She hoped the action would be something profound—washing away her state of mind and replacing it with clarity—but in the end, all she did was wet her skin. She thought about what Beth had said, "Why don't you just ask him?" In her mind, there were so many reasons why she couldn't, or why she shouldn't, or why she just wouldn't allow herself to. But when she brushed away all of the dust, and discarded the notion that perhaps he wasn't interested, or maybe he wasn't exactly who he appeared to be, or even that their lives on opposite coasts would make a relationship nearly impossible, what it really came down to, for Liz, was fear. She'd always been fearful of the unknown. When she'd read Robert Frost in college, she didn't understand how anyone could possibly take the road less traveled. Why take unnecessary chances when taking a solid path, a well-worn path, a path that promised stability in the long term, just made more sense on paper? And so that's what it was for Liz, she decided, as she looked herself in the mirror, face dripping with water, as she let the faucet continue to run. She'd never even considered what might be down that grassy, mysterious road that curved dramatically before you could see where it was heading. She'd never wanted to. She turned off the water, dried her face, and gave herself one last look in the mirror before exiting the bathroom.

Ben seemed to have settled on an old rerun of I Love Lucy but wasn't paying attention to the screen. Liz saw him on his phone, maybe shooting off a text to Joe or someone. She realized that he could have even been texting his soon-to-be ex-wife, whom she'd only heard about in passing and actually knew nothing about. She pushed that thought aside.

Ben looked up at her as she walked slowly to the couch and smiled. He motioned to the television and began to say, "Ten thousand channels and there is never anything on—" But before he was able to finish his sentence, Liz plopped herself on his lap, so that her legs were stretched out onto the cushion next to him. She turned toward him and took his face in her hands. She kissed him tenderly, but firmly, on his mouth, without thinking about what the consequence might be or what tomorrow might bring. And he put his arms around her waist, as she sat atop his lap, and kissed her back.

26.

Liz pulled away and looked at Ben. She hadn't planned to kiss him and even now, she wasn't sure it was the right move. She wanted to see his expression and get a read on how he might have felt. His eyes were cast down slightly, and she could see his feathery eye lashes for a moment, and then he looked up to meet her gaze.

"Alright, so I'm getting the impression that you aren't in an I Love Lucy mood," he said, smiling. She was relieved that she hadn't overstepped or misjudged how she thought he may have felt about her. She laughed and elbowed him, then she moved to slide onto the seat next to him, but he held her on his lap.

"Nope. Not gonna happen. I've spent the last day wondering how you felt, wondering how I felt, and now that I know, I'm not going to let you go," he said, and kissed her lightly on the cheek. The act was so delicate and careful, like he was afraid she might break if he pressed too hard. No one had ever treated her this precious before, and it made her feel something that she couldn't put her finger on, because she had nothing with which to compare it. She only knew that it felt right. So she stayed put, and found that she didn't want to move anyway, and they watched a little bit of Lucy. It was the episode in which Lucy and Ethel attempt to bake bread; it had always been one of Liz's favorites from childhood. There they sat, Liz's head nestled into Ben's neck, fingers intertwined, while Lucy and Ethel destroyed the kitchen. She wasn't sure what would come next.

And, as if reading her mind, Ben asked, "So, now what?" She sighed.

"I don't know. I'm usually a planner, and this wasn't really on my to-do list," she said, and smiled weakly. All of the boldness she'd felt earlier was slowly slipping away, and although she knew it felt right, she wasn't sure if making her feelings known was the smartest move. She curled further into him and he put his arm around her shoulder. She wished they could stay here, talk, figure some things out, but she also knew that they had to rejoin the group in a few minutes. Curtain time again.

There was a quick knock at the door, and then without waiting for an answer from the occupants within, it cracked open a few inches and Joe peeked his head in. His eyes flew open wide and he fully let himself into the room, and closed the door behind him when he caught a glimpse of Liz and Ben intertwined on the couch.

"Well, well, well, what do we have here?" he said. His face looked shocked but his voiced sounded as if he were the cat who ate the canary. She sat, frozen for reasons unknown, but Ben responded by laughing and giving him the finger.

"Well, now that seems uncalled for," Joe said, laughing, and he came into the room and sat down on the couch right next to Ben, so that Liz's feet were caught between them. Liz understood why Joe and Ben were such good friends; Joe was, for lack of a better word, always silly; always joking, always positive. He must be an easy person to be around, and she assumed Ben was around him a lot because in addition to being friends, they were writing partners. She had to smile at his complete lack of boundaries with his friend. She also noticed that Joe didn't seem too shocked to stumble upon the scene, and she wondered what had been said between the two men about her prior to this moment. Not that she was faulting him for discussing it with his friend—after all, she had spoken to

Beth about it. She just wished that she could have been a fly on the wall to hear exactly where Ben stood.

"Well, I for one could not be happier. It's not every day that Ben takes my advice about pretty much anything," he said.

"And what advice was that?" Liz asked, lightly. She didn't want to give the impression that she was pressing him for information, but she was genuinely curious. Especially because Ben hadn't taken any advice, at least not that she'd seen. She was the one who had made that move.

"I had mentioned that I thought you guys were good together, and that he shouldn't let this end. Buy you a steak dinner or something, I don't know," he said, matter-of-factly. She blushed at his frankness, and she was a little bit sorry that she'd asked. These feelings were so new, and she wasn't sure that she was comfortable talking about them, especially with a third party.

"Joe, don't you have to shower or something? Get ready to ingest a heaping pile of raw salmon or whatever the hell it is?" Ben said jokingly, but Liz could also sense that he actually wanted his friend to leave. She had the impression that he, also, wasn't ready to discuss this openly with his friend present, and she was thankful that he was pleasantly trying to send him away. "Well, I already showered. Feel free to check my armpit if you don't believe me," he said freely, and added, "I meant that for Ben, Liz. I don't know you well enough to share my armpits with you. Maybe someday." She laughed. He was an odd guy, she thought. "But, I will depart from you both in a second. I just wanted to check in, and say hello, and also inquire as to whether you know when we'll be leaving here? Because I was hoping to play a little craps before heading home."

"I'm flying home Sunday morning, early," Liz spat out, and then regretted involving herself in the conversation.

Putting an expiration date on the trip also felt like a gut punch, as she hadn't faced the idea fully, until she said it aloud, that she had such limited time left with Ben.

Ben sighed. She imagined he was feeling similarly, and she wished she could have taken back what she'd said. "Let's see if we can check out of Casa Spink tomorrow after breakfast. Then you can gamble a little bit," he said, and then he turned to Liz. "And then maybe we can spend some time. Maybe have a first date." It was a statement, but his voice went up at the end of his sentence, so that it sounded more like a question. Liz nodded and tightened her grip around his waist. There was no other way that she would have wanted to spend her last night in Las Vegas than with Ben, and a first date sounded perfect.

"Alright, I'll leave you guys now, but," Joe said, and tapped his watch, "we're due out there in the area in twenty minutes, and if you leave me out there alone with them for more than five minutes, I will cease to be your best friend. You've been warned." And he exited the room.

Ben looked at Liz and said, "I'm not ready to go, yet," and he kissed her slowly on her mouth. Liz had never felt butterflies like this, not even in her teen years when dating had been so new and foreign and exciting.

"Me, either. We still have a few minutes, though," she said.

He looked at her, and said, "That's not what I meant."

27.

Liz and Ben left the bedroom suite and walked down the hall toward the dining room. Liz found that her appetite, which had been nearly nonexistent earlier in the day, had returned. She was looking forward to pizza, but as a native New Yorker, she was yet to try pizza out of state that came close to the pizza to which she was accustomed, both growing up on Long Island and now, as an adult living in New York City. But she was hungry, and she figured it was difficult to mess up dough, sauce, and cheese, and had been known to find that even a good old Domino's pizza hit the spot every now and again.

As they strode, Liz decided to take Ben's hand. He smiled at her as she did. She figured, at least now their behavior wasn't a complete farce; she didn't have to lean on her acting skills to demonstrate some G-rated public displays of affection tonight. In fact, she almost thought the very reason she was so comfortable taking his hand, much more so than she would have been if she were on a "first date" with a stranger, or someone that she'd met, say, on a dating website, was because they'd spent the last day or so making sure they appeared to be a couple by peppering in hand-holding and whatnot. Now that the cat was out of the bag in a way, as they were clearly both interested in getting to know each other better, it made those little details that they'd already been partaking seem easier; like it was a small comfortable step rather than a giant leap.

They entered the dining room and saw that Adam hadn't been exaggerating — he did, in fact, order a whole bunch of sushi. The table was filled with platter after platter of colorful sushi. Liz only knew the most basic information about sushi, and recognized a few popular dishes that she'd seen her friends eat, but there were so many exotic-looking choices that she'd never seen before. The colors were bright and varied - from white, to bright pinks, oranges, yellows, and greens. She wished that she enjoyed the cuisine, because it certainly looked lively and inviting, but the thought of putting one in her mouth made her stomach turn. On the far end of the table, she spied four large pizza boxes. How much, she thought, did Adam think that she and Ben could put away? Even on her most hungry night, or maybe her drunkest night, she'd never thrown down more than three slices.

Joe, boisterous and jovial as always, welcomed them as if it were his own dining room. Apparently, he had been the first to arrive on the scene, and said, "Welcome friends! See this platter right here," he said, and gestured toward a large tray of seaweed-wrapped circles of rice with tuna and avocado on top, "these are off-limits. I've already coughed all over them."

Ben laughed at him, "No argument here. But I would advise you against eating all, let's see" — he counted them quickly — "thirty-eight of them. That just seems gluttonous, even for you." He turned to Liz and said, "You should know that I once watched Joe eat two twenty-piece nuggets, plus a large fry and a shake."

Liz looked at Joe. "Jesus. But you're so slim," she said, and the look of disgust on her face was not forced. She couldn't believe someone could possibly shovel that much food into their body at once. "Please don't eat that entire tray," she added, laughing.

Joe feigned offense at the line of conversation. "In my defense, I had skipped lunch that day. And you, sir, I have seen wolf down five slices of pizza on more than one occasion, so I don't need your judgment," he threw back at his friend, jokingly. Liz liked Joe very much and having his presence had been great in a supporting actor sort of way. He definitely made everything more fun.

Vivian came into the kitchen, with Adam trailing a few feet behind. To Liz, the look on Vivian's face as she walked appeared to be angry, and she guessed that they'd just had a disagreement of some sort. When Vivian crossed the threshold from the far hallway into the dining room, it was like she flipped a switch and her face changed instantly from anger to a smile, but Liz could see that it was only a smile on her mouth; her eyes still glowered with fury, and Liz could only imagine what had just transpired. She almost felt afraid, like any of them might be collateral damage tonight if anything went astray.

She made eye contact with Vivian to try to get a read, and she thought for a split second she saw her soften, but she couldn't be sure. She'd keep her distance unless she was called upon, she decided. She figured after a few drinks Vivian would probably gravitate toward her and unload, but she certainly wasn't going to push for it.

Adam, Liz noticed, seemed wholly unaffected by whatever had happened prior to their entrance. It seemed fairly consistent with the character profile that had been painted of him by Vivian; cold, narcissistic, and unapologetic. She knew that there were always two sides to every story, but she couldn't help but dislike him. Not only because of how he may have acted toward Vivian, but also because of how Ben had suggested that Spink bullied him into this weekend excursion.

"We meet again! I hope you're all hungry. We've got quite a spread here tonight," Adam said, all smiles, as he gestured grandly to the buffet set up before them. "Liz, Ben, we can't tempt you into trying? You know, not all of them are raw," he said, and pointed to the California rolls, which Liz recognized, and about five other varieties of rolls, which she did not.

She was thankful when Ben answered for them both, "They do look interesting, but that pizza," he said, and pointed toward the stack of boxes, "is much more our speed. Liz is a native New Yorker, so she knows her pizza." She was surprised that he would let this bit of information slip out, and shot him an inquisitive look, because it begged further questioning for sure, and she had no idea why he'd complicate matters further at this point. She hoped that the information would slip under the radar.

It did not. Adam's eyes perked up at this new tidbit of information. "Really! I never would have guessed it. Where in New York?"

Liz had really hoped to keep quiet tonight and just get through the last leg of the race, but it wasn't to be. She'd keep her answers short and sweet, though. "Long Island," she replied. His line of questioning was most likely just conversational, as there was no reason at all for him to have any interest in probing into the deep, dark history of Ben's wife, but her opinion of him had already become so polluted that she approached the conversation with mistrust.

"Wow! Lawn-guy-land! I wouldn't have guessed it. You have no trace of an accent at all. No cawfee for you?" he said and overemphasized the pronunciation of the words and bastardized them far worse than she'd ever heard any New Yorker do, even her Aunt Fannie who was Brooklyn born and raised and had the thickest accent she'd ever heard.

She smiled, coldly, and said, "Adam, do you know what we New Yorkers hate? When people treat our accent, or the lack thereof, like a circus act." Her smile was present, but her tone was all business. It was one of her pet peeves, after all, when people commented on her lack of a New York accent, which she'd perfected in college; it was even worse when she was tired or forgot herself for a second, and her moderate Long Island accent did make an appearance and a stranger, usually when her family had been out of state on vacation, felt compelled to comment.

It was quiet for a second, and Adam burst into laughter, clearly assuming that Liz's deadpan comment was meant to be a joke, and everyone else followed suit. "Oh Ben, you have a good one here. She had me going for a second." Liz forced herself to laugh along with the group and made a mental note to ask Ben what the hell he was thinking by bringing up New York. Why get careless now?

"Alright, well let's dig in. I'm starving. The pizza does smell good, but I've always been taught that seafood and cheese do not mix, so those pies are all yours," Adam said, and opened up one of the boxes. Liz had to admit that the pie did look good. It wasn't as large in diameter as the pies she'd typically enjoy back home, but the crust looked golden and puffy, and the cheese was nicely browned. She wondered what type of pies were in the boxes beneath the first pie, and smelling the open box made her eager to find out.

It turned out that they would be dining al fresco, and there was a large outdoor table set up with strings of lights hanging from the low-hanging tree branches; there were centerpieces comprised of floral arrangements and the table was lined with old chianti bottles filled with fairy lights. There was a wheeled bar cart beside the table that had a coppery galvanized tub filled with ice, various soft drinks, and Japanese beers, as well as several bottles of wine, both white and red. Liz thought it looked positively enchanting, and she couldn't believe that someone had set this up just for the purpose of consuming some casual takeout, as none of the items present, including the actual table, had been in the yard this morning when she'd had her spa treatments.

They each made a plate in the dining room and headed out to the back patio. Liz had settled on one slice of regular and a slice that featured all manner of grilled vegetables. She noticed that Ben only went for the plain slices, a perfectly acceptable choice, she thought. They set their plates down on the table, and Liz sat down. Ben gestured to the bar cart and said, "What can I get you? Wine? A soda maybe?" She appreciated his thoughtfulness. It wasn't something she was used to.

"I think I'll have some white wine, with ice please, don't judge me, and also a diet Pepsi if they have one," she said. She preferred a soft drink with her meal, and wine for afterward.

"Coming right up," he said, and watched as he poured the drinks and then struggled to walk back over with all four of them. She laughed and went over to help him. "Oh, you don't think I could have made it back alone with these? No faith in your husband?" he joked.

"I have no faith at all. I foresaw four broken glasses all over the patio," she shot back, and took two of the drinks herself, as they both walked back to their seats.

Joe pulled his chair next to Ben and plopped his crowded plate onto the table. It very well may have been all thirty-eight spicy tuna rolls. He grabbed a Japanese beer and attempted to twist off the cap until he realized that it required a bottle opener, which he found on the cart and utilized. He leaned with both elbows onto the table and popped one of the tuna rolls into his mouth and chased it with a swig of the beer. When he finished, he turned to Liz, and said, "So what's the deal with your friend? She single or what?"

Liz almost spit out her soda. Joe was so blunt in his delivery, and she was continually caught off guard by him. She hadn't had an inkling that Joe might be interested in Beth, and she knew that Beth had no idea, either. Although, she had never gotten a chance to tell Beth about Jennifer. She'd been too consumed with her own feelings earlier today and had forgotten to deliver the news.

"Why, you interested?" she asked, smirking. She took a bite of the plain slice of pizza.

"Would I have asked if I wasn't?" he said, and put another tuna roll into his mouth.

"Well, I'll tell you this. She did inquire about you, but she is under the assumption that you are in a hot and heavy relationship with Jennifer."

Joe seemed genuinely perplexed. He took a swig of beer and said, "Why would she think that?"

"Well, I guess because you gave your cat a human name and you talk about her a lot. She assumed that Jennifer was your girlfriend or something. I mean, I did, too."

Joe looked thoughtful. "A human name? What makes a name specifically a human name? What's your cat's name?" he asked. She couldn't believe that no one had ever questioned his cat's name before.

"Ravioli," she said.

He laughed, "Alright, so you're telling me that it's more normal to name your cat after a pasta filled with cheese than naming your cat an actual name?"

"Yes, that is exactly what I'm telling you," she said. "Anyway, she's single. Beth, not Ravioli."

"Alright. Good to know," he said.

She didn't really know what else to say on the subject. It was Friday evening and she and Beth were returning to New York on Sunday morning. What would be the point of hooking them up now, she thought? But then she thought about how it wasn't her place to edit Beth's life, and so she said, "I can text her right now, you know. If you want."

He leaned back in his chair so far that she thought he might fall backward. "Sure, give her my number. Tell her to shoot me a text. Maybe it will give me someone to chat with tonight after you two retire to your quarters," he said, and rolled his eyes in a joking way. Then he ate two more tuna rolls.

Vivian and Adam finally made their way outside. Liz wondered if there had been some more conversation between the two that had kept them from joining the rest of the party sooner, but both had unreadable expressions. Vivian went immediately for the wine and filled a glass until it almost overflowed. Adam cracked open a beer and seated himself on the other side of Joe.

"So, you like those spicy tuna rolls, huh?" he said, and pointed to Joe's plate.

"Hey, if you put out fifty tuna rolls, then I'm going to eat forty-nine of them. I'll leave one, because I won't have the public suggesting that I don't share," Joe said. Spink threw his head back in laughter, as if this were the funniest thing he'd ever heard. Vivian rolled her eyes at her husband's over-the-top laughter and took a seat near to Liz.

She whispered to Liz, "I hate that son of a bitch," and Liz nearly choked on her pizza. It was quiet outside and there were only five of them present; she wasn't positive that Vivian had said it quietly enough so that Adam couldn't hear her. Maybe, Liz thought, she didn't care. Maybe he didn't, either.

"Bad afternoon?" Liz asked, not really wanting to hear the answer.

Vivian held her chopsticks and picked up a piece of something that looked like raw salmon on a rectangular block of rice and put it into her mouth. She chewed and then took a long swig of the wine, so that nearly half of the very full glass was gone when she'd finally pulled it away from her mouth. "Yeah, bad afternoon," she said, so low that it was almost a growl. She didn't seem like she wanted to divulge any more, and so Liz didn't press for more information. She was glad, because she felt very much as if Adam could hear them, and it made her feel incredibly awkward.

Adam turned his attention toward Liz and Ben and asked, "How is the pizza? Up to your New York standards, Liz?"

Before she could answer, Vivian cut in. "Oh, stop being such a condescending dick, Adam. Let them eat the pizza without your sarcastic commentary. Asshole." Then she downed the rest of the wine, stood up, and filled another glass to the brim.

Liz, Ben, and Joe froze, unsure about how they should respond to the outburst. Liz looked at Ben wide-eyed. They all remained silent. Liz took a bite of her pizza. Adam finally broke the ice and said, smiling, but coldly, "Thanks honey. Why don't you have another drink?" Then he stood up, got himself another beer, and asked Carmen, from the door, to please put on some music. Liz was glad to have some auditory distraction. The music seemed to change the mood, at least cover it up with noise.

With the exception of the music, they all ate their dinner in relative quiet, which was fine with Liz. After he had finished his sushi, Adam sat back in his chair and then turned to Ben and Joe and said, "Spoke with Brit about an hour ago. So the acquisitions meeting is going to be soon, we're thinking Tuesday or Wednesday. Winkler is your representation, right? I'm sure Brit has already given her a call and gotten her on board. We're going to fast-track this one, at least through legal. Then, you know how it goes once it gets into first round rewrites. Might take a bit. But we'll get there. Second Chances is going to be great. I really think so."

Liz coughed hard at the title of the movie. She was struck with the notion that the name of the screenplay was some type of sign; before she left New York, she had decided to give herself a second chance—at life, at love, at putting her happiness above pleasing other people for the first time in her life, and now, here she was, confronted with the words she'd thought to herself verbatim from the mouth of the guy she thought might be the first person in forever for whom she'd felt something real.

Ben turned to her and said, "Are you okay?" He handed her a soda and placed his hand on her back. He probably thought she was choking on the pizza and had no idea that what she was actually choking on were his own words.

She took the soda and swallowed a mouthful. She cleared her throat and apologetically said, "Oh, sorry about that. Just went down the wrong pipe." She coughed lightly again, and said, "I'm alright, really. I didn't mean to interrupt."

Once he was sure that Liz had recovered from her coughing fit, Ben turned to Adam and said, "That's great, I know that both Joe and I are incredibly excited."

Ben turned to Joe, who had remained uncharacteristically quiet for the last few minutes, and said, "Aren't we? Ready to get this done?" but Joe didn't answer immediately. He stared at his plate for a moment and wiped at his brow with his napkin. Liz could see that he was flushed and sweating profusely. Ben must have noticed also, because he leaned close and said, "Are you okay? You don't look so good, man."

Joe exhaled hard and said, "You know what? I don't feel so great. I think maybe I overdid it with the tuna rolls." He looked at his host and hostess and said, "I'm just going to excuse myself for a few minutes, I think I have to go and lay down."

"Of course," Adam said. "Why don't you take this and go relax for a bit?" he said and handed him a can of ginger ale.

Joe rose, and walked toward the door, but for the last few steps he picked up his pace and practically ran into the house, and Liz could see him running through the kitchen before he disappeared down the hallway.

Liz turned back to Ben and said, "I hope he's okay."

Ben shrugged his shoulders and said, "I think maybe he just overdid it a little bit. It was a lot of tuna rolls—" But before he could finish, they heard Vivian croak out from her end of the table "oh my God," and then she tried, unsuccessfully, to cover her mouth to prevent herself from vomiting. She leaned to the side, luckily away from Liz, and lost her entire dinner all over the patio.

Liz said, "Oh no," and went to help Vivian steady herself.

Vivian looked at her, pathetically, and said, "it must have been the fucking sushi," and began to heave again, but all that came out was a watery burp.

"Let me help you into the house," Liz said, and steadied Vivian and helped her to the door.

Once inside, Vivian said, "Oh, Liz. Go back out. I think I'm going to die, and I don't want you to see any more of this," and then she bolted into the kitchen and vomited into the sink. She took a few heaving breaths over the sink before splashing her face with cold water and running for her bedroom.

Liz returned to the scene of the crime and found Ben standing out there alone. "What the hell is going on?" she asked.

"I guess it was the sushi. Adam just ran off into the pool house bathroom and I'm pretty sure he puked in that bush over there on the way," he said, and pointed to a small green shrub.

"Jeez. Should we go check on Joe? Is food poisoning from sushi dangerous? Like should they go to the hospital?"

"Believe it or not, this isn't the first time that Joe has eaten bad sushi, and if I recall, it's going to be a rough few hours for him, but it should mostly pass by tomorrow. But yeah, let's go check on him. Maybe bring him some water."

"This is why you're not supposed to eat raw fish," Liz said, and pointed emphatically at the puddle of vomit that Vivian had left on the patio next to her chair.

28.

Liz returned to their bedroom suite, as Ben thought maybe it was best if he checked on Joe alone, seeing as he might be in rough shape. She checked her phone and saw that Beth had texted her back and that, yes, it was okay to pass her number along to Joe, and that she would, having been given his number, shoot him a text as well. She texted her again to brief her on tonight's latest developments, on the outside chance that Beth attempted to reach out to Joe tonight and was disappointed at his lack of response.

Ben returned to the room and closed the door behind him. Liz could see that he held in his hand a bottle of wine, unopened and full, and two glasses. She said, "What, no cold pizza?"

"Honestly, after that scene I didn't think you'd be in the mood for food," he said, laughing.

"I'm kidding. I'm actually not. But good call on the wine. I guess we're relegated to the room here tonight, because I'm not really in the mood to overlook the pool with the scent of vomit in the air," she said.

"Look at it this way, now we don't have to play Pictionary or whatever the hell they had planned for us," he said, as he took a corkscrew and opened the bottle of wine. He poured some wine into each glass and handed her one and sat down next to her on the bed.

"I'll toast to that," she said.

He grabbed the television remote and asked, "Any preferences? Other than Lucy?" Liz was relieved that he turned on the TV. She was glad to have one-on-one time with Ben, in spite of the fact that there were three casualties of the evening in other rooms in the house, but she thought a little background noise took some of the pressure off. Any lulls in the conversation wouldn't feel as awkward.

"I don't know. Something funny. I need to distract myself from the horror we just witnessed," Liz said, and Ben settled on an episode of Seinfeld. It was almost over, but in all likelihood, there would probably be a few subsequent episodes to follow. She took off the wedding ring and placed it on the nightstand. She hated wearing it when she didn't have to. Ben noticed the gesture.

He motioned toward the ring. "So, if you tell me your story, I'll tell you mine. You know, if you want to. Or not."

Although it was still slightly raw, Liz found that she did want to tell the story. "Well, let's see. I was engaged until last week. I know this ring looks more like a wedding band, but that's just because it was a family ring." She took a sip of the wine before continuing. "Actually, the more I think of it, the more I find that the story isn't really that interesting. I was with my ex for over eight years. It was, whatever. When we first met we were both in our twenties, so the fact that I had a job and he was constantly in the market for a job didn't really matter much. But as the years went on, and his ambition never changed...well, I guess I just checked out. Going through the motions. Not that I cared about his ambition, really. I would have just liked for him to find a job, any job, because I felt like he wasn't interested in becoming an adult." She took a big gulp of wine. She wondered if this story was as boring for Ben as it sounded to her. "Anyhow, I guess it was just easier to stay than to go. And I guess I was ready to just admit to myself that life was about complacency and not about setting the world on fire. So, he proposed, and I thought, alright, I guess so. It was easier to stay and commit myself to a life of mediocrity than break out of the cycle."

Ben listened with his full attention, "So what changed?"

She thought for a second. Things had certainly changed dramatically in the last week, but she wasn't sure what the catalyst had been. She looked up at Ben and said, "I'm not sure. I just had a small glimmer of clarity and thought that it wasn't fair to myself, or to him, to commit myself to someone that I didn't really want." She finished the wine in her glass and added, "Also, Beth hated him. So, I would have signed myself up for a lifetime of her bitching." She smiled at the last part. It was a joke, but truly, Beth had seen what was best for her all along.

"Well, good for you. Not all of us know when to call it quits with someone who isn't right for us," he said. "Do you want a little more?" he asked and gestured toward her glass.

"Alright, just a half though," she said, and he poured some of the wine from the bottle into her glass. "So, that's me. What of yours?" she asked and pointed toward the wedding ring that Ben still wore on his left hand. He glanced at it, sadly, but she noticed that he didn't remove it.

He sighed and began, "Well, how can I say this?" he asked himself, aloud, and seemed to gather his thoughts for a moment. He continued, "I've spent all of my adult life, over twenty years, married to a woman for whom I've never felt an ounce of love."

Liz looked at him wide-eyed. It was a startling revelation. It was as if he had lived out in its entirety the life, she'd managed to avoid by breaking off her engagement. She placed a hand lightly on his upper arm. She couldn't imagine how he'd spent twenty years of his life with a person for whom he didn't, at least at some point, feel love.

"We met in college, she got pregnant, and we got married. I had thought it was what would be best for my son, but I was wrong. I see that now," he said, and he looked into the distance, maybe out the window. Liz couldn't see where his focus was; she was sorry that they had gone down this path because he looked broken, but then she remembered that it was Ben who started this line of conversation, so he must have wanted to unload this information.

"So what changed for you last week? How was Wednesday different than the last twenty years of your life?" she asked.

He thought for a moment. The truth was that he hadn't made that final move; Adeline had been the one to serve him with divorce papers. Who knows how long he would have gone on as they had been; maybe forever. He thought for a moment about editing his answer, but then thought better of it. He didn't want to start his journey with Liz, even if it ended up only lasting this weekend, with a lie. He hoped it wasn't only going to last the weekend.

He took a deep breath, "We've been living as roommates, hostile roommates, for years now. We don't share a bedroom and we haven't spent a holiday together in probably ten years. My son is off at college, and I know he won't return afterward. And although I've often felt like my next move would be to go it alone, or maybe bunk with Joe for a few months, it was actually her. She made the move. Left me divorce papers on the kitchen table the morning that I was scheduled to come here, to this meeting. To this life-altering meeting."

Liz didn't know how to respond. It had been a speech packed with information. Although she understood that Ben's ex-wife had clearly set out to try to sabotage his trip here, she also couldn't help but take away the fact that if it were not for those divorce papers, Ben would probably have stayed in that dead-end marriage. She wasn't sure how she felt about that.

Ben must have seen the conflicted expression on Liz's face, as he expected that his story might have elicited this reaction. "I know what you're thinking, because I'm not the one who finally ended it," he said, and Liz shrugged. "And I agree, that I should have. Years ago. But I guess I just felt so, I don't know, defeated. Like a failure. Almost like, well Ben, you failed at this marriage and now your punishment is a lifetime spent in the same house with this woman who despises your very existence. And so, I figured I would just continue on like that forever, never thinking that I deserved anything more." He stopped for a moment, then continued, "And never thinking that maybe there was something else out there for me. Something that just..." But his words trailed off. He didn't know how to finish.

Liz saw his inner struggle. Who was she to make him justify his life choices? She placed her hand on the top of his and said, "You don't have to explain yourself to me." He exhaled, and they were both quiet for a time. Ben leaned back against the headboard, and Liz moved herself over so that she was seated right beside him. He put his arm around her shoulder and they sat together and didn't mention either of their former relationships again.

As they sat together and watched television, Liz noticed that the sky, which had still been sunny when they'd attempted to eat dinner outside earlier, had changed from orange, to pink, before finally settling on a deep blue black. She wasn't sure how much time had passed because she didn't want to know. She was trying to enjoy every last moment of this trip, but she couldn't help but feel as if every second that passed took her closer to her flight on Sunday morning. Closer to home. Closer to her life back at home, which now seemed like an empty shell, or maybe more like an unfinished novel that she was no longer interested in picking up. But, she didn't feel excited for what may come next. She felt a little scared and mostly sad. She wanted to continue to see Ben after this weekend, to see where the road took them, but she also couldn't imagine being in a long-distance relationship. It seemed so daunting.

* * *

"YOU ALRIGHT?" he asked. The two had been sitting in silence for a time, save for the sound of the television, but Liz must have been lost in her own thoughts, because she'd sighed so loudly that it had startled Ben out of his own private reverie. They hadn't really had closure on the conversation that he'd brought up earlier about their respective relationships. He chastised himself and wondered why he thought Liz might want to hear about his ex-wife. He wished now that he would have just kept his mouth shut. It was clear to him now that he'd ruined the mood and he wasn't sure how to go about fixing it.

She turned to him and nodded vaguely and smiled weakly. She almost looked as though she might cry, and it was all he could do to refrain from scooping her up onto his lap, but he realized that despite the part they'd been playing, this was all brand new for both of them, and he had to remember that. He barely knew this woman and, yet, he felt her sadness in the pit of his stomach. He racked his brain. He knew he had to break this spell, because he couldn't ruin any of the minutes that he had left here with her.

"You know what? I'm going to check on Joe. See if he's still in agony," he said.

"Yeah, that's probably a good idea. Hopefully he's getting some rest at least," she answered, halfheartedly.

Ben got up and left the room. He knocked lightly on Joe's door, and when there was no answer, he entered anyway. He looked around the suite, which looked very similar to his, and didn't see Joe. It concerned him slightly, so he walked to the bathroom. There was Joe, sound asleep and snoring loudly on the bathroom floor next to the toilet bowl. It wasn't a scene with which Ben was wholly unfamiliar, as in their younger years Joe would often drink to the brink of vomiting, and more often than not lose the battle. Ben didn't want to move him—he may, after all, require use of the toilet again before the night was through—but he did retrieve a pillow from the bed and a fleece blanket to make sure that his slumber was a little more comfortable. Joe, exhausted from whatever had transpired over the last two or three hours, only murmured unintelligibly in his sleep and allowed Ben to assemble a makeshift bed for him. Then Ben exited the bedroom and walked into the kitchen area, hoping that Carmen or someone else might be around.

He entered the kitchen and there Carmen was, cleaning the top of the huge gas range. She looked up when Ben entered the kitchen and smiled. "I see you're up and about, are you feeling better?" she asked with genuine concern.

"Oh, Liz and I are fine. We only at the pizza, thankfully," he said.

She nodded sympathetically, "Good move. I never eat the raw fish myself. I don't trust it."

Ben wasn't sure how to broach the subject with Carmen, but he also knew that if he lurked around any longer she was going to feel uncomfortable. He jumped right in and said, "Carmen, earlier today Fred, the driver, was nice enough to take us into town—do you think he might be around still? I'd love to take Liz to get some ice cream or something."

He could tell from her expression that Fred must have already gone for the day. "Oh, no, I'm so sorry. Mr. Spink was so sick that he told Fred he wouldn't be needing his services tonight for sure." She looked at him pointedly and said, "I can call an Uber for you, if you'd like." He felt like a moron. An Uber. Why didn't it occur to him?

"Carmen, that would be fantastic. Thank you so much," he said.

She pulled her cell phone out of the pocket of her apron, and after about thirty seconds looked up and said, "Alright, they should be here in about ten minutes."

"Awesome. Carmen, really. Thank you so much. I don't expect that we'll be out too late. I thought maybe just an ice cream cone, stroll around a bit," Ben said.

"It is my pleasure, Ben. Don't rush back. I'll leave the front door unlocked until I leave around two a.m.," she said, and turned back to her work.

Ben returned to the room and Liz was sitting cross-legged on the bed looking at her phone, probably chatting with Beth, he presumed. He could only imagine how Liz had phrased it all to her friend. He hoped that she realized that he was truly no longer attached to his wife, if he'd ever been. This trip had been eye-opening and life-changing in so many ways for him.

"Wow, that was like ten minutes. Is he okay?" She looked concerned.

"Oh, yeah, he's fine. He was passed out on the bathroom floor, so I made him a little more comfortable."

"Oh, OK. That's good. I hope the other two are alright. I know for sure neither of them are checking on each other," she said.

"Yeah, probably not," he said, and then changed the subject, because he was anxious and excited to be out and about in the world with her. He wanted to be normal with her, just be regular Ben. This charade was very tiresome. "So, you want to get of here for a little bit?" he asked.

She raised an eyebrow, slightly confused. "Really? What did you have in mind?"

"I thought we could go get some ice cream," he said, and he smiled that same shy smile that he'd shown to her after their very first encounter at the Lily Bar.

"Alright," she said, and smiled. He was so relieved to see the smile.

Ben sat down on the bed, so that he was facing her. It was as good a time as any to make some changes in his life, he decided. And so he took off his wedding ring, and placed it on his nightstand, much in the same way that she had placed hers down earlier. She saw the gesture and looked at him wide-eyed and perplexed.

He wasn't sure what to say, exactly. He didn't want to be dramatic and he certainly didn't want her to think he was jumping into a situation with her too quickly, or that she was a rebound, because honestly, he wasn't thinking like that. He was just thinking that in that moment, with that girl, was where he needed to be. And so he just said, "Well, I just know there's something else out there for me."

He stood up and stretched. Then, he extended a hand to her and helped her up and onto her feet. He thought that maybe his last course of action was a little too much — after all, they'd only actually known each other for two days, and they'd only made their feelings known to each other a few hours ago. So, although he meant every word, he chose his next words wisely and said, "Just going to put out there that if you're a rainbow sprinkles person then I'm not sure that we can go on that date tomorrow night."

Liz laughed. She said, "Actually, all sprinkles are just a waste of money and calories. If I'm going with a cone, and

I haven't committed to that yet, then I'm going with chocolate crunchies."

"Alright, those are acceptable. Joe gets rainbow sprinkles and vanilla ice cream and I've nearly ended our friendship over it," he said.

"Wow, look at Joe ordering like a bitch. Ending a friendship over it would be totally understandable. Oh, and I should add that I stand up and leave a room if anyone dares to order rum raisin. Why are you going to get raisins all tied up with delicious ice cream?" she responded.

"Totally agree. And I extend that to cookies as well. No raisins, please," he said, and Liz laughed and nodded. "Alright, let's hit the road. I had Carmen call us an Uber for us," he said, and took her by the hand.

As they left the room, for the first time without the artifice of their wedding rings, the air was almost pungent with anticipation about what might come next.

* * *

"ALRIGHT, I HAVE ONE. So, you either have to stand up in a crowded movie theater and announce, loudly, that you have herpes really bad, or you have to approach a random child on the street and tell him that Santa doesn't exist."

Liz slapped the table. "That one is not fair at all! Like I'm going to be responsible for ruining someone's childhood. Guess I have the old herp. But that one wasn't fair. You gave me one choice that wasn't even possible," Liz said, and erupted in laughter.

"Totally fair. I didn't complain when one of my options involved making out with Judge Judy," Ben threw back at her.

"Which was the option that you chose!" Liz interrupted.

"I'd do it just so I could tell the story at parties," Ben said, and put his hands up in the air as if he were surrendering. Liz laughed. They had finished their ice cream a while ago, but they had stayed at the table chatting, and she couldn't remember when she'd last had such a naturally great time with someone. "It's getting a little crowded in here and I think those guys over there are eyeing this table with impatience," Ben said, and gestured to a group of three well-dressed guys who seemed to be waiting for a table with annoyance.

"Alright, but you know part of me feels like we should stay another hour because I just don't care for their attitude," Liz said, kidding.

"There's the New Yorker in you coming out," Ben joked back, and it earned him a punch in the upper arm. "Oh, and there it is again!" he said. She laughed.

They stood up and tossed their garbage into the can, and then left the ice cream parlor. Ben put his arm around Liz's shoulder, and she in turn put her arm around his waist. "Should we stroll a little bit? It's such a nice night," she asked. She was glad she'd brought along a sweatshirt, because as the night wore on it had started to get chilly.

"You sure we won't run into your friends? I don't want to put you in an awkward position, and I don't really think that I can pull off the role of Aunt Lorraine," he said.

"Nah, they're at some bar tonight. We should be good. Let's walk down to MGM and get a look at the big cats inside," she suggested. They walked for a while in easy silence, the kind of silence that usually only feels comfortable after you've known someone for years. After a time, they approached the MGM Grand and walked into the lobby, and found that they no longer had lions, and in fact, they'd been removed in 2012.

"Oh well, it's for the best. I always hate when I see wild animals stuck in cages, " Liz said. "Why don't we sit in here for a few before we walk back," she said, and pointed toward some seating in the lobby area. Ben nodded.

"So, I hope you don't think this counts as our first date. This was like a half date at best," Liz said, smiling.

"Wow, alright. Now I feel some pressure about tomorrow," Ben said. "Any suggestions?"

Liz thought for a minute. "To be honest, I don't really care for Las Vegas. I'm not a gambler, and all of the bars and lounges are so loud. Maybe there's something quiet. Maybe a casual dinner and then something, I don't know, that doesn't have a bunch of drunk idiots acting a fool."

"Well, that is a tall order. I'll think about it. Quiet in Vegas. It might be a challenge, but I will make something happen. Maybe there's a library or something," Ben said.

Liz looked away for a moment, and then looked back at him. "It'll be our last night." She put the statement out into the world, she wanted to see how he might respond. She knew how she would like him to respond.

He took both of her hands in his and said, "No, it's just our last night here." She wasn't sure what it meant for the day after tomorrow, or the ones after that, but she knew that those were the words that she'd hoped for tonight.

* * *

LIZ AND BEN DIDN'T make their way back to the Spink's house until well after one in the morning, but fortunately Carmen had left the door unlocked for them as she'd promised. They were as quiet as possible, and on their way back to the bedroom they stopped in to see how Joe was feeling. Liz only peeked her head into the room, but she could hear loud snoring and saw that he was sound asleep on the bed. Ben picked Joe's phone up off of the floor and plugged it into a charger sitting atop the nightstand, and quietly closed the door.

When they got back into their room, Liz excused herself to the bathroom to wash her face, brush her teeth, and change into pajamas. She looked in the mirror, face wet from the cleanse, and thought about how she felt as though she were looking at an entirely different person than the girl who looked in this very mirror not twelve hours ago. She felt like she'd lived a whole year in the last two and a half days; like her skin was the only thing keeping her from going a hundred places at once. She dried her face and walked back into the bedroom. Ben was already changed into pajama pants and was settling in on the couch, as he had previously. It wouldn't do. She wasn't quite ready to get too physical — after all, she was fresh off of a breakup — but she knew she had to have him next to her, close to her.

"Plenty of room over here, if you want company," she said, and almost before she'd finished the sentence, Ben was on his way over. He kissed her on the forehead, and she curled her head against his chest. They were both quiet for a few minutes. There was so much that should be said, that could be said, but that they were both afraid to mention.

"What are we going to do, Ben?" she asked. She almost felt like she was living someone else's life. Who has an experience like this? No one that she knew. No one in the real world, she thought.

He sighed. "I don't know, but we'll find a way." He pulled back a few inches and looked at her in the dim light, as the only light that now filled the room came from the slightly ajar bathroom door. "I've lived my entire life without feeling the way I've felt for the last two days, and I'm not about to abandon it because of a pesky 2700 miles.

Right?" he asked, as if he needed assurance that what he was feeling was a real thing.

She smiled and said, "Right." Then she added, "Weirdest two days of my life. Best, but also weirdest." He laughed.

Then she curled into him, and they both fell off to sleep.

29.

Liz wasn't sure if it was the mattress or the company, but she couldn't remember when she'd slept more soundly. The light began peeking through a gap in the curtains and seemed to make a beeline directly for her forehead. She flopped onto her belly and tried to shut out the morning, but next to her she could feel that Ben was beginning to stir, and she knew that if he awoke, she'd have a hard time staying asleep. She was generally a light sleeper, and any movement in the room would prove to be too much for her to overcome.

Before either could fully awaken, there was a knock at the door. Sure enough, before waiting for a response from within, Joe strolled right into the room, and although she was face down on her pillow, she could feel him plop right down on the bed.

"Good morning, honeymooners," he said. Ben kicked at him from under the covers. Liz could not understand how someone who had been completely incapacitated hours before could be so perky that early in the morning. She reached blindly for her phone on the nightstand. She gasped when she saw the time— it was already after eleven in the morning. She'd assumed it was hours earlier; she hadn't slept that late since college.

"Why are you here?" Ben asked, without emerging from under the blanket. She guessed he also had no idea how late it was.

"Because it's nearly lunchtime and I want to leave this fucking prison already," Joe said. "And I've been texting you for the last two hours without reply, so you've left me no choice but to invade your little lover's nest here."

Ben sat bolt upright. "What time is it?" He reached for his phone. "Jeez, its 11:08!" They'd slept away the whole morning. "Sorry man, I guess I had it on silent. Alright, where is everyone else? Did you guys have breakfast or anything?"

Joe leaned on his elbow across the width of the foot of the bed. Liz could not believe his complete lack of self-consciousness at the scene he'd walked into, but she didn't feel awkward. He really seemed like an old friend. "I had some coffee with my friend Carmen, but so far I haven't seen anyone else. I took a little stroll out in the yard. Tried to peek in your window."

Liz broke in, "Joe, I realize that you have absolutely no boundaries, but I am in my pajamas and I'm going to need you to avert your eyes so that I can run to the bathroom."

Joe replied, "Wow, Liz. I thought we were past that point, but fine," and he buried his face in the comforter until Liz has safely retreated to the bathroom.

* * *

WHEN THE DOOR OF the bathroom clicked closed, Joe sat upright on the bed. "Well, I'm going to need some details," he whispered to Ben.

"There aren't any. It wasn't like that. We went out, got ice cream, walked around, and then we slept." Joe raised an eyebrow. "I'm serious."

Joe said, "Well, my condolences to you, my friend." Ben shook his head at his friend's comment. "Hm, what is this?" Joe said, as if something caught his eye, and he stood up and walked to the nightstand. He snatched Ben's wedding band and held it up to one eye and looked right through the center.

Ben wasn't quite sure how to reply to Joe's discovery. He found he was at a loss for words, which, as a writer, wasn't something to which he was accustomed.

"Nah, I'm teasing you. This is all good as far as I can see. You should pawn it while we're here. Put the money on black, like Adeline's soul."

Ben couldn't help but laugh. But he had no intention of selling the ring. He had grand plans of signing the divorce papers and leaving them on the kitchen table, as they'd been left for him, topped with the empty symbol of his wedding band. Carol, his lawyer, had taken a quick glance at the papers yesterday before possibly referring Ben to a more qualified colleague. As it turned out, because they had so few assets to speak of—just Ben's truck, a savings account, as well as both of their retirement accounts, the dissolution of the marriage wasn't a complicated matter. Adeline wasn't even asking for more than her fair share; she wanted no part of Ben's truck, which surprised him. He'd thought she'd want to force the sale and split the money because she knew how much he loved the truck, but she hadn't. It seemed as if she just wanted out of the marriage, and fast. She requested half of the value of their joint savings account, and that he be removed as beneficiary on her retirement account.

Carol had mentioned that he was lucky that the split seemed so amicable, and it perplexed him because there was nothing amicable about their relationship as it stood. It was evident that Adeline hated him; after all, she'd served him with papers with the hope, he assumed, that it would ruin this business trip. When he'd told Carol about these details, she said matter-of-factly, "Well, then my guess would be that she already has a boyfriend and just wants to move on with her life." It wasn't something that he'd considered before, but once he did, all of the hours she'd spent outside of their home, at the beach or wherever she'd been going, seemed to make more sense. Ben found that he felt nothing at the thought of his wife with another man, other than some pity for the poor son of a bitch who would be inheriting her. In fact, if it made their divorce as quick and painless as possible, then he'd be willing to officiate at their wedding someday, maybe gift them with a nice blender.

Knowing that his divorce could be final sooner rather than later, and without a long and drawn-out legal battle, had made his decision easy. He'd return home on Sunday, sign the papers, leave them on the table with the ring, and then after he'd driven Jack back to school that evening, he planned on staying with Joe until he figured out his next move. He actually felt lighter after hearing Carol's news and making the decision to move forward with the divorce immediately. It wasn't something that he'd shared with Joe, or Liz, as of yet because he hadn't had time alone with Joe, and he didn't think this type of heavy news was something that he wanted to pile on top of his fledgling relationship with Liz. He'd dropped enough info about his wife on her yesterday; he wasn't going to make that mistake again.

"Alright, give us like twenty minutes to get dressed, and then we'll figure out how to get the hell out of here. But you know, tonight, I know you want to play a little craps..."

Joe interrupted, "Oh stop. I can read the writing on the wall. I know I'm flying solo tonight. Maybe I'll hunt down Beth and the royal wedding party. See what those chicks are up to."

* * *

LIZ POKED HER HEAD out, "I heard that. Beth said they'll be at the Palms tonight."

"Ugh, forget it. I don't have the patience to deal with a gaggle of twenty-one-year-olds. I guess I'm on my own tonight," he said, and then he turned to Ben. "Twenty minutes. Kitchen. I'm ready to bust out of here already. Now I'm going to go find Carmen, see what she's up to tonight." He left the room, and when Liz heard the door shut, she stepped back out into the room.

"How do we get out of here if Vivian and Adam are missing in action? Won't they feel slighted that we left? I mean, I don't really care, but I'm just thinking about how it could affect your situation?" she asked.

"Yeah, I don't know. This whole weekend has just been weird. Hopefully Joe is out there now laying some groundwork."

"Alright, let me get changed and then we'll head out there. I have to get in touch with Beth and see where all of the girls are today. I guess I'll head back to my hotel, get changed and everything, and then we'll meet back up?" She hated wasting her time today with her friends, and she felt bad even suggesting in her inner monologue that time with her friends was a waste, but it was true. And although it was selfish, she didn't care. Logistically she had no idea when she'd see Ben again after today, but she knew she'd be able to see Beth and Jenna and Sonia and all of the other mateys anytime she wanted.

"Yeah I guess. I hadn't really thought about the activities between now and our big date tonight," he said, and smiled at her. He stood up and stretched, and then he sauntered over to where Liz stood just outside of the bathroom and enveloped her in his arms. "I've gotten used to spending the whole day with you, though."

She looked up at him, "Well, how about I drop my stuff off, and shower, and then we meet back up for lunch? We can make it a foursome if you want. I'm sure Beth would love an update. Then we can break off from them, maybe? I don't know. I'm just spit balling."

"I like it," he said and kissed the top of her head. "I'm going to throw on some clothes out here while you get ready in the bathroom, and when you're done in there, I just need like 5 minutes."

She nodded and let herself back into the bathroom to finish getting ready.

* * *

LIZ COULDN'T BELIEVE what Joe told them when they'd entered the kitchen. Although she didn't really know Vivian well, she had to admit she almost felt a little bit betrayed. She had been under the impression that they'd formed a kind of friendship, albeit one based on false pretenses. Now she felt like maybe she was the one who had been duped.

"What do you mean, they're gone?" she asked.

"What I mean is that, apparently, the king and queen boarded six a.m. flights back to Los Angeles this morning without nary a goodbye or best wishes," Joe repeated.

"They just left us here?" She was so confused, she looked back and forth from Ben to Joe. "They just left a bunch of, for lack of a better term, strangers in their house after pretty much forcing us to stay here all weekend?" She sounded more annoyed than she anticipated, but she couldn't believe how rude it was for the host and hostess to depart without so much as a note. Money or no money, it was poor manners in her opinion.

"That is the news on the street. Although I don't know why Carmen waited until now to tell me when we had coffee together earlier this morning. I was beginning to think I had a special bond with her, and now I just don't feel like I know her anymore," Joe said, in mock offense.

"Well, I guess that saves us the trouble of making up an excuse about why we have to leave so early," Ben said, and shrugged. He poured himself a cup of coffee; he was afraid if he didn't get some caffeine into his body that he might start to develop a headache. "I guess we have to call ourselves an Uber or something, right?" he asked, as he grabbed a danish from the tray on the island; he realized that he felt ravenous and figured why not take advantage of the free food.

"Well, since we're all alone here for the most part, why don't we eat something, think about what our plans are for the day, and then get our stuff and get the hell out of here," Liz said, and eyed the tray of pastries as well. She turned to Joe. "I'm going to see if Beth wants to meet up for lunch a little later. Do you want to join?"

"Sure, now that Carmen has done me dirty I guess I'm free this afternoon," Joe replied. Then, he strolled over to the gigantic sub-zero refrigerator and opened it up, "I wonder if they have any orange juice up in this bitch." He found that they did, in fact, have orange juice and poured himself a tall glass before returning it to the fridge. Then he sat down at the table and sorted through the pastries with his fingers. Liz had to laugh; Joe made himself at home wherever and with whomever he happened to be.

"I'm going to pack my stuff up and give Beth a call. I just want to make sure she's good with lunch and let her know I'm heading back to the hotel for a little while," Liz said, and excused herself to the bedroom. She had kept all of her clothes in her duffel, and so she only had to gather up the contents of her toiletry bag. Knowing that it would only take her a minute to complete the task, she sat at the edge of the bed and called Beth.

Beth answered after one ring. "Tell me something good, lady," Beth opened with. Liz laughed at her lack of salutation.

"I don't really even know where to begin," Liz said. "So, our stay at the resort over here is coming to a close. I'm going to be back at the hotel tonight."

"And that's it? It's not done, right?" Beth asked. She didn't articulate what she meant by it but Liz could surmise.

"Oh, no. It's not done. Was thinking we could have lunch today, catch you up on things or whatever," Liz said.

"Yeah, but please no more Denny's. It's my last day in Las Vegas, and I want to get liquored up and make some questionable choices, so can we please go someplace where I can have a drink for the love of God?"

"Yeah, that's fine. Maybe there's a Mexican place or something off the Strip that isn't swarming with people. What's the vibe like over there with everyone? Are they super pissed off that I'm MIA?" Liz asked. She knew that her reappearance today, and then subsequent absence again tonight, would probably raise some eyebrows. Why would she leave her dying aunt only to return to her house for a few hours that evening? It didn't make sense. She didn't really care. She was going to do what she was going to do tonight.

"Not really. They've been keeping themselves occupied with all kinds of fun activities like pretending they're younger than they are, dancing up against men who are clearly disinterested, talking extra loudly when we're out to make sure everyone can hear their conversation, those sorts of things. So, they're a little too self-involved right now to think about where you've been. I can tell you, though, that your absence has ruined my life and now, when we get home, I'm taking full possession of your brown Ferragamo boots," Beth said in a tone that Liz knew was only mock annoyance.

"You know what? They're all yours. You've earned them," Liz said back, and Beth laughed.

"Wow, willing to give up the boots for some time with this guy? Must be something pretty special," Beth said, and Liz could feel herself blush at the comment, like she would have in seventh grade if someone would have let the name of her "crush" out of the bag.

She changed the subject. "Anyway, I think I should be back at the hotel around noon, so please come down and meet me. I feel so awkward walking in there alone for some reason."

"Yeah, yeah, I'll meet you down there. See you in a bit," she said, and Liz ended the call. She gathered all of her items from the bathroom, added them to the duffel bag, and went back out into the kitchen. "Almost ready to head back?" she said.

"Let me get my stuff together, and then I guess we can roll," Ben said. "I don't have much here, so it'll take me a minute." He left the kitchen and walked toward the bedroom. Joe was seated at one of the chairs adjacent to the island and had his feet up on another chair while he sipped at a cup of coffee and scrolled through his phone.

He looked up at Liz and said, "So, what are you guys going to do after today? Keep this up?" She was shocked by his candor. She knew he was forward, but this seemed to border on invasive. She felt her cheeks flush, and she wasn't sure how to answer.

"I mean, I would like to," she said, but it came out more like a question.

"Maybe that was a little too personal, but you know. Ben is...well, it's just good to see him happy for a change. I guess I would just hate to see that end. That's all," he said, and went back to his phone, as if the conversation had been about something as innocuous as the weather.

Ben walked back into the room and said, "Alright, I'm all set. Uber should be here in like fifteen minutes." Liz offered a smile. While she was glad that her brief conversation with Joe revealed that Ben was as interested as she was, it still brought up those feelings of — Confusion? Dread? — about the idea of a long-distance relationship. She just kept telling herself that life has a way of working itself out.

"So, are you guys good with something off the Strip for lunch? Beth wants to get tanked apparently," Liz said. Joe's ears perked up at this tidbit of information.

"I second a drunk lunch. Finally, somebody on the same page as me on this trip," Joe said, and stood up. "Let's hit the road."

30.

When lunchtime rolled around, they found themselves at an off-the-beaten-path Mexican restaurant called The Furious Burrito, about a five-minute car ride from the Strip proper. It wasn't swarming with tourists, and it offered bottomless margaritas, which Liz knew her friend would take as a personal challenge. It seemed like a quiet place to pass the afternoon, and Liz always appreciated a burrito, even if it turned out to be a furious one. She had to admit that it was freeing that she was no longer being held to the pretense of acting like someone's wife. She had put the wedding ring into her wallet that morning and did not plan to fish it out and place it back onto her finger again, ever. She was further pleased to have noticed that Ben seemed to have followed suit with respect to his wedding band.

Once, years prior, when Liz and Beth had been to a bottomless Mimosas brunch, Beth had thrown back so many drinks before the food had arrived that she somehow ended up spilling her entire crepe entree onto her lap. She had been so drunk and indifferent to this mishap at the time, that she'd simply taken her fork and knife and began eating the entree off her lap, as if it was supposed to be there all along. That day's luncheon seemed to be shaping up to be a similar experience, and by the time the waitress had finally gotten around to refilling their basket of chips and salsa, they'd already gone through three pitchers. And although Liz and Ben were both on their second drink, Liz noticed that Beth and Joe seemed to be keeping pace with each other and were downing the drinks at breakneck speed. Liz wondered if she should place a napkin, or maybe a plate, on Beth's lap to prepare for the chimichanga she'd ordered.

"Wait, wait, wait. Are you telling me that Sonia was making out with some guy last night? This is not computing for me at all," Liz said incredulously. Sonia had been married for eight years and had two little kids at home. She felt like this news was akin to hearing that the sky was green when you knew that it was blue.

"Yes, I tell, you, um I told you that it is tr-ue," Beth said, with speech that was way too slurred for one thirty in the afternoon. "Look, I even took a pick-chur." Beth leaned in and showed Liz not a picture, but an actual video of what was most definitely the back of Sonia's body clearly wrapped in an embrace with an unknown man. Beth cleared her throat and said, slowly and emphatically so as to get the words correctly, "Sonia said that Jon had slept with a coworker while she was, um, pregnant this last time and now she feels, um..." Beth closed her eyes and searched for the right word before deciding on, "vindicated."

Liz was stunned. Poor Sonia. She imagined her feeling insecure and pregnant, with another little one at home, and finding out that her husband had been canoodling with a coworker. Was Sonia also scared of upsetting the apple cart, the status quo, and leaving her cheating husband? Was an embrace with a total stranger on a trip truly vindication, or was it just more writing on the wall that perhaps their marriage had run its course? It wasn't Liz's business. She had her own chaotic situation to worry about.

The waitress, after nearly forty-five minutes, finally brought their entrees and set them down before each person. Liz had already stuffed herself sufficiently with chips and she wasn't quite sure she could even take one bite of her combo platter. She stared it and said, "I'm not sure I can fit any of this into my body after the mount of chips that I ate." She hadn't thought she'd had that much to drink, but when she realized that she'd said "mount" instead of "amount" she burst out in peals of laughter, and Beth, probably not even sure why Liz was laughing, joined in as well. Liz couldn't articulate why she found it so amusing that she'd eaten a "mount" of chips, but for some reason it really tickled her, and she made a mental note that she should cut herself off and try and get some heavier food in her body.

Joe interrupted her thought with a loud burp, and the entire table burst into hysterics. "Pardon me," he said. When they finally composed themselves, Joe said, "So, is it weird for you two ladies that you have the same name?"

Liz and Beth both looked at him confused. Beth asked, "What do you mean?"

Joe looked perplexed at their confusion. "You know, because you're both Elizabeth, right? Liz, Beth? No?" He looked from Beth to Liz for an answer.

"She's Elizabeth. I'm Bethany," Beth said, first placing her finger against Liz's cheek before digging it hard into her own nose.

"Huh, Bethany. That never even occurred to me," Joe said. "Did it occur to you?" he asked Ben. Ben just shrugged his shoulders. He actually hadn't given a second thought to what Beth's full name might be. He actually just assumed it had been Beth.

"Yup, it's Bethany," Beth said, and took a bite of her entree.

"Well, Bethany, we know that these two" — he gestured between Liz and Ben — "are probably going to blow us off at some point this afternoon. And I am itching to play some craps. Care to join me? Blow on my dice or something?" Beth found the last line of this proposition particularly funny, and nearly spit out her drink.

"Joseph, I would love to blow on your dice. Thank you for asking," she replied. Ben and Liz looked at each other across the table.

Liz, feeling slightly concerned for the lowering inhibitions of her friend, said, "Maybe Ben and I will walk around the casino with you for a little bit." She turned to Ben and asked, "Is that ok with you?" with wide eyes. She knew that her friend openly noted that she wanted to make some bad decisions today, but she didn't necessarily want Joe to become one of those bad decisions. That could prove to be awkward for all of them in the long run. Ben seemed to understand.

"For sure. We've been in Vegas for three days and I haven't set foot in a casino," Ben said.

"Uh-oh, Bethany. I think our friends are concerned that you might fall victim to my irresistible charms," Joe said, and tipped back the rest of the drink in his glass. Then he attempted to wink at her, but it looked more like a facial spasm, and they descended into hysterics again.

* * *

THE LUNCHEON HAD lasted nearly three and a half hours before they finally stood up and left the restaurant. They took an Uber back to Bellagio so that Joe could play some craps, and Liz presumed, so that Beth could blow on his dice, whatever that might turn out to mean. Liz didn't expect that it could mean much, as she knew that Beth was expected that evening at the Palms with the rest of the crew. Liz knew that as much as Beth might like to, she was not the person who would blow off Jenna and their other friends. Apparently, that was Liz's job, she thought to herself with a bit of remorse.

They entered the casino at Bellagio and Liz found that the cacophony of various slot machines, in combination with the twinkling and flashing lights, was an assault on her brain, which still felt sufficiently buzzed from their long luncheon. She almost couldn't focus and leaned against Ben for support. He leaned into her asked, "Are you okay?"

She looked up at him and said, "Actually, I think I need to sit for a little bit, and maybe have some water. Believe it or not, I don't usually have three really strong margaritas with lunch every day. I think it went to my head a little bit."

He sat her down at a slot machine and said, "Alright. Wait here one sec and I'll tell Joe we'll meet up with them in a little while." She nodded and watched him approach Joe and Beth, who were a few steps ahead of them. She couldn't hear what was being said, but she saw him take out his phone, presumably to look at the time, and saw Joe nod in agreement at something Ben had said. Beth waved to her, and she waved back. Then, Ben started walking back toward her.

"Alright, they're going to go play for a little while. Well, he is at least. I think she's just along for the ride. We'll meet them back in here in an hour. I figure we can go sit by the pool. Detox a little bit," he said, smiling.

"Perfect. I probably should have eaten a little more than chips while we were there, I guess. I could really go for a soda," she said, and leaned against him as they walked toward the pool. They took two chairs in a shady part of the pool area close to the building, and Ben walked to the bar and came back with two sodas.

"Here you go," he said, and twisted it open and handed it to her.

"Thank you," she said, and took a long swig and then exhaled deeply. "That really hit the spot. Sorry about this. Although I realize my performance this weekend doesn't really support what I'm about to say, I'm really not a big drinker. Especially during the day."

"Well, you probably should have taken more than two bites of your food," Ben said, and pushed a piece of hair behind her ear. "Should we have second lunch?" he said, half joking.

Liz laughed, "Actually, I could probably go for something in a little while, but right now I kind of just need to sit."

"Alright, then let's sit," Ben said. "If you get hungry, I think they have some food right out here," he said, and pointed to an area with a sign that read "Pool Cafe."

"In a little bit for sure. Could use some fries probably, but let's just chat for a little. Like, let's go over some of the basics. I feel like we haven't really had any moments to just talk. Ask the little questions. You know, like the first-date questions," she said, and took another long drink of her soda.

"OK, so what's your plan? Do you want to ask me questions? I haven't been on a date in over twenty years, so I'm a little out of practice about how this all works," Ben said.

"I'll share something about me, and you can share, like, a matching fact about you. Then you can tell me something about you and ask me a similar question. I don't know. I'm no dating expert, either," she said, laughing. "I just want to sit here and talk until I feel like some of the margarita in my body is dried up."

"OK, I'll let you take the lead then. And if you want me to go and order fries to help soak up that alcohol, just say the word."

She laughed. He was so nice. "OK, how about five simple facts about me. Let's see," she mulled it over for a few seconds. How, she wondered, do you start to reveal to someone who you really are? What are the important pieces, and what do you leave by the wayside, at least for now? "This is actually really hard."

He laughed with her and said, "Should I just get the fries?"

"No, no. I want to know Ben, so now you're going to be forced to know Liz. Alright, a few random facts. Well, I'm from Long Island, but moved into the city two years ago. Just made the commute easier. I'm an only child, but I wanted a sibling so badly as a child that I used to dress my cats up in baby doll clothes. My favorite dessert is a good jelly doughnut, but the kind with sugar, not powder. I have an irrational fear of elevators, and yet, I still take them every single day even if there is another option. And I hate country music with a fiery passion. Like, hate."

"Wow, you are a complicated person, aren't you?" he said, but she could tell by his tone he was being playful. "How do I follow that up? Well, I'm Ben. Nice to meet you. Born and raised in Southern California, but I can't really give you a specific town or county even, because we pretty much moved every other month." Liz's eyes opened wide; she'd lived in the same home until she was in her mid-twenties, the home her parents bought during their second year of marriage; it was still the home in which she spent every holiday. She couldn't imagine not having solid roots. He continued, "I am not an only child. I have an older sister, who, coincidentally, liked to dress me up in her clothes as a toddler because she really wanted a sister, so I feel some camaraderie with your cats. I am not afraid of elevators; however, I do have an odd fear of, and please don't judge me here, that if I sit on an airplane toilet, and the toilet flushes for some reason, that it might suck my organs right out." Liz couldn't help but laugh at this statement. She'd actually never sat on an airplane toilet before; did they really have that much power? He continued, "How many was that? Three? Let's see what else I have that might scare you away... Well, Joe and I met junior year of college in an advanced expository writing class, and we've been best friends and partners ever since. Please don't ask me what expository writing is. And I know I've mentioned him before, but I have one son. He's twenty now and he's away at college," he finished, and sat back in his chair, and exaggerated exhaustion at sharing the information. "Have I scared you away yet?" He realized that in the last two minutes he shared that he had an unstable upbringing, he'd had a child at a young age while he was still in college, and he had a weird fear of his colon being forcibly sucked out of his anus. Probably not his finest hour, he reflected.

 She laughed. "You have not scared me away. But I will certainly be more cautious when sitting on high-powered toilets going forward, that's for sure."

 He was glad she was so easygoing. He hated to compare, but Adeline had always been so uptight. When Joe would be over at the house, which was a rarity because they'd made no secret that they had not cared for each other from the start, she had continually rolled her eyes with disdain at any off-color remark that might escape his mouth. He also remembered that she had been angry with Ben when he'd brought home a whoopee cushion for Jack when he was about seven years old because she just didn't think that type of crass humor was funny.

 "I feel like I have to one-up you now, though. Hm." She rubbed her hand along her chin, as if she were stroking an imaginary beard. "OK, well, about a year or so ago, maybe two years tops, Beth and I had been shopping all day trying to find dresses for a friend's baby shower. Well, I don't know how Los Angeles is, but in New York, public bathrooms are few and far between. I guess I'd had a giant coffee earlier in the day, and then a bottle of water, and then Beth tried on this dress. It was orange, with these weird brown vertical stripes, just something that should never be on a garment. And something about the way Beth had described herself as a deflated pumpkin...well, at the time, I could not keep it together. And I legit pissed myself right there in the fitting room." She looked at Ben to see if this was an amusing story, or if she had just disgusted him, because she reasoned that urinating in a department store fitting room could really go either way, but when she saw his laughter, she thought it was safe to continue. "And, like I said, I'd had quite a bit to drink, and there was nothing I could do. So, I took off my underwear and left them in the puddle of pee right in the middle of the fitting room. And I haven't been back to that store since. Thank God I'd worn a skirt that day, because I could not have pulled off that maneuver with pants." She laughed at the memory and thought about telling Beth about it as she'd rushed her down the escalator and out of the store. Wait, how big of a puddle? Like, was it a tinkle or a kiddie pool?

"Maybe they have your picture up by the fitting room. If it were me, I would have printed it on yellow paper, to really drive the point home," he said, laughing.

"Anyway, so, you didn't scare me away. Why did we both share toilet stories, though?" she said, and laughed. "You know what? I think I could go for some fries. Let's walk over," she said, and started to stand up.

"No, no. You sit. I'll get them. I'll be right back," he said. Ben stood up and made his way over to the Pool Cafe. She figured she would take the opportunity to send Beth a text and see how her casino time with Joe had been going. She assumed that they were going to play some table games, as Joe had suggested, but if they ended up making out in some dark corner of Bellagio like two amped-up teenagers, then who was she to judge? She had a story to go home with, so why shouldn't Beth write one as well?

By the time Ben returned to the table, Beth still hadn't replied, so Liz put her phone into her purse. Casinos were incredibly noisy, and Beth was incredibly drunk, so she conceded that she probably wouldn't hear back from her until it was time to meet back up. Beth was a big girl, and could handle herself, Liz reasoned.

"Oh, these are perfect, thank you," Liz said, as she eyed the boat of fries. Her stomach rumbled at the smell of salty potato, and she popped one into her mouth. She gestured to Ben that he should partake, and he waved it away.

"I'm good for now. I ate my whole lunch and about a pound of chips, but maybe in a few I'll grab one. You enjoy for now," he said.

"You know, I didn't want to come on this trip. I didn't feel like taking the time off of work. I didn't want to spend the money. Beth and I both thought it was obscene that Jenna was forcing us to do this for a second time, because this is her second wedding in less than five years. I felt bad leaving my cat"—she stopped and ate another fry before continuing—"but I am so glad that I came, because you are my favorite unexpected thing that I've come upon in quite a while."

Ben moved his chair closer to Liz, so that their knees were touching, and he kissed her lightly on the mouth. "That is quite a high compliment," he said.

"I'm going to ask you something, and you can say no. I'm feeling forward, because I still have quite a bit of liquor in me, so if it goes south I will blame it on the alcohol," she said. She could tell from his perplexed expression that he had no idea where she might be going with this line of conversation.

He seemed tentative, but curious, and said, "Sure, ask me."

"Would you be my date for Jenna's wedding in August? I know it would be a trip for you, but I have so many rewards on my credit card that I think I could cover the cost of the plane ticket," she said. "I hope I didn't... I hope that isn't too much. But, I would also just like to know that I'm going to see you again." She looked up at him through her lashes and the hair that he'd pushed behind her ear earlier fell forward.

"I would love to be your date for the wedding," he said, and she smiled, and she took his hand, and intertwined her fingers with his.

"Well, now that makes leaving tomorrow a little easier. A little," she said, with a weak smile. She ate another few french fries, and said, "Have you heard from Joe? Are we supposed to meet back up with them soon? I've lost track of time."

Ben pulled out his phone and looked at the time. "No texts from him, but you know, it's loud in there. We can start walking over, if you feel up to it. We were actually supposed to meet them, oh let's see, three minutes ago."

"Yeah, we should. Beth was pretty tanked. I'm hoping that she didn't pass out on him, or puke all over the casino. I'd feel better knowing that she's still alive," she said. She'd held Beth's hair back more than a time or two as her friend puked over a toilet. She hoped that Joe didn't have to share in the experience. Ben helped her to her feet, and she found that the combination of soda, french fries, and conversation did, in fact, make her feel much better than she had when she'd walked into Bellagio a little over an hour ago.

* * *

IT TURNED OUT THAT Joe and Beth hadn't been at the designated meeting spot when Ben and Liz reentered the casino. Granted, they were about six minutes late, but Liz doubted that they would have abandoned their post after such a short period of time, and without even attempting to text either of them. So, they took a stroll by all of the craps tables, and then the roulette tables, and then they covered most of the casino floor. There was nary a sign of them. Liz said, "It's not like Beth to not respond and not meet me. Why don't we check out by the pool? Maybe they're out there looking for us." And so, they did.

They weren't there, either.

A quick survey of the restaurants in Bellagio also turned up empty. "Well, what should we do? I don't really feel like walking around forever. I imagine they're someplace. She's thirty-five years old, so I'm pretty sure she can take care of herself. And my feet hurt," Liz said, and wished she'd chosen a more sensible pair of shoes as she looked down at her sky-high ankle-wrapped espadrilles. She just felt like they were the right fashion choice for a Mexican luncheon earlier when she'd picked them; they were decidedly the wrong choice for a manhunt around a casino that had to be, she imagined, a hundred thousand square feet.

"Alright, what should we do? We can go and hang out in my room until we hear from them, if you want. And I'm not suggesting that with any questionable intentions, I promise," he said. He was smiling, but she believed him.

"That sounds good to me. I would really love to put my feet up for a little while."

As they approached the elevator bank, Ben turned to her and said, "You're good with this, right?"

She laughed, "I'm not, but I am. I told you I realized it was irrational. Well, not the fear, but the fact that I continually make myself face it, but to no avail." They waited for an elevator to come, and stepped inside. Ben could feel her tense up as the elevator car made a swift ascent, and he realized she hadn't been joking. She certainly did have a visceral reaction to the elevator. She didn't release her grip on the elevator rail until the car came to a halt and the doors opened.

* * *

THEY EXITED THE elevator car and walked down the hall, toward the room that Ben had been sharing with Joe, although, he mused, they'd only actually slept in the room for about four hours total since they'd arrived, and, yet they were paying through the nose for it. If he'd known in advance how the weekend was going to go, they could have saved themselves hundreds of dollars and stayed in a Motel 6. The best-laid plans, he thought, and rolled his eyes inwardly.

They came to the door, and Ben held his key card in front of the sensor. He entered first, a step ahead of Liz, and stopped short when he saw the unmistakable sight of people and movement beneath the bed linens on the bed closest to the bathroom. Joe's bed. He didn't know exactly what had been going on in the room, but he could put together the pieces and he knew he didn't want to witness anymore of the action, nor did he want to catch a glimpse of Joe's bare ass, or worse. He turned around abruptly, stifling a laugh, and ushered Liz out of the room. He hoped that the occupants within hadn't noticed there had been a momentary intruder, because he hated to bust up his friend's good time.

Liz looked confused, "What is it? What happened? Housekeeping?"

Ben laughed and leaned against the wall. "Not exactly. How can I put this? The missing person cases of Beth and Joe can officially be marked case closed."

Liz put a hand over her mouth and held back a laugh. "Wow," she said, and looked at her watch, "and it isn't even 5 o'clock yet."

* * *

THEY HEADED BACK toward the elevators, because they couldn't very well wait outside the hotel room door. "I guess we'll hang around the lobby or the pool until they're, um, done? I guess?" Liz had to laugh at the situation. She wondered if they'd ever even made it to a craps table, and if Beth had gotten the chance to blow on any dice. As they waited for an elevator to arrive, she took out her phone and composed a text to Beth: Text me when you get this. Details please, you hussie. Xoxo

As they navigated the lobby, and found a couch to sit on, Liz found that she was slightly at a loss for words. She hadn't been given any indication to the contrary, but she wondered if Ben was expecting anything before they parted ways tomorrow morning. Truthfully, it had been on her mind, and it wasn't that she wasn't attracted to him, but she felt like after two days it was just too soon to take that step. Probably. It was different for Joe and Beth, she reasoned in her mind. That was only intended to be a fling, a single drunken afternoon exploit never to be revisited again. It wasn't what she hoped for with Ben. He hadn't pushed for it, or even hinted at it, so she assumed, or at least hoped, they were on the same page in that regard.

She started to say to Ben, "I wonder how long they'll be up there—" and before she could finish the thought, she heard that she had a text notification. It was Beth. It said,

Craps was boring and I couldn't think of anything else to do.

"Well, that was quick," Ben said, smirking.

"Maybe they were up there the whole time we were at the pool. Who knows," she said and laughed. She messaged Beth, We're in the lobby. Are you coming down anytime soon? No pressure.

"Did Joe message you at all?" she asked. She hoped she didn't come across like a gossip. She just wanted to do something other than sit in a hotel lobby, and it seemed like Ben's hotel room was the right place to go. Also, she did want to hear a little bit of gossip, but she was positive that Beth would fill her in.

Ben pulled out his phone and took a look. Liz watched him smirk when he saw the message. She could only imagine what it said. She surmised something like, "The eagle has landed." He shook his head at whatever it he saw. Liz realized that was never a dull moment with Joe. She hoped that this latest development wouldn't make things awkward, but she knew that Beth typically took this type of thing in stride, and from what she'd seen from Joe, he seemed similar.

Ben did not offer to share the messages with Liz. He merely looked up from his phone and said, "They should be down in a few minutes. Then we can go and hang out up there, unless you want to stay with them for a while. Totally your call."

She exhaled. She would have much preferred to spend the time alone with Ben, especially as the minutes ticked away, but there were other factors she had to consider. First of all, she didn't necessarily want to leave Beth alone with Joe after what they'd just done; she'd have to read the room and see if the vibe seemed awkward. Second, she'd hoped to change before her "first date" with Ben tonight into something a little more memorable than a knit romper and espadrilles. Maybe the better plan would be to go with Beth back to Treasure Island and change her clothes. "Let me talk to Beth when she comes down and see what's what."

She put her legs over Ben's lap and said, "So, what's our plan for tonight? Find any quiet places in noisy Vegas?" She knew it was a tall order. The city was just loud, in both volume and appearance.

"Actually, I do have a plan. But I'm not going to tell you, yet," he said with a mischievous smile.

"Oh really? Well, my interest is piqued. Can I have a hint?" she said, playfully.

"Nope, no hints," he said. "Well, I will tell you that we have someplace to be at eight, and then afterward we'll get something to eat."

Liz looked up and saw Joe and Beth making their way across the lobby. Both were clearly still stumbling, and Liz wondered if they'd had more drinks before they'd retired briefly to the boudoir. Beth was waving wildly at Liz, while Joe trotted to keep up. When they finally made their way to Ben and Liz, still seated on the small lobby couch, Joe gave Beth a loud slap on the rear that almost echoed in the lobby. Beth giggled and pushed him away. At least there wasn't a feeling of awkwardness, Liz thought.

"So, what'd we miss?" Beth said. Liz had to laugh at the situation and the complete lack of self-consciousness in the group in spite of what they all knew had just transpired upstairs.

"Oh, you know, nothing much. Soda and fries, Liz asked me to the prom, I mean to the wedding of the year in August," Ben said.

"Aw, that's adorable," Joe said. Then he turned to Beth and said, "I give you my body and I didn't get an invite. Not cool, Beth."

"Joe, I don't bring sand to the beach," Beth said, deadpan, and Joe pretended to cry.

"Damn, you are a sibyl," Joe said. Beth threw back her head laughing. Liz looked at Ben.

"Did you guys have more drinks?" Liz asked, laughing.

"Let's get more drinks!" Beth said and pulled Liz off of the couch.

"Beth, wait!" Liz said. Beth stopped in her tracks, "Stop. Wait a minute." Liz pulled her to the side. She watched Joe sit down next to Ben, and when she was sure they had fallen into conversation, she turned back to Beth. "Well, one thing is that I want to run back to the hotel and grab some stuff. So, you have to come with me for that. And like, are you planning on hanging with Joe tonight? Or are you going with the girls?" Liz hadn't quite expected this plot twist.

Beth, clearly still quite intoxicated, pointed across the lobby back at Joe, and said "Joe's coming with me to the Palms tonight!" Joe heard her and shaped his hands into two guns and fired them both toward them. Liz wasn't sure what that meant, but she assumed that it was a positive reaction. She had no idea what Jenna would think of Beth bringing a date to their last night of slay. She almost wished she could observe Joe interacting with her friends.

"Well, it's about five. Can we go back there now, so I can get in and out, and back here? Then you and Joe can go and do God knows what? How was it, by the way? Just curious," Liz asked.

"Well, I'm pretty drunk, but actually, it was really good. I think. Maybe I'll find out again later," she said, and winked. Liz laughed. She was glad to see that Beth was finally having a good time on the trip.

They walked back toward the guys. "Why don't the four of us walk toward our hotel so I can grab a few things, and then if you all want we can have a drink at one of the bars before we part ways tonight," Liz suggested. She held her hands out toward Ben, as if he needed help hoisting himself up from the couch. He stood up and put his arms around her.

"Sounds like a plan," he said.

Joe stood up and once again gave Beth a slap on the rear, and she followed suit and smacked him so hard that Liz winced watching it. Joe said, "Oh, Bethany, you know I like it when you reprimand me." Liz opened her eyes wide and looked at Ben. She had no idea how Joe and Beth had become so familiar in such a short period of time. Then she thought of her own words from the night prior. Weirdest weekend ever. Best, but the weirdest.

31.

They walked back from Bellagio to Treasure Island. Fortunately for Liz's bleeding feet, the walk wasn't very far. She'd fully considered removing her shoes completely and walking barefoot on the sidewalk, but when they'd exited Bellagio, she spotted a blood-stained Band-Aid and a used condom on the concrete; it was then that she'd decided that she'd prefer blistered feet to some sort of weird infection. She'd made Beth call Cara to see where the slay crew was at the moment, as Liz was intent on keeping up the Aunt Lorraine pretense. Why stray from the story now? It was the home stretch. Fortunately, they were already seated and dining at Margaritaville, despite the early hour. Cara explained that they wanted to be fully digested before heading out for the night so that they wouldn't have giant belly bloat. Beth rolled her eyes when she explained this to Liz. Only Jenna and Cara would micro-manage a trip to the point where they took into account how many minutes were needed for proper digestion. Beth said, "They literally suck the fun out of everything."

When they arrived at Treasure Island, they started to walk through the lobby and approach the elevators. Ben stopped and said, "We can wait down here."

Beth said, "The room is empty, so you guys can come up and hang while Liz does what she has to do." Liz would have preferred that the guys waited downstairs, as she hoped to mull over which outfit she wanted to wear tonight but didn't see how she could uninvite them without sounding like a jerk. So, the foursome entered the elevator together, and then after they walked down the hallway Beth opened the door into the suite.

"Wow, this is large," Joe said, and walked from room to room. "Two bathrooms. Sweet."

He plopped down on one of the beds and turned on the television. Liz just shook her head. She could only imagine what Jenna and Cara would think if they knew a strange man was laying across their bed. She was used to him by now, but he still amused her. Ben sat down next to him on the bed.

"Is it OK if we hang here?" he asked.

"Sure, make yourself at home. We're going to head into the other bedroom and get beautiful," Beth answered. Then, Liz and Beth entered the room they'd been staying in, and pulled the door slightly closed.

As they closed the door, Liz could hear Joe say, "I feel like you were looking for a compliment there, but I support old-school feminism so I'm not going to take your bait, Beth." Beth rolled her eyes, playfully, as she heard the door nearly close.

Liz whispered, "So, can you fill me in on the whole Joe thing? How did that go from, like, zero to um, what happened in an hour?" She started to rummage through her duffel bag, which had been wheeled in and out of the suite more times than she wanted to think about. She had no idea what to wear tonight. She wanted something that left an impression. She thought that if this was the last thing Ben saw her wearing until he saw her next, presumably in August, she wanted that mental picture of herself to be as perfect as possible. There was nothing in her luggage that struck her. There was also the fact that she had no idea what they would be doing that night.

"Well, alcohol helped, obviously. But he's cute and I figured I'd lay some groundwork. You know, so if you decide to fly to California on a whim and I tag along I'll have something to do," she said, and took her shoes off and threw them onto the floor. "Now I just have to get rid of pesky Jennifer."

Liz stopped what she was doing. She realized that she'd never revealed to Beth the true identity of the infamous Jennifer. She put down the dress that she had in her hand, and sat down on the bed next to Beth, as if she was about to deliver some very serious news. Beth actually looked concerned as Liz said, "I have something to tell you about Jennifer."

"What is it? He's engaged, isn't he. What a son of a bitch. I placated my very slightly guilty conscience by telling myself that they were an on again, off again sort of thing. That bastard," she said.

Liz started laughing at her, and Beth said, "Tell me! Now you're getting me annoyed!"

Liz calmed herself down and said, "Alright, but part of me really wants to take video of your face as I tell you this information." Liz could see by her facial expression that Beth had no idea where the conversation was headed, but also that she was growing impatient and probably wanted to know the punchline immediately.

"OK, ready?" Liz asked.

"Just tell me!" Beth said, seemingly trying to keep her voice down so that the guys in the next room couldn't hear her.

"Alright, well the truth about Jennifer is that...well, Jennifer is Joe's cat," she said, and almost couldn't finish the sentence without laughing.

"What?" Beth looked as if she wasn't sure what to do with the new information. "So, you're telling me that this guy is constantly talking about and looking at pictures of a cat?" She sat back against the pillow. "I'm not sure if that's better or worse than him having a girlfriend. Don't you think it's odd? Like, you're not getting texted photos of your cat. And who is sending him these photos?"

"Well, word on the street is that his parents are cat sitting and they send him photos to let him know she's doing okay," Liz said. "I think its endearing, actually. I would have thought you'd be relieved."

"I guess. But now I'm wondering if he thinks this might be more than it is. You know? I didn't really intend for this to stretch beyond tonight."

"But you literally just said you wanted to get her out of the way and that you might want to see him again in California! Make up your mind, you psychopath," Liz said, and threw a pair of her socks at Beth's head.

"You're right. You know what? I'm just going to have more drinks and see where the night takes me. Lots. More. Drinks," Beth said, and stood up and started rummaging through the clothes with Liz. She picked up a navy-blue strappy sundress and said, "This. Wear this. It's your best color for sure." Then, she started packing the rest of Liz's clothes back into the duffel bag.

"Why are you packing for me?" Liz asked, laughing.

"Because you're not going to come back here tonight," Beth said, matter-of-factly.

"Of course I am. We have to be at the airport at like seven in the morning," Liz said. She was flying home with Beth on a separate flight from the other girls, who wouldn't be leaving until the afternoon. Liz had promised her family she would not miss Easter dinner, although she now wished she had a few more hours tomorrow before her flight departed.

Beth stopped and looked at her. "So, you're planning on going out with Ben tonight, and then, what? Having him drop you back off here at the hotel at midnight? Spending your last night in this city alone in this bed, because you know I won't be home until at least three, maybe later. How pathetic would that be? You're here, all alone in this bed, while I'm out there doing God knows what, or God knows who, knowing full well that Ben is in another hotel in the same city. Think, Lizzie. You're not coming back here. I forbid it."

Liz had no response. She hadn't thought about any of that. "But Ben and Joe are sharing a room. It's not like we'll have privacy."

Beth put her hand over her heart and said, "My pledge to you, as your best friend, is that I will make sure that I keep Joe out of your hair until at least three. Plenty of alone time. And I'm not even saying you have to sleep with the guy, but you know, at least sleep with the guy. I don't want to see your face until tomorrow at the airport. And then we have five hours to fill each other in on the flight home. Or maybe I'll just be asleep the whole time." Beth extended her hand as if this were a business deal on which they had to shake. Liz laughed and shook her hand. "Let's wrap this up, because I feel my buzz starting to wear thin, and I'm afraid if I get too undrunk, I'll just want to go to sleep."

"Well, I wouldn't want you to become undrunk, that's for sure," Liz said. "Alright, let me change into this and then we can go."

"I guess I should put on something clubbier than this," Beth said, and gestured toward the shorts and tank top that she'd been wearing since lunch. She looked through her suitcase and pulled out a swingy black mini dress. "I guess this will do," she said, and pulled off her clothes, tossed them onto the floor, and pulled the dress over her head.

"Wait!" Beth said and thumbed through Liz's luggage as if she were looking for something in particular. She pulled out a pair of lacy black underwear and threw them at Liz. "Those, too. You never know." Liz rolled her eyes, but she did take the underwear into the bathroom, along with the dress, and changed.

When she was finished, she zipped all of her belongings into the wheeled duffel bag, and opened the door to the other part of the suite.

Joe looked up as they entered and spied the luggage. "Moving out?" he asked.

Beth cut him off before Liz had to answer. "Shush."

"Beth, you continually cut me to the bone. I'm not sure how much more of this treatment I can take," Joe said and put his hand to his heart, as if Beth had shot him with an arrow. "But I do like that dress," he added.

"Staying with me tonight?" Ben asked, and he stood up to help her with the small piece of luggage.

"Is that okay?" she asked.

"Of course it is," he said.

"It's ok with me, too. I'm also in that room, by the way," Joe interjected. "Beth knows. She was there."

"I know all about your cat," Beth said.

Joe turned to Beth and said very seriously, "You know nothing about my cat, Beth. Maybe in time you will, but right now I'm keeping you at an arm's length."

"Well, this is starting to feel kind of weird, so maybe we should go back, drop this off, and have that drink," Ben said. Liz agreed. She was glad that Beth and Joe were obviously hitting it off, but their strange aggressive, sarcastic banter wasn't something in which she necessarily needed to be an active participant. They could work out their dynamic tonight, over a hundred drinks, in a loud club with the rest of her friends. As for right now, Liz sort of just wanted them to stop talking. Maybe shoving another drink in both of their faces was the best and quickest option, she decided.

"Yes, let's get out of here," Liz said. They left the room and she gave one last glance around the suite before leaving it for the last time.

* * *

AFTER SOME CONSIDERATION, and after leaving Liz's luggage in the room that Ben and Joe had been sharing, they agreed that the best place for their final drink as a foursome was to return to the original scene of the crime, the Lily Bar in Bellagio. Liz couldn't believe that it had been three nights ago, Wednesday night, when Ben had come to her rescue and this crazy scenario began to unfold. It seemed like a year ago, but at the same time it also seemed like minutes. Liz and Beth settled into one of the couches, while Ben and Joe went to the bar to order drinks for the group.

"This is weird, right? Coming back here?" Beth said.

"No, you're right. It does feel a little strange," Liz said, laughing. "It is definitely not how I expected that this trip would go, believe me."

"It's good, though. This was good for you," Beth said, and Liz could see that either the alcohol was wearing off, or that it wasn't and it was making Beth a little sappy. She was right. This trip was exactly what Liz needed in many ways, and she didn't believe it was because she met a guy. That was great, and she hoped that it was the beginning of something extraordinary, but it was really secondary to the fact that she fulfilled her self-imposed goal of proving that she wasn't boring—proving that she was fully capable of doing things because she just wanted to, not because it was what may have been expected of her. She could do things just because it felt right in the moment. She suspected that's what Beth meant, too.

"So, what are you thinking about this Joe situation? Just a Vegas thing? Or a keep-in-touch kind of thing," Liz asked, changing the subject. She was already feeling a bit melancholy that she would be back in New York at the same time the following day, and she didn't want to descend into some kind of "last night blues" abyss. Beth perked up at the mention of Joe, and Liz wondered if there might be more to it than just a vacation hookup.

Then, she shrugged nonchalantly and said, "I don't know. I like him, but he might be a bit much. Like, he's always got something to say. And, coupled with the fact that I also always have something to say...we just might be too much together. But who knows. I'm just going to see how tonight goes. Maybe he can make the trip for Jenna's wedding with Ben. But I'm not going to commit to any of that yet." Liz could tell that Beth really had thought about it, and this told her that Beth probably didn't want it to be a onetime thing. At the same time, Liz figured that Beth probably also understood the disadvantages of starting a long-distance relationship with a person that you barely knew.

"That's probably smart. Just have fun tonight. Do the others know you're bringing someone along?" Liz inquired.

Beth laughed, "No, I'm going to just show up. I didn't feel like hearing some crappy girl code or sister-bridesmaid-matey slay crap about how it's a girl's trip tonight. I was a good sport on this entire trip, but today I'm going to think about myself."

"That's fair. You deserve it. You totally saved my ass this trip for sure," Liz said. "You and Aunt Lorraine, the amputee." She could see that the guys were on their way back over with drinks.

"Yeah, well, that's because there's a pair of boots in your closet with my name on them when we get home," Beth said, and laughed, as Joe handed her a pinkish drink. "You think I'm kidding, but I'm already planning an outfit for Monday that centers around them, so say your goodbyes." She turned to Joe after taking a sip of the drink and asked, "What is this, exactly?"

Joe said, "I have no idea. I told the bartender, 'See that pretty lady over there? I'm going to need her to make some bad decisions tonight so mix me up something real good' and that is what he handed me. Also, you're welcome."

Beth raised an eyebrow and took a sip, "Thank you."

Joe said, "Or maybe, it's just vodka and cranberry." He sat down on a chair that sat adjacent to the couch, next to Beth, as Ben settled into an identical chair on the opposite side of the couch, next to Liz, and handed Liz a drink.

"I did not have a similar conversation with the bartender. I just ordered you a rum and diet coke, because I'm pretty sure that's what you were drinking the last time we were here," Ben said.

"I was, but how did you know that?" she asked.

"Well, you had what looked like soda with a wedge of lime in it, and you've only had diet soda since then, so I assumed," he said. "Was I wrong? I can drink that and get you something else."

"Nope, I'm just surprised you noticed and remembered," she said, and took a sip. Then she added, "Thank you," and smiled.

Joe said, "I feel like we should have a toast or something, shouldn't we?"

"You're right. To what shall we toast?" Beth asked.

"You know what? I didn't expect much from this trip, other than sealing our screenplay deal, which now seems like it happened weeks ago. But this turned out to be a pretty good time. Thanks ladies," Joe said, and raised his glass. They all clinked their glasses.

"To Jenna's Last Slay," Liz said.

* * *

AFTER TWO DRINKS at the Lily Bar, Ben looked at his watch and saw that it was already nearly seven. His plan for him and Liz that evening began at eight, and he wasn't quite sure how long the drive would be. He assumed about a half hour, but traffic in Vegas, it seemed to him, was nearly as bad as in Los Angeles and he didn't want to be late.

"I hate to break this up, but I have a little something planned tonight, and we should probably hop in an Uber sometime soon," he said to Liz.

"What time is it?" Beth asked, and then, when Ben informed her that it was just about seven, she turned to Joe and said, "We're not meeting up with the girls until nine, so we can actually try craps again, if you want. Maybe there will be more than one person there this time."

"And by craps, do you mean..." Joe said, with a mischievous smile.

"I mean let's go into the casino and actually play craps," she shot back.

"Hey, can't blame a guy for trying," he said, and finished his drink. "How about I buy you one more before we head out there. I'm pretty comfortable sitting here." Beth nodded.

Ben stood up and helped Liz to her feet. "I'm so curious about this mysterious plan of yours," she said.

"Now I kind of think I oversold it a little bit," he said, "I hope it's not a letdown." He didn't think it would be. He hadn't had much time apart from Liz, but he managed to do a little research on the sly and came up with what he hoped was something a little different. And quiet, which was her one request. Still, he felt slightly nervous as he said goodbye to Joe and prepared to leave on his first date with Liz.

* * *

LIZ TURNED TO BETH and said, "I guess we're going to hit the road. You're good, right?" She wasn't sure why she even asked. Beth was always good. She had no issues exerting her independence, nor did she have reservations about going after what she wanted. Beth would be just fine tonight, with Joe, without Joe; with her friends, or without them. Liz had warmed up to the notion of Beth and Joe together, and if nothing else it made her feel better that Beth wasn't out and about in Las Vegas by herself looking for her friends at a crowded club.

"I'm great," Beth said, and she stood up to talk to Liz, so that only Liz could hear her. "I don't want to hear from you until I see you at that airport tomorrow. Have a good time, and for God's sake I hope you show this poor son of a bitch that underwear tonight," she said. Liz laughed and pushed her playfully.

Liz leaned in and whispered in Beth's ear, "panties." Beth cringed but laughed. She hugged her friend, and then sat back on the couch with Joe. Liz turned to Ben, "Ready?"

He held out his arm, and she hooked hers through, and the exited the Lily Bar and walked toward the lobby.

32.

One of Liz's most favorite childhood memories was probably her first trip to the planetarium. She had been in third grade and it had been a field trip with her class. At the time, she'd had no idea or expectation as to what a planetarium was, and she recalled how delighted she had been with every aspect of the trip. She'd relaxed into the high-back seat, and had leaned back as the soothing voice, probably a graduate student, had pointed out various constellations on the dome above. Her favorite part of the show, she recalled, involved watching a storm on the dome, and feeling actual raindrops on her face. It had been, for young Liz, a positively magical experience. She'd begged her parents to take her back, and in the subsequent years they'd often made a Saturday afternoon trip up to the Vanderbilt Planetarium and walk the grounds, and then take in a show. Even as an adult, when she was still living on Long Island, she would sometimes think about taking a drive to the north shore to see a show, but she never seemed to make it happen. It was, unfortunately, just one of those causalities of adult life, when the daily grind seems to snuff out anything remotely whimsical, or even just out of the ordinary.

In light of this, Liz had trouble containing her excitement when, to her surprise, Ben's mysterious plan had been to see a show at the Planetarium at CSN. Liz hadn't even thought for a moment that there might be a planetarium in Las Vegas. In fact, it had probably been years since she'd even given the planetarium at home a second thought. Ben had looked at her side eyed, as if he'd thought her joy might be inflated for his benefit, but after she'd explained how much she'd love going as a child, he had realized that her excitement was genuine. She thought that he must have been relieved, because he had admitted that it had been a wild card choice; it had been number seventeen on the list of "Twenty Quiet Things to Do in Vegas" when he'd googled it earlier that day, and had won out over an evening at the Clark County Library and a way-off-the-Strip dive bar, numbers nine and fourteen, respectively.

They sat down and waited for the lights to dim. Liz took Ben's hand, and said, "Honestly, I feel like a total nerd, but this is the best place you could have taken me. I know that you couldn't have known this, but it's just so special that you brought me here. I love it." He leaned in and gave her a kiss on the mouth.

"I'm so relieved, because Joe completely made fun of me when I told him my plan," he said. "Afterward we can walk around and find someplace to eat if you're hungry. I'm pretty sure I'll be hungry. I'm actually already hungry," he said.

"Sounds like a plan," she said, and gave his hand a kiss as the lights went down. A woman's low, husky voice welcomed them, and directed them to look to the dome above. The show was titled A Journey through Our Solar System, and featured facts about all the planets, as well as important satellites, moons, and the asteroid belt. Liz was fascinated, and she imagined Ben was bored out of his mind, but when she stole a quick look at him, he did seem involved in the show. She wondered if he truly appreciated a science-lesson first date as much as she did; she couldn't imagine that anyone possibly could.

After nearly an hour the overhead lights began to illuminate again and Liz was slightly disappointed that it hadn't fake rained on them, but she was still incredibly happy with Ben's choice of venue. It was so not Vegas and she really appreciated it; it almost made her believe, for forty-five minutes, that they weren't even in Las Vegas at all, but that they were elsewhere in the world, maybe New York, but maybe not, just doing everyday things like a regular couple might do.

She stood up and stretched. "So, what did you think? Be honest," she asked.

"Actually, I've never been to a planetarium before. It was pretty cool. Definitely something different to do. Thanks for the suggestion, internet," he said, as they walked toward the exit.

"So, what should we do now? I'm actually pretty hungry," Liz said, and looked at her watch. "Wow, its nine. I guess the show started late. It didn't feel like a whole hour."

"Well, we could stop someplace and eat on the way back, if there's something that you're in the mood for," he offered, and pressed open the door that led outside. A car was expected to pick them up at nine o'clock and return them to the Strip.

Liz mulled it over and did the calculations. By the time they arrived back on the Strip, decided on a place to eat, sat down and whatnot, she thought that having dinner out at a restaurant might consume more of their remaining time than she preferred. She didn't need to be fancy, and she certainly didn't need to be wined and dined. Actually, she'd had enough wine and liquor that weekend to last her awhile.

"What about if we just get McDonald's and bring it back to the room?" she suggested. It had been a while since she'd enjoyed a good nugget, and it would allow them to maximize their time together. "I feel like I just want to change out of this," she said, and gestured to her outfit and shoes, "hang around, and not, oh, I don't know, be around other people I guess," she finished. At heart, Liz was a homebody and mostly enjoyed spending her time at home, on the couch, sometimes with Beth, watching a movie; sometimes with Ravioli, sharing a bowl of vanilla ice cream. She wanted a little bit of that type of downtime tonight with Ben.

"Really? I don't know. I'm a little bit of a health nut," he said, smiling. For a few seconds Liz thought he was serious, then she took a mental inventory of all of the French fries and alcohol and ice cream that they'd consumed over the last four days and laughed.

"For a split second you threw me, and then I recalled that giant steak that you ate at the Spinks', after, you know, like six empanadas and some wine," she said, as the car pulled up.

As they sat down on the back seat of the car, Ben said to the driver, "Good evening. So, we just want to make a pit stop at McDonald's before we head back to Bellagio, if you don't mind."

"You got it, man," the driver said, and they were on their way.

* * *

"I WISH WE WOULD have gotten some apple pies, because I'm still kind of hungry," Liz said, as she wistfully noticed that she was nearly done with her fries. She was always so disappointed when it came down to those last two or three fries in the box; she almost felt like she could eat two large fries, not that she'd ever allow herself to try.

"Nah, their apple pies stopped being good years ago when they started baking them instead of deep frying them," Ben replied, as he dipped a nugget into barbecue sauce.

"Wow, health nut indeed," Liz said, and eyed Ben's remaining fries.

"I see you looking over here, and I am really getting to like you, but I don't share food," Ben said, and he covered his fries with his hands.

Liz laughed. "Well, that might change everything." She finished up her fries and took a sip of soda. "I wonder what Beth and Joe are up to now. I wish I could see Jenna's reaction when Beth shows up with a random guy. Jenna is, well, she likes to be in control of everything."

"Beth doesn't seem like someone who would deal with that kind of bullshit," Ben replied.

"And I do?" Liz asked.

"Well, I bet you'd spare someone's feelings and go with the flow more easily than Beth. And that's not a bad thing, if you ask me. Trust me. I go along with Joe's flow more often than I would like to admit, mostly because I just don't feel like hearing it," he said, laughing.

"Yeah, you're right. For sure. But I'm trying to be more, I guess, aggressive with making my feelings known and not just being passive all the time," she said. "I mean, all of this," she said, and gestured around the room, and back and forth between the two of them, "I would never have taken chances like this before. But now, I'm so glad that I pushed myself."

"Me, too," he said, and fed her one of his French fries.

"Oh, so you do share. I will make a mental note of that for next time," she said, but then she wished she hadn't, because she wasn't sure when the next time might be. She pushed the thought away. She picked up all of the empty containers from her dinner, and brought them over to the garbage, then she walked back over to the bed and sat beside Ben and hugged her knees to her chest. "So, now what?" she asked, and smiled at him. She wasn't sure how they should spend the rest of their evening. Maybe watch some television, maybe have some more chit chat. She actually didn't really care, she was just happy to be in a quiet space with Ben, even if it was only for the next seven hours, and she assumed part of that would involve sleep.

He cocked his head to one side, like a puppy who hears an odd noise, and said, "I hadn't thought about it. I just wanted to be here with you. Doesn't matter to me what we do."

"You know, I specifically wanted to change out of this dress and into my pajamas, but then I got distracted by food and never changed. So, maybe I'll do that now," she said.

"Sure, be comfortable. We're not leaving again until the morning," he said. The plan was for Ben to ride with her to the airport, and they knew that they had to leave around six in the morning. There was no way in hell, barring the apocalypse or some sort of alien invasion, that Ben would be leaving that room tonight. Unless, of course, they needed ice from the machine.

"Alright, I'll be right back," she said. She hopped off the bed and grabbed a pair of cotton shorts and a tank top out of her luggage and retreated into the bathroom. She stripped off her dress and stepped into the shorts. Before she pulled on the top, she looked in the mirror to make sure she didn't have food in her teeth or ketchup all over her face, or something equally egregious. She looked fine. Her makeup was still intact, her hair wasn't a wreck. She thought to herself that she looked happy. She felt happier than she had in a long time. In fact, when she tried to put her finger on when she'd last felt so positive about life in general she couldn't even remember the last time she'd felt such peace and optimism. Maybe never, as an adult.

It seemed to her that all of her split-second decisions over the past week, all of the boundary testing, jump-and-don't-look-back moments that she'd embraced since she'd been in Las Vegas, but also in the week preceding the trip when she'd laid the groundwork to make sweeping changes in her life, had changed her. Made her a better, stronger version of herself. And so, without overthinking and without second-guessing herself, she decided to live only in the moment and do what felt right to her. She didn't know when she'd see Ben next after tonight. She hoped she'd see him in August, but one never knows what cards fate might decide to deal. She stepped back out of the shorts and gave herself another once-over in the mirror. There she stood, in the black underwear that Beth had insisted upon, and a simple black cami-bra, and she was pleased with herself. She wasn't perfect, at least by Hollywood's standards, she conceded, but she liked who she was in that moment.

She closed the bathroom light and stepped back out into the hotel room. Ben looked up when she entered the room and she saw his eyes fly open wide. "I had an idea about something we can do," she said.

* * *

LIZ LAID HALF ON her side, half on her stomach, with her left leg intertwined with Ben's right leg. She propped herself up on her right elbow, and said, "Wait, say that again. I zoned out for a second there, I think." She smiled as Ben played with the piece of her hair that had fallen in front of her eye.

"I asked if you wanted me to turn the temperature up a little bit. Because now that we're, um..." He searched for the right words, because he thought now that she didn't have any clothes on, she might be cold, but he didn't want to state the obvious. "I just thought you might be a little chilly now." He decided it was better to be vague.

"I'm good. It's warm under the blanket," she said, and pulled it up a little further so that it covered a bit more of her back.

"OK, because Joe keeps it arctic in hotel rooms and I'm used to it by now, but I wouldn't want you to get frostbite," he said. Ben's head was reeling. On Wednesday morning, not four days ago, he felt as if his entire life had been spiraling out of control. He was on the precipice of a professional high with the possibility of selling his screenplay, and at the same time his home life, which had always been a train wreck in progress, but one he had grown used to, was about to completely crash and burn. And now, here he was, on Saturday evening, with this unexpected woman who had brought everything into focus for him in a way that he could never remember feeling in his life. And as if that wasn't enough chaos for half a week, tomorrow they both left for their respective corners of the country, and the thought of not being able to see her and hold her, especially now, was like a gut punch.

He must have looked forlorn because Liz asked, "What's up?" Her face looked concerned.

He smiled and said, "I'm just not ready to leave you tomorrow. I guess, I don't know. I just want this to be my everyday life. All of this." He combed his hands through her hair and looked at her.

Liz inched her body up so that her head nestled into his neck, and she pulled the blanket over them. "I know," she said. She kissed him on the neck and said, "I think I'm going to have to get a second job so that I can afford all of the plane tickets we're going to need." He was happy she was being optimistic, and he realized he had to shake off this mood. It was not how he intended to spend his last few hours with her in Vegas.

He pulled her on top of him, so that her face was an inch from his. "Well, I'm coming to you in August, so why don't you come to see me in June? I can't possibly wait four months to see you again," he said. "Use your miles for June, and I'll handle my own ticket in August. Deal?" he asked.

She smiled and replied, "You have yourself a deal." She offered her hand for a handshake, but he pulled the blankets over both of their heads and pulled her down and kissed her.

33.

They managed to stay awake talking until a few minutes past three, before they finally curled into each other and succumbed to sleep. Liz had her alarm set for 5:30. She figured she could take a ten-minute shower before making her descent to the lobby, and then finally leave for the airport. She noticed that by three, Joe still hadn't returned to the room, and she wondered, briefly, how he and Beth had fared at the Palms. Maybe Beth and Joe ended up back at the suite, although she couldn't see how that would be possible with all of the other ladies there. Although, she reasoned, if anyone could finagle their way into that suite full of ladies it was probably Joe. He was funny, and pretty charming, she had to admit. She was sure that Beth would have an interesting story for her.

Liz nearly jumped out of her skin when her alarm went off; it seemed as if she'd only been asleep for minutes. She looked over at the other bed and saw that it was still neatly made. Joe hadn't come back to the room. She gave Ben a kiss on the forehead, and figured she'd let him sleep another ten minutes while she quickly got ready and got the rest of her belongings together. She grabbed the outfit she'd laid out on the chair the night before— leggings, a tee shirt, and a hoodie—and tiptoed to the bathroom in the early morning darkness. She quickly brushed her teeth and turned on the shower.

She stepped in and let the hot water beat against her head. She felt exhausted and would have given nearly anything to crawl back into bed and sleep for another five or six hours. She heard the door open, and Ben walked into the bathroom. She had tried to be as quiet as possible, but she supposed that the sound of the shower had awoken him. She cracked the shower door open and said, "Good morning." He looked as tired as she felt, but he smiled.

"I'm going to brush my teeth, and then I thought maybe you'd want some company before we head out," he said, and winked. He stepped into the shower and held Liz close. They stood, silent, under the steaming hot water for about a minute, until their moment was interrupted by three loud knocks at the bathroom door. Liz jumped, concerned that the intruder, obviously Joe, might just take it upon himself to enter the bathroom. She was familiar enough with Joe by now to know that this was a strong possibility. Ben stepped out of the shower, grabbed a towel, and cracked the door open a sliver.

"What?" he asked.

"Are you alone in there?" Joe asked. Liz couldn't tell if he was exhausted, or still drunk, but he was speaking extra slowly.

"I'm not. Why don't you go lay down? You look like shit," Ben said, trying to get his friend to go away.

"Hi, Liz!" Joe called from behind the door. Liz covered her eyes with her hand in exasperation, although she knew Joe couldn't see her.

"Hi, Joe," she called back.

"Alright, I'm going to lay down, because the room is spinning, and I think I might fall. But I'm coming to New York in August. Liz, I'm going to come to New York in August. Jenna invited me personally. I think I'm a matey now," he said, but his words came out more like per-sin-olly and may-tee.

"Alright, that's great, Joe. We'll talk about it all on the flight later. But you need to get some rest now," Ben said.

"Fine, fine. Bye, Liz!" he called, and she could hear a loud thud as he obviously fell hard onto the bed. She hoped he hadn't missed the bed and fallen directly onto the floor.

Ben closed the door and reentered the shower. "Sorry about that. I guess we have to think about getting dressed and going," he said, frowning.

Liz looked up at him and said, "This just sucks. I hate today." She turned off the water and they both stepped into the cold bathroom. He wrapped a towel around her shoulders before securing one around his waist. She gathered up the few items she'd taken out of her cosmetics case last night and put them away and zipped up the case. She looked at her phone, which she'd also laid on the counter. 5:45 a.m. They had fifteen minutes to get dressed and get downstairs, as they had a car arriving at six. She dried off her body and put on the clothes she'd brought into the bathroom and pulled her wet hair back into a ponytail. Ben dried off and had to go into the room to find clothes to put on. Liz followed him out, and saw that Joe was passed out and snoring, still in his clothes and shoes, on his bed. It must have been some night, she thought.

She closed her toiletry case into her luggage, and retrieved her tote, and left both bags by the door. She sat on Ben's bed, and looked at him sadly. "I guess I'm ready to go when you are."

He sighed. "I guess it's time." He grabbed clothes off of the floor, probably the ones he had worn the evening before, Liz thought, and they headed to the airport.

* * *

THE RIDE TO THE airport was short and silent. At that time of the morning, the seven-mile drive only took them about ten minutes, maybe a bit more, and Liz sat as close to Ben as she possibly could, seat belts be damned. She wasn't typically much of a crier, and she had been doing everything in her power to keep the tears at bay that day. June was less than two months away, she reasoned. It was not insurmountable. At least, for now it wasn't. In a far back area of her brain she thought about the long term—they couldn't possibly go on with periodic visits forever. Eventually they'd have to be in the same location. She pushed the thought away for now. She had no interest in self-sabotage, especially not this early in the game. She gripped his hand harder, and he squeezed back.

As they drove into the airport, and the car pulled over to let them out, Ben leaned down near the driver's side window and spoke to the driver. "Are you able to circle back around in fifteen minutes? I'll need a ride back." Liz couldn't hear what the driver said, but she did hear Ben say, "OK, great, thanks." Ben hoisted Liz's duffel onto his left shoulder, despite the fact that it was on wheels, and held her hand with his right hand. As they entered the very empty airport, they spied Beth sitting alone in a bank of chairs, with her luggage on the seat next to her. She waved to them, and they walked over. She, like Joe, looked exhausted; the countenance of someone who had been up all night and had probably imbibed way too much.

"Hey, guys," she said. She looked pretty down, Liz thought. Maybe she was sad that the trip was over, or maybe she was sad that her fling with Joe had come to a close. Or, Liz thought, maybe she just needed sleep. Liz was sure she'd get the full story on the flight home, if Beth felt up to it. "We don't have much time. I think once we go through security you'll have to break off from us, Ben," she said, and Liz could hear the pang of sadness in her voice.

"Yeah, I know. But I still had to come," he said, and then he turned to Liz and continued, "to see you guys off." He addressed it to both of them, but both women knew that it was really only meant for Liz.

Beth said, "I think I'll walk ahead so you guys can have a moment alone. I'll see you soon, Ben." She gave Ben a hug, and she walked ahead with her rolling duffel bag trailing behind her.

Liz looked at Ben, "I hate this. I hate all of this." She blinked her eyes and pressed her face into his chest, because she was sure she was about to lose the battle and that tears would break through. He kissed the top of her head.

"I know, I do, too." He placed his hand under her chin, and he tilted her face up so that their eyes met. "But we have a plan now, so this isn't goodbye. This is more like, I'll see you in about forty two days. Right?" Despite his optimism Liz felt a tear escape. She cursed it.

"I guess. It's just that, you know. I am feeling all kinds of big feelings, feelings that I don't think it's smart to give a label to yet," she said. "And yet, here I am, feeling them full force. Do you know what I mean? I hope you do. God, I'm so tired I hope I'm making sense."

She felt that Ben knew what she implied, and she also knew that after only four days it was dangerous to even suggest that they might be falling in love, and as much as she wanted to tell Ben that she loved him before she got on the plane, she knew that she wasn't ready to say it aloud, or even admit the feelings to herself.

"Liz, I feel all of those big feelings also. And I won't give them a label yet if you don't want me to. But you know. Yes. I feel that thing you're thinking," he said, and they both smiled weakly. They were exhausted, they were sad, but they were also both hopeful. And that would have to do for now.

She stood on her toes and took his face in her hands and kissed him long on the mouth. "All the big feelings, Ben. I can't wait to see you in June."

"All the feelings, Elizabeth. All of them."

34.

It turned out that Beth wasn't in the mood to chat on the flight home. Liz couldn't tell if she was tired or sad, but she didn't inquire because truthfully, she felt both tired and sad herself, and she mostly wanted to nap and wallow for at least the first half of the flight. She closed her eyes and leaned her head against the window. After an extremely turbulent takeoff and ascent, Liz hoped to try to force herself to sleep away at least a chunk of the flight. She twisted and turned and tried to shove her sweatshirt against the side of the plane, but she could not force herself to get comfortable. Her movement must have annoyed her friend, because Beth stood up, opened the overhead compartment, grabbed a pillow, and shoved it on Liz's lap. Liz was afraid to ask if she was upset about something, so she just said thank you, and found that the pillow did help, and she was able to doze off for a while.

She was jolted out of a sound, but dreamless, sleep, by the vibration of her phone beneath her thigh. She had been in such a deep sleep that she woke up confused about her whereabouts, just as she had the other night when Peter's nonsense text had awoken her, and it took her a few seconds to put the pieces together. On a plane home from Vegas. With Beth. She looked at the phone. It was a text from Ben. It didn't have any words, only a single red heart. She swallowed hard and closed her eyes, but she was unsuccessful in preventing a tear from escaping.

"What did it say?" Beth asked. Liz hadn't even realized Beth was awake. She tilted the phone toward her so that Beth could see. Beth just smiled when she saw it. "So, do you want to tell me about last night? Or do you just want some quiet?"

Liz turned to her and gave a half smile and shrugged. "I don't know. Why don't you tell me about you. I think maybe I need a little distraction."

"Honestly, it's a little bit fuzzy and I almost feel like there are whole chunks of the evening that I don't recall," Beth said, and rubbed at her temples. "I could use some ibuprofen. Do you have any?" Liz handed her one, and Beth tossed it in her mouth and chased it with half a bottle of water that the flight attendant had given her earlier. "So, we ended up having a few drinks at Bellagio before we finally headed over to the Palms to meet all of them. And you can imagine that we were pretty tanked. But you know, Joe has basically zero inhibitions and no problem talking to complete strangers, so he just introduces himself to everyone and tells them that we've just come from eloping at the Elvis chapel." She paused to take another drink of water.

Liz interjected, "You didn't though, right?"

Beth laughed, "I don't think so. I feel like I would have remembered that. Anyway, they were all so flirty and taken by him, because you know how he is. Kind of a charmer, kind of a talker. I don't know. It just pissed me off. I was sorry that I brought him there."

Liz looked at her, confused. "Wait, so he was hanging out with them, and that pissed you off? I think I'm missing some pieces."

"No, not at all. I don't know," she said and she buried her face in her hands. "I will say that they were all super flirty toward him, because he was really the only guy that was in the vicinity, but he mostly deflected. He was pretty attentive, actually." Liz was even more confused as to why Beth was so annoyed today. Her face must have belied her confusion. "I know, I'm all fucked up."

"I am trying very hard to follow all of this. Maybe I'm just too exhausted to understand. Joe didn't come back until almost six this morning. Was he with you?" Liz asked. She could see Beth's neck and face turn a crimson red, and she had a guilty smile. "Alright, so he was. But where were you guys?"

Beth laughed to herself as she recalled the events of a few hours prior. She leaned her head back on the seat and turned to Liz. "I waited until the other girls fell asleep and then I snuck him in." Liz covered her mouth with her hand in shock. "Then, I snuck him back out around five. I guess it took him a while to figure how to get back to his hotel." She smiled as she recounted the recent memory.

"I still don't get why you're annoyed, though," Liz said.

Beth turned back to her. "I'm not going to tell you that I'm in love with this guy or anything. Like, I look at you right now and I see those white picket fences all over your face." Liz made a face, then Beth continued, "And that's perfect. For you. Like, you two just look like you were supposed to find each other on this trip, and I know you're going to find a way to work that out. But that's not me. I'm not there yet. I just... It was nice to meet someone that I just could stand to be in a room with for more than a half hour. And the other stuff was good, too. So, if this had happened in New York, I'd say to you, 'Hey, I met this guy and he was really cool and I can't wait to have another date with him' but unfortunately that can't happen, and I'm just so pissed off about it," she said, and Liz could hear that her voice cracked a little in the last few words that she spoke. Liz understood. It was hard to find someone that you liked and now that she opened herself up a bit to the idea, there was no logical reason to even continue to pursue it.

"I'm sorry. I'm not even going to offer advice, because look at the mess that I'm in right now. How could I?" she said, trying to joke through their shared misery.

"It's nothing. I just need a few days, I think. But it was a pretty wild trip," she said.

Liz said, "Yeah. I'm glad you got to bring home a story, too." She looked out the window, and then turned back to her friend. "But how did you end things last night? He said he's coming to Jenna's wedding." Beth rolled her eyes.

"Well, I don't know if that will happen. Jenna invited him when he revealed to them that we were married, so, you know. It wasn't really based on reality. If he comes, he comes. But it's not like I'm going to take a vow of celibacy or tie a ribbon around a tree or some crap until he returns. Ugh, I just need this headache to go away right now," she said, and closed her eyes. Liz couldn't imagine how it felt to be hungover on a five-hour flight.

"Maybe she'll come around with some ginger ale," Liz said, looking up and down the aisle to see if a flight attendant was around.

"I just can't wait to be home at this point," Beth said. "So, what about you? How was last night?"

Liz blushed a deep magenta color, "It was great."

"See, I bet you're glad I made you wear the underwear," Beth said, laughing. Then added, "Oh damn, it hurts my head to laugh."

"I don't know. I don't want to be dramatic, but this is just different," Liz said. "So, I'm going to visit in June. We haven't worked out the details yet, but we'll see."

"Good for you, Lizzie. I like him. I don't like where he lives, but hopefully we can work on that. And what about Peter? When are you going to return the trinket?"

"I thought about it. I think I might do it tonight. I feel like I have to return it immediately. Rip it off like a Band-

Aid. I need that last piece of the past gone as soon as possible. You'll drive with me?"

"Yeah, of course. Tell your mom I'm coming to dinner. My family was doing brunch this year, so I'll be about seven hours too late," Beth said.

Liz sighed. "Beth, how did I fall so hard for this guy so quickly?"

Beth patted her on the knee. "You don't get to choose these things in life, Liz. You think you have your boring-ass life under control, and then, nope. Surprise. You fall in love with a mysterious stranger from California, I hook up with his comedic sidekick. And we both have a shitty flight home. Way of the world, my friend."

35.

Getting Joe up and coherent in time for their two o'clock flight home had proven to be more difficult than Ben had anticipated. Ben had no idea how much Joe'd had to drink, but he had slept like a rock until about nine, and then he'd spent the rest of their time vomiting in the bathroom. Ben had been concerned that they might miss their flight, but miraculously by a quarter to eleven, Joe had seemed to come around and had proclaimed that he needed a soda with ice, and that all would be well afterward.

To Ben's surprise, Joe had been right. A large soda with ice did seem to be the antidote to whatever he'd thrown down his throat the night previous. When they'd finally boarded the flight, Joe spent nearly the entire hour and change prattling on about his evening with Beth.

"You seem quite taken by her. I thought it was just a vacation thing," Ben said.

"I don't know. She's pretty cool. I dig the New York thing. She says what she wants. She's not a bullshitter, like all of these California idiots," Joe said.

"I like Beth," Ben said, nonchalantly.

"Me, too. Maybe I'll go visit my brother and pop in to see her," Joe said.

"Really? When was the last time you saw your brother?" Ben asked, surprised. Ben had known Joe for over twenty years and could count on one hand the number of times he'd seen Joe's brother Jonathan. Joe may have visited his brother a time or two in the last ten or twelve years when he'd had other professional matters to take care of in New York City, but he certainly never seemed interested in jetting across the country to visit him.

"OK, let me rephrase that. Maybe I'll find out when my brother will be traveling out of the country next and crash at his apartment. And then pop in to see her," Joe said. Ben wasn't clear about Jonathan's occupation, but he did glean from conversations with Joe and his parents that Jonathan often traveled out of the country for weeks at a time. His professional base had been New York for as long as Ben could recall, and he rarely made the trip back to California to see his family, even on holidays. It made no sense that Joe might want to visit him; it made perfect sense that he might want to make use of his empty New York apartment.

"Sounds like you have it all figured out," Ben said, laughing at his friend's plans. He doubted that Joe would take off for a few weeks to New York all alone, and without his cat. But he kept those thoughts to himself.

"And what about you?" Joe asked.

"What about me?" Ben returned.

"Oh stop. You know what I'm talking about," Joe said, and opened up a fun-size candy bar that he had been hiding somewhere on his person.

"I don't know. I think she's going to come to visit in June, and then obviously I'll go there in August. I don't really want to think about it yet," Ben said, and hoped that his friend would sense that he wanted to change the subject.

He didn't. "Well, you need to think about it. Because obviously you're in love with this girl. Don't look at me like that. I said what I said," Joe said, and popped the tail end of the candy bar into his mouth.

"I'm going to make it work. Not sure how yet, but I will," Ben said. "But in the meantime, after I bring Jack back to school tonight, I'm going to crash with you if that's cool. Nothing left for me back at my place other than some clothes and my laptop."

Joe put his hand on Ben's shoulder and said, "Of course, man. Best move you've made in a long time." Ben nodded. He didn't feel like talking for the rest of the flight, and for once, Joe seemed to understand and closed his eyes for the last few minutes until they landed.

* * *

BEN HAD GONE OVER his course of action about a thousand times in his mind. He planned on packing his scant belongs—mostly clothes, his computer, a few photographs and some old sentimental items from his college days, but nothing more—and loading them into his truck. There was nothing in the condo, a rental that had come fully furnished, that either belonged to him or spoke to his heart. He had no trouble leaving it all behind. Then, he'd planned to sign the divorce papers, and leave them on the table with his wedding band. Case closed.

He opened the laptop, which had been sorely neglected over the past few days in Vegas, as he had no need or time to use it, and looked at the wallpaper. The family photo of himself, Jack, and Adeline. A beautiful artifice, and nothing more. And then he did something quite spontaneously. He opened the photo itself in the editor program, and cropped Adeline out of it completely. All that remained was a crowd of strangers enjoying the day at Disneyland, and himself, with Jack upon his shoulders. There was nothing fake or contrived or manipulated in this version of the photograph. The love between these two was real and true, and not a lie captured on film all those years ago. With this change made, he closed the laptop and moved on to more pressing business.

When he'd gotten home the condo had been completely empty. He assumed Jack and Adeline went to see her father, or perhaps they went to have a quiet dinner, just the two of them. Alone in the house, his packing went as planned, and he loaded three large rubber tubs into the back of his truck, along with the luggage he'd used in Las Vegas and one larger suitcase. He opened the yellow envelope which contained the divorce papers. He glanced at them, despite the fact that his lawyer had already advised him that they were fairly innocuous, and he could feel comfortable signing. He planned on going to the bank tomorrow and opening up a separate account in his name so that he could transfer half of their savings, which was about $30,000, into his name. It was nearly all money that he'd earned without the help of his now soon-to-be ex-wife, but he was at peace with it. Fifteen grand seemed fair in the grand scheme of things for all of their shared years of indifference, and he just wanted out.

He signed the papers, returned them to the envelope, and left them, as planned, in the middle of the table with his ring on top. She could sell it, flush it down the toilet, toss it into the ocean. He didn't care. It was just a circlet of useless metal.

At nearly eight in the evening, he heard the deadbolt on the door open, and Jack entered, alone. Maybe as Carol had suggested, Adeline already had a boyfriend. "Hey there," Ben said, and Jack walked over and gave him a hug. "How was your Easter?"

Jack said, "Well, I just came back from Mike's house. I had dessert over there. I had an early dinner with Mom, and then she left."

"Probably just didn't want to be here when I got home," Ben said.

Ben saw Jack laugh, and he knew that not only was he correct, but Adeline had probably vocalized that exact sentiment. He wasn't offended. He didn't want to be around her, either. Now that he had packed all of his worldly belongings into his truck, he was anxious to leave the condo and never return. He looked at his watch and turned to Jack, "We should probably get on the road soon. What time is your first class tomorrow?"

"Not until eleven actually, but I'm packed and ready. I'll just grab a water and a piss, and then we can head out," Jack said. Ben smiled at his son's choice of words. Sometimes, because he'd had Jack at such a young age, he felt like they'd grown up together and he liked that Jack often talked to him like a peer and not as an old fogey. At age forty-one, he definitely didn't feel like an old guy. When Jack returned a few minutes later with a huge bag slung over his shoulder, plus his backpack, Ben took one last glance around the condo. He wouldn't miss this place. It had never felt like home and it only held terrible memories for him.

Once they got onto the freeway, they had a nearly two-hour drive ahead of them, maybe less given the time of night, and Ben knew that he'd have to fill Jack in on some things on the way. He wasn't nervous that Jack would be upset about the divorce, or any of the news, really, but he still wanted to deliver everything he had to say in person. He wasn't sure how to approach the subject, so he figured he would dive in headfirst.

"Just so you know, I signed the divorce papers. My lawyer said it seemed like a very straightforward case, and I figured that I didn't want to prolong it," Ben began. "Are you OK with all of that now?" He turned to face him slightly for a second to see his reaction.

Jack sighed. "Dad, honestly, you guys should have done this years ago. I'm not sure why I was so upset the other day about it. I guess I thought it would happen, but I also never thought it would, if that makes sense. But this is better. You're better apart."

Ben breathed a sigh of relief. "Good. I know it hasn't been good for a long time in the house. Maybe ever. And I hate that you were somehow shaped by all of that."

"I think I turned out okay, in spite of it all," Jack said, smiling slightly. "I feel better not being in the house with you guys, though, I will admit." Ben laughed. It was an honest answer, and he couldn't fault the kid for that.

He patted him on the knee. "You turned out alright." Then he said, "After I drop you off, I'm going to go and stay with Uncle Joe for a while until everything is final and I get another place, which, by the way, will always have a bedroom for you. I'm not going back to the condo. I'll shoot your mom a text and let her know. Not that she's going to stay up waiting for me to come home with a lit candle on or anything like that."

Jack snorted and said, "That's for sure."

"There's another thing, though. And I'm not sure how you're going to feel about it, but I've always been honest with you about pretty much everything, and you're an adult," Ben started.

Jack was quiet and Ben began to second-guess his decision to tell Jack about Liz. Maybe it was too soon; maybe it wasn't necessary. But he felt as if he had already popped open the can of worms and there was no turning back.

Ben exhaled hard. "Well, I'm just going to say it. I met someone."

Jack was quiet for another few seconds and then his only response was, "Really." He didn't quite phrase it as a question, it was more of a statement. Ben wasn't sure how to interpret the response.

"How do you feel about that?" he prodded.

Jack exhaled hard and said, "Dad, I saw mom with some old guy at Taco Loco the other day." He spat the words out like they left a bad taste in his mouth. "He was like, I don't know, sixty or something."

"Not exactly the response I was expecting, but alright. If you think that I'm offended that she has a boyfriend, I'm not. My lawyer guessed she probably did based on her divorce demands, or the lack there of."

"No, I know. It was just weird. To see it, I guess. They were holding hands and shit," Jack said, and looked out the window. "Like, I think I'm okay with you meeting someone, but it's kind of gross when it's your mom. I don't know."

"I'm sorry you had to find out that way," Ben said. "As for me, it's something that just happened, and I'm just letting you know because I think it's right to keep you in the loop. Who knows where it will go."

"This happened while you were away? Or it's someone here in California?" he asked. There wasn't any accusation in his voice. He sounded curious.

"Met her in Vegas. Totally unplanned. Literally four days ago."

"I guess that's cool. Honestly, I want you both to be happy, but I also feel very weird talking about any of this, if you know what I mean," Jack said. Ben did know. It felt very weird to discuss his new romantic interest with his son. Jack continued, "So, she's from Vegas?"

"New York," Ben said.

"New York. Wow. That's a little far," Jack said.

Ben shrugged. "I know. Definitely makes a second date a little bit difficult." He tried to lighten the mood.

"So, why don't you go there? Can't writers basically work out of their car if they wanted to?" Jack asked.

Ben wasn't sure how to respond to this statement. "Well, I can't exactly up and leave my whole life here. You're here," Ben said.

Jack paused for a minute or two before choosing his next words. "Alright, I'm going to talk out of turn for a second here. But, like, Dad, do something for yourself for a change," Jack said.

"That is all well and good, but you'll be home for the summer in a few months, and then back at college in the fall, and even if it was on the table, I'm not about to put myself in a situation where I can't see you if I want to," Ben said.

"Dad, I'm not coming home this summer. I know I haven't mentioned it, but I'm going to go with Noah to spend some time at his dad's ranch in Wyoming. And, actually, I'm thinking about doing next semester abroad in Ireland. So, please. I'm going to be okay. You know I hate the beach, and I just don't see myself staying in California long term."

"Ireland?" Ben was confused. They weren't Irish and Jack had never voiced an interest in Ireland before. He was always the contrarian child who refused to wear green to school on St. Patrick's Day. It seemed like an unusual choice to him.

"Yes, Ireland. I just want to explore, get out in the world, and see what else is out there for me. I have more than enough money saved from working last summer to pay for it," Jack said.

"How much are we talking?" Ben asked.

"Dad, don't change the subject."

"Jack, I really don't even know what you're suggesting. I'm going to go and visit her, for sure. And she'll come here.

Because that's how adults do things," Ben said, and then he regretted that the last sentence sounded condescending. "I'm sorry Jack. I just have to be smart about this."

"You do what you want. I'm only twenty, so I don't have life experience, but what I do know is that when I decide on something, like this summer, or next year, or whatever it is, I throw myself at it with everything I've got. Because I can handle fucking up and failing, and then trying something different, but I can't handle regret. And, not to be a dick, but I have a feeling you know a thing or two about regretful decisions," he said. Then there was silence, because Ben didn't know what to say. His son was right. His life had been full of regret, and full of chances not taken and decisions never made.

He sighed. "You're a smart kid. Much smarter than I've ever been."

They drove in silence for the duration of the trip, and when they had parked the truck, and had nearly reached Jack's dorm room, Ben hugged his son and said, "You're not going to pay for Ireland. Use your money for something fun while you're there."

Wednesday, April 26th

36.

Since her foray back into her regular life nearly two weeks prior, Liz had been making a concerted effort to live more intentionally and without fear, and on a normal work day what this meant for her was that she would try to force herself to stand apart from the elevator wall, hands nowhere near the rail, for a few floors each day. For the first three or four days she found that she wasn't able to go more than two floors, or one lurch, before she grabbed onto the rail and held on for dear life. After about eight days of this self-imposed therapy, she was feeling good about her ability to steer clear of the rail until about floor five, a total of fourteen floors, she was proud to say. She'd told Beth about her experiment, and Beth only looked at her and said, "Oh Liz, you are certainly one odd little ducky sometimes."

Ben, however, had been completely supportive from afar of her new elevator venture. She suspected that inwardly he probably thought she was immature or dramatic, but he never let on in either his texts or his daily video chats with her. Yesterday he had said, "Just a few more weeks and we can try the elevator together at the Wilshire Grand Center" and it made her so excited that she'd be seeing him soon, although she'd never heard of that particular building. She'd booked her flight the day after she returned home and counting down the days on her desk calendar certainly helped ward off her separation sadness.

As they strolled toward the elevator, en route to their traditional extended Wednesday luncheon and errand run, Liz composed a text to Ben. About to enter the box of doom with Beth. Hoping to make it all nineteen floors today. Wish me luck. She sent it before they entered the aforementioned box of doom, and she stowed her phone away in her tote.

She turned to Beth, "Well, I don't have any returns to make today, strangely enough. But I did want to stop and pick up some more body butter if you don't mind. My legs look like those gross images of dry, cracked landscapes. Do you know what I mean?"

Beth curled her lip, "Gross. Yeah. We can get your butter. I could stand to do some browsing, I guess. But I'm dead set on an eggplant parm hero today. I'm not even going to debate it with you."

Liz shrugged. "Fine with me. There's a pizza place right by the store, so we can stop after. Or before. I don't really care either way." She pressed the lobby button on the elevator, as she was the closest occupant to the control panel, and the doors closed. She felt a little lurch but she didn't reach for the bar. She refused to let herself fail until, at the very least, floor twelve.

Beth eyed her, "You alright over there? Shock therapy working wonders for you?"

Liz laughed. "Distract me with something stupid so that I'm not paying attention, please and thank you." Beth obliged by launching into a juicy piece of gossip that she'd overheard earlier. It concerned their coworker Jay, and their boss, Martin. Beth had long ago developed pseudonyms for several of their coworkers, and she had proclaimed them Marco and Polo, respectively. It was a poorly kept secret that Marco and Polo had been seeing each other under the radar for at least two years. And while their relationship outside of the office really wasn't their concern, Polo was still, as far as they knew, married to his wife of nearly twenty years. This caveat made it an especially interesting topic to whisper about in the office. As it turned out, Polo had tried to break it off with Marco, and the unfortunate scene of the breakup had been a local bar. Marco hadn't handled it well, and had gotten very loud, and was apparently extremely drunk, and unfortunately for Polo, unbeknownst to him, the bartender was a good friend of his sister-in-law and had recognized him from social media. The bottom line was that Polo was now involved in a very messy triangle between himself, his wife, or soon-to-be ex-wife, and his boyfriend.

Liz already knew parts of the story, but Beth had a talent for spinning a yarn in such a way that Liz often nearly peed her pants laughing. Sure enough, by the time the doors finally opened for the final time on the lobby level, Liz realized that she hadn't reached for the rail once.

"Am I your best friend or what? A perfect nineteen-floor run," Beth said, and held the doors open with her hand as Liz and the other occupants emptied out.

"You're the best around," Liz said, in a singsong voice.

"So, did you break your fourteen-floor record today," a voice from behind them said. Liz turned and was dumbstruck. Ben stood casually, leaning against the marble wall, with one knee bent so that his foot rested on the wall as well. She hadn't seen him in two weeks. He'd had a haircut and he looked so handsome standing there in the middle of the lobby in jeans and a button-down shirt. She almost didn't know how to react—she was so confused as to how and why he was standing in front of her.

She took the two steps toward him and embraced him. "I'm so confused, what are you doing here?"

"Well, it's a bit of a story," he said. Then he turned to Beth and handed her what looked like a piece of lined notebook paper torn from a spiral book and said, "I was told to hand deliver this to you, Beth."

"Thanks," she said, and took the note cautiously. She, too, looked as perplexed as Liz. She unfolded the note and read it to herself. She smiled and laughed at the contents, which she didn't reveal, but Liz could see a blush rise from her neck to her cheeks. She folded it again and dropped it into her bag.

"Let's sit here. Tell me the story. I'm just... I'm happy and confused and, oh by the way, yes, I shattered my record," she said.

"All thanks to me," Beth interjected.

Liz directed him to a seating area in the lobby, and Beth followed. "So, like, what is happening here?" she asked, and grabbed his hand. She could feel that she was speaking uncharacteristically quickly.

Ben blew air between his lips and said, "Well, I've been told that writers can work anywhere. So, here I am."

Liz shrugged, "You've got to give me more than that. I talked to you this morning and you said you had a meeting with Joe."

Ben smiled and said, "Well, on the one hand I lied about the meeting. But on the other hand, I did see Joe this morning." Liz stared at him blankly. She needed a few more of the details to fall into place to make sense of this, because at that very moment she almost felt as if she were hallucinating.

Ben exhaled, "Alright, I'll lay it out there. So, the day I got home from Vegas I moved out and stayed with Joe. I had some business to take care of over the next week, you know, the legal meetings with the screenplay and all of that, and of course, the other issue." Liz assumed the other issue was his divorce. "I had to move some money around, but after a great talk with my kid, and some unconventional advice from Joe, and you both know how Joe is by now, we made a crazy decision."

Liz and Beth were both hanging on his words. "What's the decision?" Beth interjected.

"Well, Joe's brother lives here in New York. I'm not going to pretend to know neighborhoods or anything, but it's in Manhattan someplace. Joe can tell you that. Anyhow, he's in South Africa on business until the end of the summer. Usually, he leaves his place empty while he's gone because it's a doorman building so who cares I guess, but Joe reached out to him to see if he would sublet it to us for a while, and he was down. So the three of us hopped in my truck on Saturday and drove here, with some stops along the way obviously." He leaned back in the chair, as if the story took a lot out of him.

"The three of you?" Beth asked dubiously.

"Yup. The three of us. Myself, Joe, and of course, your arch nemesis, Jennifer," Ben said, smiling. "I can tell you that four days in a car with a cat is not an experience that I would recommend."

Liz smiled. "So, you're here until the fall?"

Ben said, "I might have to fly back for a meeting or two if things progress with the movie, but in all honesty, sometimes those things take years to make, if they ever end up getting made. I can tell you they did pay us out our first chunk, so Joe and I will be good for a bit financially. But, again, I'm a writer and I can write anywhere. So, here I am, in New York. Ready to write. I already feel inspired," he said, and his eyes crinkled up as he smiled and looked at Liz. "I thought I could take you on a second date tonight, if you're free?"

Beth interrupted, "She's free right now. Take her to lunch."

Liz looked at Beth. "But it's Wednesday. I'm not going to bail on you."

Beth shook her head and said, "Oh no no no. There's no way I'm going to be the one who screws up this little fairy tale thing you two have going on here." She turned to Liz. "I'll pick up the body butter for you. I'll see you back upstairs at two thirty." She turned to Ben and winked. "Have her back on time, please. We wouldn't want her to have to take that elevator ride alone." Then she blew Liz a kiss, picked up her tote, and exited through the revolving door.

Liz turned to Ben and said, "So, what now?" She smiled at him, and she almost forgot they were seated in the middle of the crowded lobby of her office building. She felt like they were the only two people in the city.

He stretched his arms above his head and said, "I guess you should cancel your plane ticket for June."

She laughed. She hadn't even thought about that. She was glad she'd stifled her initial urge to cheap out and buy the nonrefundable ticket. She thought to herself that when she got back from lunch today, she'd trash her desk calendar, too, the one on which she'd been marking off the days until she left for California. She wouldn't need it anymore. She also thought that she'd wished she'd run the vacuum and made the bed that morning. Her apartment was an absolute disaster, which was out of character for her, and she'd hate for Ben to think she was a pig. She made a mental note to tidy up as soon as she got in from work that day in the hopes that she would have company that evening.

"Well, now I have an extra seven hundred dollars burning a hole in my pocket. Can I buy you lunch?" she said.

He stood up and offered his hand to help her up. "I could eat. Know any place around here with good fries?"

"You're in New York now, where lunchtime is for pizza. Plenty of time tonight for fries," she said.

"Alright, Elizabeth. Your city. You lead the way," he said.

She pulled him by the hand, through the revolving doors, and before they set out so that Liz could show Ben how pizza was supposed to taste, she stopped, right in the middle of the sidewalk bustling with people on their lunch breaks. She took his face in her hands, and said, "Best surprise ever. All the big feelings, Ben," and kissed him.

Acknowledgements

The input of each of these people helped me make this the best novel possible, and I thank each of them from the bottom of my heart for their contributions.

First and foremost, to my husband Tom, who listened to me talk about writing this novel for eight years before I finally sat down and got the job done, and who literally listened to each chapter aloud as I wrote it. Thanks for your unfailing support, always.

To my first readers, Lee-Ann, Nicole, Christine B. – your thoughtful input on my raw novel was invaluable. Thank you for taking the time to closely read and thoughtfully critique. Your notes helped to shape this into a better story.

Krissy, many thanks for your sage industry advice, and for connecting me with Elaini, who's input and commentary on my novel are, I believe, imperative to its success (I hope.)

Erika, for all of your "hella" awesome California expertise. You helped make Ben's half of the story more authentic and I greatly appreciate you!

About The Author

Heather Melo is a freelance writer and blogger from New York. She currently lives, and writes, from her home on Long Island which she shares with her husband, son, and glaring of very spoiled female cats.

She loves to interact with readers and other writers, and you can find her online at the following sites:

(blog) www.thelitkitty.com
(Twitter) @hmelowriter
(Instagram) @hmelowriter
(Goodreads) Heather Melo

Printed in Great Britain
by Amazon